QUEEN *of the* ROAD

QUEEN *of the* ROAD

HEIDI HEATH TONY

Cover art by Marco Marella

Paperback ISBN: 979-8-218-41194-7
eBook ISBN: 979-8-218-41195-4
Library of Congress Control Number: 2024909419

For Rick, Erica, Jordan, & Jillian
You fill my life with joy.

"Home is what you take with you, not what you leave behind."
— N.K. JEMISIN

"Every day is a journey, and the journey itself is home."
— MATSUO BASHŌ

chapter

ONE

DEE LEVARI LOVED HER HOME THE WAY SOME PEOPLE love their pets. Like a neglected shelter pup, the run-down center hall colonial she and her husband bought as newlyweds had required a lot of love and attention. To call it a fixer-upper was an understatement—the previous owner fancied himself a do-it-yourself handyman and left half-demolished walls and sketchy wiring in his wake. But that had suited Dee just fine. Once the structural problems were addressed, she'd set about hiring contractors to turn it into the cozy family home of her dreams—refinishing the floors, restoring the old claw-foot tub in the master bath, converting the fireplace to gas so she could warm up by simply pointing a remote as she sat on a deep-cushioned sofa. Dan let her make all the decorating decisions. A distracted "Sure, sounds good," had been his reply whenever she'd asked for input, until last year when he himself suggested updating the kitchen they had renovated twenty years earlier. This time, Dan had opinions: "I've heard this is the best granite." "A six-burner Wolf range is what we need." "Two dishwashers, yes, we definitely need *two* dishwashers."

Dee wondered if he'd begun watching HGTV in the middle of the night. So their kitchen was a little showy, but whatever, it was fine.

Home was an oasis of calm to buffer the noisy and disruptive events life tossed her way. Not that she was agoraphobic. She *could* leave the house. But she always breathed a sigh of relief on returning home and closing the door behind her. *Home.* Simply whispering the word helped her relax. She had systems in place to keep everything running smoothly: meal planning and a trip to Wegmans on Monday, laundry on Tuesday, and cleaning the entire house herself on Wednesday—no maid service she'd ever tried met her standards of cleanliness. Some people, including her own husband, called her rigid and predictable. The rigid criticism stung a bit, but what was wrong with being predictable?

Unpredictable things are the real problem—tornadoes, the stock market, and reliable men who wake up on a Tuesday morning and decide their lives need to change.

Dee stood in the basement laundry room, smoothing one of her husband's golf shirts on top of the still-warm dryer, a trick she'd learned from her mother-in-law early in her marriage. It really cut down on the ironing. As she had every day of her married life, Dee had risen before her husband to style her hair in a neat French twist and apply her makeup. She wore tan wool trousers and a cream sweater set—the classic, or as her daughter so helpfully pointed out, *boring* style she'd worn forever. She smiled when she heard Dan coming down the stairs behind her.

"Hey, stranger! How are the muffins?" she said. She thought he'd come to thank her for making them, a new low-carb banana nut recipe she'd found that fit into his ketogenic diet. She'd gotten up extra early to make them, even taking an additional five minutes to toast the walnuts. It was the least she could do. He'd been working such crazy hours since his practice merged with the Children's Hospital of Philadelphia. Last night she'd fallen asleep before he even got home.

"I don't have time for breakfast this morning."

Dee's sunny mood evaporated. She understood he was under a lot of pressure, and she tried to be supportive. Couldn't he at least express some appreciation for all the things she did to make his life easier? Was a little gratitude too much to expect? She blew out a breath and turned to look at him. "Okay. I'll wrap a couple up for you to take. You know you shouldn't skip meals."

His hair was damp from the shower, the thinning but still-dark waves slicked back from his receding hairline. He waged a perpetual battle against the twenty extra pounds around his middle, but his sport coat hid it well. Men were so lucky. A little padding in the shoulders and skillful tailoring at the waist and *boom*, any one of them could grace the cover of *GQ*. A spot of blood glistened near Dan's ear where he'd nicked himself shaving and, without thinking, Dee reached out her finger and dabbed it away before it dripped onto his shirt. That's the kind of thing you do when you've been married for so long, some evolutionary remnant, like those apes on the Discovery Channel that groom themselves by picking nits out of one another's fur.

Dan took a step backward. "We need to talk."

Never, in the history of human communication, have those four words been followed by anything positive. Dee racked her brain. Had she dinged the car door at the supermarket? Was he angry because she didn't apply for that position on the hospital auxiliary board? Did she buy the wrong brand of low-carb bread?

Forgetting the blood on her finger, Dee smoothed her hair back and pasted a smile on her face.

"What's up?"

"I'm going to be moving into an apartment in the city, closer to the hospital."

This wasn't such terrible news. She wouldn't mind being on her own a few evenings a week.

"So, you won't have to drive home late like last night? I guess that makes sense, I mean, I do worry when you're on the road at that hour. But can we afford it? Is the practice going to pay for it? Ooh! Can we use it when we go into the city to see a show? What's that called? A pied-à-terre?"

"Stop." Dan closed his eyes briefly and took a breath. "Are you intentionally trying to misunderstand me? I'm leaving you."

And just like that, Dee's carefully orchestrated life imploded.

Dan's voice sounded the way it did when he was on the phone late at night with the parents of feverish children. He spoke in the same measured tones, in a placating even rhythm meant to make things less emotional. But she couldn't make sense of what he was saying. He was leaving her. Why? Their life was perfect. At some point, he claimed that since Katie left for college they'd grown apart and "developed different life goals." Life goals? What the hell are life goals?

She walked up the two flights of stairs to their bedroom while he talked, like a wounded animal retreating to her den. Her husband followed her, droning on, but all she could hear was the sound of her own voice saying no, over and over and over.

Dan finally dropped the calming routine. "Jesus, quit doing that." He looked at his watch. "Do you want me to call someone?"

Dee stared at him, mute.

"Oh, for God's sake." He crossed the room and grabbed the bottle of Ambien from his nightstand. "Don't go doing anything stupid, okay? You need to come to terms with this."

From some deep-seated need to please, Dee found herself nodding her head in agreement. Yes. She'd come to terms with this and then her husband would be happy, and he wouldn't need any new goals and life could get back to normal.

Dan paused at the bedroom door. "I'm sorry, Dee. I just can't do this anymore."

At the mechanical sound of the garage door opening and closing, Dee crossed the room and watched his car drive out of the neighborhood. Then she sat on the unmade bed, staring out the window at the pure white clouds scudding across a perfect blue sky. Her cell phone began ringing downstairs, but she couldn't summon the energy to move. She lay down and closed her eyes. She didn't need Dan's sleeping pills. The shock hit her like a two-by-four to the back of the head.

SHE WOKE TO THE SOUND OF CHILDREN GETTING off the afternoon school bus. Fighting the urge to close her eyes and escape again into the oblivion of sleep, she sat gripping the edge of the mattress and willing herself to take deep breaths. Not that she thought it would do any good. When she was supposed to be connecting with her breath in yoga class, she mentally compiled her grocery list. Really, the idea that controlling your breathing somehow makes things better had to be some sadist's idea of a joke.

Averting her gaze from the gallery wall of family photos, she forced herself to go downstairs to the office, where her phone sat plugged into the charger. Ten missed calls from her daughter and one from her nosy neighbor. Her stomach dropped. Had something happened to Katie?

"Hi, Mom! I just called to say good morning," Katie's voice chirped on the voicemail. "I wish you'd keep your cell with you like a normal person. Anyway, I'm on my way to class, so don't bother calling me back. I'll talk to you tonight. Love you."

No cause for alarm. Katie's phone must have been un-locked and redialed automatically somehow. Dee's phone seemed to do that to people all the time. *Butt-dialing*—ugh, she despised the phrase. Her sense of panic subsided. Then she checked her text messages, one from Katie and one from Susan across the street.

> Pls answer. I know ur there. Dad called. What is wrong w him? OMG. Pls call me!

> Dan just called and told me what's going on, so if you want to talk, I'm here.

What the hell was he thinking? Did he call everyone they'd ever known? Why on earth would he call Katie and upset her like this? With a deep centering breath that would have made the staff at the Yoga Loft proud, Dee picked up the phone and returned her daughter's call. Katie answered on the first ring.

Her words tumbled together in a rush. "Mom, are you okay? Where have you been?"

It felt as if someone had reached into Dee's chest and grabbed her heart. Then she did what any loving mother does when confronted with her child's pain. She lied.

"Oh, honey, I'm okay. Everything is going to be okay. I mean, it was a shock when . . . well, I was shaken up, but I didn't mean to worry you."

"But where were you? Why weren't you answering your phone?"

Dee scrambled to think of something reassuring. "I just took a long walk to clear my head."

No response, just sniffling.

"Sweetie, really, it's okay. This kind of thing happens to people all the time, and everybody lives through it. So, we'll get through it too."

"Not to me," Katie cried. "This kind of thing doesn't happen to me. I mean, I thought we were a happy family. And then Dad called this morning, and you weren't answering your phone and I was afraid you did something like . . . oh my God, Mom, I'm so sorry. I know this isn't about me. I was just so worried, and I didn't know what to do."

Katie could be, by turns, self-centered and then compassionate—as if she were two people inhabiting one body.

"I'm sorry I worried you. I'll keep my phone with me from now on," Dee said.

"Do you want me to come home?"

"No, sweetie, that won't help anything. You'll just end up falling behind in your classes." Dee had no intention of letting Katie see what a mess she was. It was all she could do to keep it together on the phone.

"So, what? We're just going to pretend everything is fine?"

Dee ignored the bitter tone in Katie's voice. "I'm sorry you're upset. I'm upset too."

Katie sniffed. "I can't believe this. God! Why are all men such jerks?"

"Is that a rhetorical question?"

"It's not funny."

"I wasn't really joking." It occurred to Dee that being a mother meant this heartbreak wasn't hers alone. And sharing the pain didn't lessen it so much as compound it.

"I better go. I'm supposed to meet some people at the library. I love you, Mom."

"I love you too, baby. Everything is going to be okay. I promise."

She ended the call and spun around in the chair only to receive another unpleasant shock. Her neighbor Susan stood on the porch with her hands cupped around her face at the office window.

chapter

TWO

SUSAN GRABBED DEE IN A HUG THE MOMENT SHE opened the front door. "Dee, honey, are you okay?" Susan's voice shook with emotion. "I was just about ready to call the police."

"Why?" Dee found herself locked in an uncomfortable embrace, a wine bottle digging into her ribs.

"Well, you weren't answering my calls or texts. And I didn't see any . . . signs of life." Her voice dipped ominously.

Dee concentrated on not rolling her eyes. Murder documentaries were Susan's favorite topic of conversation.

"I'm fine, really," Dee said. "I don't know why Dan called you."

Susan squinted down at her. "Why, you're not even crying." She set her things down on the foyer table and pulled a tissue from her purse to clean up the mascara tracks on her cheeks.

Why was Susan crying? This had nothing to do with her. Dee didn't trust people who cried at the drop of a hat. *Pull yourself together*, she wanted to shout.

With a final swipe under her eyes, Susan turned away from the mirror and examined Dee critically. "You're in shock. Yep, that's it. I know all about this. It's the first stage of grief. Come on, honey, you just sit right down and tell old Susan everything." With that, she grabbed the wine bottle and herded Dee into her own kitchen.

They sat at the massive island in the center of the room, where the basket of muffins Dee baked that morning sat untouched next to a mug with the dregs of Dan's coffee.

Susan lifted the edge of the napkin on the basket. "Oh my, these look delicious. Mind if I have one?"

Dee shook her head.

"You know I can never resist your baked goods." Susan bit into a muffin and sighed. "Mmm. So good."

This was impossible. Her life just blew up in her face and now she was being forced to play hostess to her obnoxious neighbor.

"So, what did Dan say when he called you?"

Susan licked a crumb from her finger. "Well, he said he was going to be moving out and you, um, were having a hard time with it. And then he asked me to check on you. And I immediately grew suspicious because in *Murder So Deadly*—"

Dee cut her off. "What did he think I was going to do?"

Susan shrugged. "He really did sound worried."

So that's why he took his sleeping pills with him. Does he think I can't live without him?

"You weren't going to take them, were you?"

"Take what?" Had she really said that out loud? Before the night was out Susan would have the entire neighborhood thinking she was suicidal.

"Dan's sleeping pills."

"No, of course not." She bit her cuticle. In for a penny, in for a pound. "Is Ambien even lethal?"

"I don't know. He's the doctor." Susan hesitated for a moment. "Do you know who the other woman is?"

"You think he's having an affair?" Dee's voice rose an octave.

"Oh no, I just assumed . . . I mean, that's usually the reason men leave, isn't it?"

"I can't imagine him doing something like that." Dee turned the mug around and studied the faded image of dolphins painted on it. They always used their old souvenir mugs in the morning instead of the ones that matched the dishes. This one was from a trip to Florida when Katie was just ten years old; they'd swum with the dolphins in Key Largo and then drove all the way to Key West in a candy-apple-red Mustang convertible. Dee could still see Katie's joy-filled face as she clung to the dolphin's fin and was pulled back to the dock. Did Dan think about that trip when he poured his coffee this morning? Or had it become just another dusty memory he no longer cared about?

"I think he's just tired of our life. Tired of me, I guess."

Susan raised her eyebrows and gave a little half snort. "If you say so. But to me this sounds like a run-of-the-mill midlife crisis. You just let it run its course, and I bet he'll come around and the two of you can work things out. Why don't you ask him to go to marriage counseling with you?"

Dee looked out the French doors. Late afternoon sun reflected off the maple tree's bright orange leaves, bathing the backyard in amber light. She and Dan had planted it when they first moved into the house.

"I don't think he'll want to do that. He sounded like he had his mind made up."

"Well, it never hurts to ask." Susan patted her arm and rose from the table. "I think it's time for some wine."

Dee sat in silence and watched her neighbor move around the kitchen, finding the wineglasses in an upper cabinet and grabbing them with ease. Dee herself needed a step stool to reach them. But then, she didn't drink wine that often. After rummaging through the drawers, Susan waved the corkscrew in the air with a triumphant flourish and gave the drawer a shove with her hip. She smiled with satisfaction as the soft-close mechanism took over and louvered it shut.

"It's lucky you redid the kitchen." Susan ran her hand along the Azul Aran granite countertop and swept her eyes around the gleaming appliances and creamy white custom cabinets. "If you need to sell, buyers will go wild for all the granite and stainless steel. And this oversized island is to die for."

"Sell it?" Dee had the sudden sensation that the room was spinning around her. "But it's my home." Would she really have to leave this house? It felt like something that lived and breathed, another part of the family. The thought of losing it hit her almost as hard as the thought of Dan leaving.

"Oh, honey, I'm sorry." Susan's eyes welled with tears again. "I don't know why I even said that. Sometimes my real estate instincts take over and I start preparing for a listing. I tell you, I do it in my own home all the time. I look around and think about what phrase I'd use to describe such-and-such a feature. Don't pay any attention to me. You and Dan are going to be just fine."

Dee scraped her chair back and stood. She had the absurd impulse to run from the room. "I think you'd better go now, Susan. I, um, need to get dinner on." God, she was a terrible liar.

Susan seemed about to say something, but instead she just gave a small nod of her head, set the corkscrew down and walked over to give Dee another hug. Without the wine bottle, it was almost comforting.

When the front door shut, Dee opened Susan's bottle of Cakebread pinot noir, filled a wineglass and gulped half of it down. Then she grabbed a block of cheddar from the refrigerator and a box of crackers from the pantry. She didn't want to drink on an empty stomach. Or did she? Getting drunk might shut down the swirling thoughts in her head.

Out of habit, she drifted into the dining room. Most afternoons she enjoyed curling up in one of the upholstered dining chairs, watching the sunset through the bay window. With its floor-to-ceiling red silk drapes, the view resembled a stage set. But today, she sat with her head in her hands, staring at the Lenox plate that held her cheese and crackers. Place settings for twelve and every matching serving piece filled the china cabinet. Most had been wedding gifts. Even now, Dee could remember the thrill she'd felt as she'd opened each ornately wrapped package.

Now she sat forward and looked closely at the multicolored flowers circling the plate. Such a fussy pattern. Why hadn't she registered for something more classic, maybe just a band of silver around the edge? She took another gulp of wine and then set the glass down. She shouldn't be drinking it like a glass of iced tea. What had that wine steward said? You must *experience* the wine. At least, that's what she remembered from the one and only wine tasting she'd ever attended.

They'd been on a cruise, celebrating their tenth anniversary, and she convinced Dan to sign up for the two-hour Wines of the World course on board. They weren't big wine drinkers.

Dan preferred scotch, and Dee drank nothing but the occasional glass of white zinfandel. She tried to remember the five *s*'s the sommelier had demonstrated—see, swirl, sniff, sip . . . and what was the fifth one? Whatever. Four *s*'s were good enough. She could *see* that it was red. Easy-peasy.

Picking up her glass, Dee swirled the wine around, sloshing some onto the table. Okay, so her swirling might be too aggressive. She'd have to work on that. Next, sniff. She inhaled deeply over the rim. Then she took a sip and let the fruity liquid roll back over her tongue. After swirling, sniffing, and sipping her way through a generous glass, she decided Susan's pinot noir was far superior to the white zinfandel she normally drank. Who knew what other good wines she may have been missing out on all these years?

"I think it's time for another wine tasting," she announced to her empty glass.

Returning to the kitchen, she yanked open the doors of the newly installed dual-temperature wine cabinet and began carrying the bottles into the dining room. Dan had stocked it with a list of wines one of his colleagues recommended. On her third trip to the kitchen, it struck her—the wine refrigerator and all the other outrageously expensive appliances Dan had chosen made their kitchen look like it belonged to someone else. They hardly drank wine. *Had* he designed it for someone else? Her stomach suddenly felt empty. Time to eat more cheese and start drinking in earnest.

She grabbed a bottle of white with a screw top. Kim Crawford sauvignon blanc. That seemed promising. There used to be a supermodel named Cindy. Maybe this was her sister. She swirled and sipped her way through a glass while pulling the corks out of the other bottles. After sniffing the open bottles, she decided to stick with the Kim Crawford. Thanks to Google, she learned that the winery was owned, not by a model or even a woman. Just some guy in New Zealand.

The bottle was empty by the time Dan got home. He flicked on the kitchen lights and then stood in the doorway to the dining room, his shadow looming over her. When had it gotten so dark?

"What are you doing?"

Dee saluted him with her glass. "Having a wine tasting."

"Did you have to open every bottle?"

"I'm letting them breathe." She congratulated herself on pulling out this bit of wine lingo. She was a natural. Maybe she'd take some classes and become a sommelier herself.

He picked up one of the bottles and grimaced. "This is a $600 Château Margaux."

She held her glass out to him. "I'll try it."

Dan set the bottle down and walked back to the kitchen.

Where did he think he was going? She filled her glass with Château Margaux (how could it be worth $600?) and took a sip. Wrinkling her nose, she followed him into the kitchen and stood watching as he fixed himself a scotch on the rocks. He dropped an oversized ice cube into a cut-glass tumbler, then poured amber liquor from an important-looking bottle. Scotch on the rocks was such an attractive yet serious sort of drink. Maybe she should quit being a wine connoisseur and start drinking scotch.

"How was your day?" She grabbed the edge of the counter to steady herself.

Dan narrowed his eyes at her and rattled the ice in his drink. "Fine."

She took another sip of her wine and hiccuped. She preferred her supermodel wine to this Château Magoo stuff.

"You should eat something," Dan said.

He pulled leftover roast chicken from the refrigerator, along with lunch meat and hard-boiled eggs. Dee watched as he ate the assortment of cold proteins and a side of pork rinds on the island between them. No wonder he was unhappy. He never ate carbs.

Dee sat on the couch with her wine while Dan sat in the recliner, clicking the remote. She turned from the television and stared into the kitchen full of luxury appliances and high-end finishes. "Is there someone else?"

"What?"

"I asked if there was another woman."

Dan kept his eyes on the screen. "No." He paused to clear his throat. "Look, this has nothing to do with you. I've just realized that I want something more out of life. I don't want to simply sit around this house with you and grow old."

"Oh!" Dee exhaled like she'd been punched in the gut.

Dan clattered the remote on the side table and scrubbed at his face. "I'm sorry. I didn't mean for it to come out that way."

"What about our cross-country trip? Remember how we talked about buying a motor home when you retire? I saved magazine clippings of all the places we could visit. I still have them in the office." She knew she was begging, embarrassing herself, but she couldn't stop talking. "We could start doing that now. You could take some vacation time, and we could rent an RV to try it out."

Dan finally looked at her, shaking his head with his eyebrows knit together.

"That never *ever* appealed to me. You're the one who was always talking about it. I can't think of anything worse than sitting behind the wheel all day and sleeping in a trailer every night."

Could it be true that she was no better at listening than him? Had they just been sharing a house all these years, rather than sharing a life? Dan lowered himself onto the couch next to her, and she struggled to avoid leaning against the once-comforting bulk of his body.

"I'm sorry," he began. "I swear to God I hate hurting you like this. But I've done what was expected of me my entire life, and at this point, I want something more."

"More than me, you mean."

"Ah, Dee. Don't do this."

"But I don't understand," she said, her voice breaking. "I thought we were happy."

He took a deep breath and blew it out.

"We *were*," he said.

"I can be different." Dee clasped her hands as if in prayer. "I want to be different. Tell me what to do, and I'll do it!"

He shook his head and looked away.

"You haven't done anything wrong. Listen, we had a good life together, and we raised a beautiful daughter, but it's not the same anymore. I don't know what else to tell you." He then drained his glass, set it on the coffee table, and left the room.

So that was it. Her marriage was over.

Dee picked up the tumbler and wiped at the ring of condensation on the table with her hand. Then she set it back down. It didn't matter. Let the damn table get watermarks. She pulled an afghan around her, lay down, and passed out cold.

AS SHE STOOD IN THE KITCHEN THE NEXT MORNING emptying wine bottles, hungover and consumed with self-loathing, Dan came in and poured himself a cup of coffee. Then he stood at the counter drinking it. Why didn't he just put it in a travel mug and leave? Did he enjoy seeing her humiliated?

"I, um, I lied to you last night," Dan said.

Dee shut off the water, but she didn't look up from the bottle she'd been rinsing.

"The truth is . . ." He paused to clear his throat. "I'm dating someone."

"'Dating,' Dan?" A line from *The Princess Bride* popped into her head. *I do not think that word means what you think it means.* "'Dating'?" She felt bile rising in her throat. "Don't you mean *cheating*? *Screwing around?!*"

"Okay. Poor choice of words. I've met someone else."

"Who is she?" Dee, still staring into the sink, appeared to be directing her question to the faucet.

"Well, you remember the case I had last year, Adam Berger. He was hospitalized here for weeks, and his mother seemed to have me on speed dial?"

Dee turned to her husband in a cold fury, holding a dripping bottle in her hand. She remembered. She'd been beside herself thinking of that little boy suffering through one medical procedure after another. And so relieved when he made a full recovery. He'd been four.

"A patient. You're sleeping with the mother of one of your patients. What is she, twenty-five, thirty?" She spoke in a tight, strangled voice.

"What are you talking about? Stop being melodramatic."

"Why not a nurse?" She continued her rant as if he hadn't spoken. "Why aren't you screwing a nurse? Wouldn't that have been enough of a cliché for you!?"

"Calm down." Dan spoke in his I'm-the-only-grown-up-in-the-room manner. "I'm trying to be honest with you here."

At that moment, some violent, shrewish instinct took hold of her, and she hurled the wine bottle at his head. Lucky for Dan, Dee had never been much of an athlete. The bottle sailed past him and exploded against the refrigerator. Shards of glass flew everywhere.

"Are you out of your mind?" His composure finally left him. "You could have killed me!"

The sick realization of what she might have done intensified her queasy stomach. What if she *had* killed him? Visions of herself rolling him in a carpet and dragging it out to her car in the middle of the night flashed through her mind. She would never have been able to lift his lifeless body into the back of the Volvo. She couldn't even manage to roll him over in bed when he was asleep and snoring. And what was this? She was thinking of ways to cover up her near-murder. Self-pity and anger swirled together inside her like an existential food processor. Before she knew what was happening, she had vomited all over the smashed bits of wine bottle on the floor between them.

Dan backed away from the mess, his mouth twisted in disgust. "You have to pull yourself together."

"Get out." She wiped the back of her arm across her mouth. "Just get the hell away from me."

Without another word, Dan walked out of the house, glass crunching under his shoes all the way.

Dee stood for a moment, surveying the mess, before turning toward the pantry to get a broom. The top of the bottle had rolled in front of the door. She picked it up by the neck and stared at the jagged end. It looked like a dagger. She could end everything with one swift movement. Then he'd be sorry.

chapter

THREE

SITTING IN THE LIVING ROOM WITH THE DRAPES closed to block the sun, Dee swallowed some ibuprofen and sipped at a glass of Gatorade to settle her stomach. Aside from her hangover symptoms, she felt kind of numb. What was she supposed to do now? The life she'd thought lay ahead of her had vanished, and she couldn't imagine what would take its place. Dan's so-called life goals sounded like bullshit to her, but maybe that was her problem. She'd never consciously set *any* goals for herself.

When Katie left for freshman year, Dee made a half-hearted attempt to return to her career in pharmaceutical sales, but after a handful of interviews and no offers, she gave up. Then she bought out the self-help section at Barnes & Noble. Anything that promised to help her find a purpose in life was fair game. *What Color Is Your Parachute, Finding Your Perfect Work*, and *What to Do with the Rest of Your Life* all found a home on her bookshelves. Unfortunately, all the books assumed everyone had some underlying ambition. *Follow your bliss*, they commanded. Dee had been stumped. Her only passions had been her daughter and husband. And the house, of course. Instead of finding a new career, she'd spent the last year and a half scrolling social media for glimpses of Katie's life at school, changing out pillow covers on the sofa, and forcing herself to go to yoga.

She joked about the empty-nest syndrome, but truthfully she didn't miss those years of constant doubt—measuring herself against other mothers, other wives. How much time had she wasted second-guessing herself? When she and Dan used to socialize with his colleagues who had children, she'd felt defensive about leaving her career. And on the days when staying home with a small child became monotonous, she beat herself up for not being constantly engaged.

Then the school years came along with more things to compare and second-guess. She agreed to be a room mom so that Katie would see her doing something useful outside the home and ended up serving consecutive terms in PTA executive positions. Even now, she couldn't quite remember how it happened. What she did remember was her sister sniping that it wasn't real work and Dan complaining it made her irritable. Of course she'd been irritable. She worked at a series of unpaid, thankless jobs that didn't end until her child graduated high school. A twelve-year sentence of indentured servitude. No one tells you that when you're the bright-eyed parent of a kindergartener shooting your hand in the air to volunteer.

Her cell phone began ringing and she debated whether to even pick it up off the table. But what if it was Katie? She didn't want to worry her like yesterday. She reached over to grab it, then groaned when she saw the caller. Marian. Her older sister lived across town, but they weren't close. Hadn't been since they lost their father. Dee tried to remember the last time they'd spoken. Had it been at Rebecca's wedding in the spring? Maybe Rebecca was pregnant, and Marian was calling to crow about becoming a grandmother. Not that she'd see much of any grandchildren she might have. Both of Marian's kids had gone to college and taken jobs on the West Coast, probably to get as far away from their mother as possible. Dee relished this thought. And hated herself for having it. Compelled by both guilt and curiosity, she answered the call.

"Hello, Deirdre." Marian always insisted on calling Dee by her given name. "What are you thinking about Thanksgiving this year? Do you want to host, or would you rather do Christmas?" Marian had no time for idle chitchat. Dee could picture her, pen in hand, ready to check this chore off her list.

The holidays. Her once-favorite time of year now loomed like a dark cloud on the horizon. "I'm not sure, Marian." She paused. She should call back when her pulse stopped throbbing in her temples. No. Better to get it over with. Maybe Marian would surprise her and offer some words of comfort. "I don't really feel up to planning anything at the moment. Dan is leaving me."

"I'm sorry to hear that." Classic Marian. She might have been reading from a cue card—parroting the expected phrase without any emotion.

"You're sorry to hear it?" Dee closed her eyes, surprised at the tightness in her chest. Even after all these years, her sister's coldness still stung. "How about, 'Oh, Dee. That's terrible! Is there anything I can do to help?'"

"Is that what you would like me to say? You know I think it's terrible. The divorce rate in this country is just awful, and I hate to see you and Dan become another statistic, but there you have it. If you recall, I asked you two to join Allen and me at our church's weekend marriage retreats many times, but you were never interested."

"Oh my God! Are you kidding me? I'm practically begging you for sympathy and instead you decide to blame me?"

"I understand you're upset, but I don't appreciate you taking the Lord's name in vain," Marian sniffed.

"You know you sound like that church-lady character from *Saturday Night Live*, right? Except you're not funny. Could you maybe just focus on the fact that my life is falling apart?"

Marian barked a laugh. "Oh, come on. Your life is hardly falling apart. You'll come out on top, just like you always do."

The throbbing in Dee's head had grown progressively worse since she answered the phone. She wondered if rage could bring on a stroke. "I'm sorry, Marian, I really don't have the energy for you today. Thanks for nothing." She ended the call and stared at the screen saver photo of her daughter. For years, Dan's mother had taken every opportunity to hint that they should have more children. "Don't you want to give Katie a little sister or brother? She'd have a built-in playmate. Wouldn't that be nice?" No, Linda, it wouldn't be nice. Because when your onetime best friend becomes a stranger to you, it hurts like hell. Better to have never had that friend at all.

A text from Marian flashed on the screen. You and Katie are welcome to come here for both Thanksgiving and Christmas. Please bring a pie. The woman had less compassion than a robot.

Her friend Jancee, who minored in psychology and therefore considered herself an expert in mental disorders, believed Marian suffered from a martyr complex brought on by their parents' early deaths. Their mother passed when Dee was a child, and their father died suddenly when she was in college.

Jancee had been on hand to witness the falling-out Dee and Marian had after their father's funeral. The three of them were drinking stale coffee in the church basement and packing away the photos they'd displayed at the viewing when Dee held up a snapshot of their mom and dad on a beach. "Look how happy they were," she'd said. "I hope I find someone who loves me that much someday."

"Be careful what you wish for," Marian replied.

"What's that supposed to mean?"

Marian crossed her arms. "It means you don't know what things were really like."

Dee remembered saying it wasn't true and Marian snapping back that she was the one who had dealt with everything, so she ought to know. It escalated into a screaming match, each of them saying the worst things they'd ever thought of the other. Total war. Sherman's March to the Sea. You really can't come back from that.

Suddenly, Dee knew what would make her feel better.

DRIVING THROUGH THE LITTER-STREWN STREETS and graffiti-covered buildings on the way to meet Jancee for lunch, it dawned on Dee that she had never really liked the city. *Filthy-delphia*, her father used to call it. Yet she'd lived in or just outside of it all her life, not even leaving when she had the chance in college. Attending Temple had been a foregone conclusion, simply because Marian went there before her.

She pulled into the Penrose Diner parking lot and saw Jancee striding toward the entrance. With her platinum-blonde pixie cut, bright red lipstick, and black-winged eyeliner, she was hard to miss. They'd met in their freshman year, sneaking out of a sorority rush party.

"What the hell was that?" Jancee had whispered.

"I don't know. It's all Greek to me!" Dee had replied. Their shared appreciation for corny jokes and aversion to sororities set the stage for a lifelong friendship.

After parking next to the 1950s-era sign featuring a chef with a jaunty green scarf, she hurried across the lot to catch up to her friend. Even though they were both just over five feet, Jancee seemed much taller thanks to her exuberant personality and confident posture—and the fact that she rarely wore a pair of shoes without a heel of at least three inches.

"Jancee, wait up!" Dee called.

"Hey, girlfriend." Jancee gave her a quick hug, then leaned back and frowned at her. "Are you okay?"

Dee shrugged. "Not really."

"Come on." Jancee pulled open the door. "Let's see if we can get a booth."

They slid into their seats, and Jancee waved away their server's offer of menus. "I'll have the pastrami on rye with a side of coleslaw and iced tea. What do you want, Dee?"

"Cheeseburger, fries, and a Coke." Dee wondered why they were rushing. Hadn't Jancee said she was free?

Their waitress nodded as she jotted down the order. "Okay, girls, I'll have these out in a jiffy."

"Thanks," Jancee said. She glanced at her phone and dropped it in her purse.

"I'm sorry," Dee said, swallowing her disappointment. "I know this is your busy season. We can make it quick." Jancee had a thriving jewelry-design business, and the months leading up to Christmas were always crazy.

"What do you mean? I'm not in any hurry."

Dee raised her eyebrows.

"Oh. You mean putting the order in like that? I just figured we can talk now without getting interrupted. We always get the same thing anyway."

"True." The diner had been their favorite late-night stop in college, and with a sense of nostalgia, they still met there for the occasional lunch.

Jancee took a sip of her water. "So, what's going on?"

"Dan's leaving."

"Leaving what?" Jancee's face was blank.

"Me. Dan's leaving me."

"Oh my God! But you guys . . . you're like . . . I thought you were—" Jancee leaned back in the booth, eyes wide. "How could he do this?"

Dee shrugged. "I don't know. I guess he's bored with me. Yesterday, he told me our marriage was over and left for work. Very cut and dry."

"What a jackass."

"Yeah." Dee busied herself taking the paper off her straw. "Marian thinks it's because we never went to her church's marriage retreats."

"Oh please. Marian doesn't know anything about anything. Is there another woman? There's always another woman."

"Yup. Nobody I know. She's the mother of one of his patients."

"No! Isn't that unethical, or against the medical code, or . . . something?"

"Who knows? It sure seems sleazy to me."

They were silent for a few moments while the waitress set their plates in front of them.

"Jesus. I don't even know what to say."

Dee picked up a french fry and forced herself to eat it. "There's not much *to* say about it. I just need to figure out what I'm doing with the rest of my life, I guess."

"So, what do you think you'll do? Are you going to stay in that big house by yourself?"

"I don't know. I feel kind of unhinged, like I'm not even sure I know who I am anymore."

"What's that supposed to mean? You're the same person you've always been. My careful, dependable bestie."

"Careful and dependable, huh? I sound like a household appliance."

"There's nothing wrong with being dependable."

"Remember back in school when we read *Welcome to the Monkey House* in American lit?"

Jancee shook her head. "The only thing I remember from that class is that it was the only one we ever had together, and it was way too early. Wasn't it, like, eight o'clock on a Friday?" Everyone at Temple had griped about early Friday classes because the student body believed the weekend started on Thursday. But Dee hadn't minded missing a few parties. She'd loved her literature classes.

"It was by Vonnegut. One of the short stories was about this guy who starred in his little town's local theater productions; he sort of turned into the characters he played, but when he wasn't playing a role, he had no personality."

"Oh yeah, I remember. You used to talk about it all the time after you'd been drinking."

"I did?" She didn't remember that. Which made her wonder if she'd been some kind of blackout drunk back then. "Well, now it's like I'm that guy, only I've been playing the same role for twenty years. If I'm not Dan's wife or Katie's mom, who am I? I'm just one of those people who reflects what others want to see, like the moon or something."

"Oh God, Dee. Don't go off the deep end on me."

"It just feels like I wasted all these years being married to someone who I didn't even know. Like, what was the point?"

"You know what I think? I think you need to get to know *yourself.*" Jancee set her fork down and pulled out her phone. "There, I sent you my therapist's contact information. She's wonderful to talk to."

Dee shook her head no, but Jancee had already hit Send. "Thanks," Dee said, "but I'm not interested in digging around in my past. The present is bad enough."

"You don't need to talk about anything you don't want to, you can just—"

Dee cut her off. "Really, Jancee, it's just not for me."

Jancee shrugged. "Okay. Then maybe you could take a little road trip and stop anywhere that looks interesting. Or go to a spa or a yoga retreat. I'd love to do any of those things with you after the holidays. If nothing else, planning a trip will give you something to look forward to."

"Maybe I'll take you up on that." Dee stirred the ice in her Coke and made herself smile.

"Wait!" Jancee smacked her hands on the table, making the silverware and Dee jump. "I've got a great idea! Let's go to Florida and watch the surfers! Maybe we'll get lucky and see some good waves."

Dee set her glass down. "I actually love that idea."

"Remember that time we went down to New Smyrna Beach on spring break? This time, we won't have to sleep in a crappy motel and eat off the McDonald's dollar menu."

"Are you sure you'll be able to take off?"

"I'm the CEO. I do what I want." She said this waggling her finger back and forth like a diva.

"It's good to be the queen, huh?"

"Well, maybe in a couple of months. Right now, I'm pretty crushed. In fact"—she stopped and glanced again at her phone—"I need to get back soon. Are you ready to pull the trigger?"

"What?"

"Let's do it! Let's book our trip right now."

"Really?"

"Yes! I've got like a million miles on American. I'll book the flights, and you find us a hotel."

Dee bit her lip. Impulsiveness was not her strong suit.

Jancee looked up from her phone. "My calendar is wide open in March. Does that work for you?"

"March?" Dee picked up her phone to check and then stopped mid-scroll. She had no obligations anymore. "Yes." She nodded slowly. "Let's do it."

Both women hunched over their phones, barely looking up when the waitress stopped to check on them.

"How's this one look?" Dee held her phone up.

Jancee squinted through her funky retro reading glasses. "Ooh, The Salty Mermaid! And it's right on the beach! Is it available the week of March 8?"

"Let me check." She entered the dates and held her breath. Now that she'd agreed to the idea, it felt like a lifeline. "Yes!"

"Okay, I've got the flights. Ready? Let's book this bitch."

Dee's finger hovered over the phone. "Dan's going to freak when he sees this bill."

"Fuck him." Jancee flashed Dee a wicked grin. "Make sure you book a nonrefundable rate. Then he can't cancel it on us."

ON THE HIGHWAY HEADED HOME, DEE CAME DOWN from her momentary high. Especially when she hit bumper-to-bumper traffic on the Northeast Extension. This section of the Pennsylvania Turnpike always seemed to be under construction. She tuned the radio to a classic country station and settled in for the monotonous drive.

Maybe she *should* take a trip. She could leave right now. Just keep driving north until she hit Canada. She could stop home, grab her passport and some clothes, and be in Niagara Falls for dinner. A very late dinner. She had no idea how long it would take to get there. And what if there were no hotel rooms available? Spur of the moment sounded good in theory—for other people—but Dee liked a sure thing.

Still, she'd always loved road trips when she was a kid. Before her mother got sick, summer vacation always meant a two-week family trip towing a travel trailer. Every year had been a different destination—Disney World in Florida, Dollywood in Tennessee, the Outer Banks in North Carolina. The drive itself had been a big part of the adventure. Would they stop for ice cream? Would the campground have a pool? Would she make a new friend? Once the wheels were rolling, anything seemed possible.

Dee found herself studying the tractor trailers as she crept along beside them on the interstate. To pass the time on their family trips, she and Marian used to have competitions to see who could get more truckers to honk. It was hard to believe that her bitter sister had once been a fun-loving partner-in-crime. They'd lean out of the back-seat windows pantomiming pulling on an air horn and then collapse with giggles when the drivers complied. What would happen now if she put down her window and motioned for them to blow their horns? They'd think she was a lunatic. They probably saw all sorts of crazy things out on the road. She'd be just one more.

The truck ahead of her had a huge sign emblazoned across the back of the trailer: "Join Our Team! King of the Road – A Company That Cares! Competitive Rates and Signing Bonus! Will Train!"

Dee mulled it over. She imagined herself sitting up in one of those cabs, surveying the landscape and traveling around the country. Maybe blowing her air horn to entertain little kids who signaled to her. Did children still do stuff like that? Probably not. They all seemed to be glued to portable electronics nowadays.

As if summoned by the thought, Dee's phone pinged, and she glanced over to where it lay on the passenger seat. She knew better. Of course she knew better. How many times had she nagged her daughter and Dan to put their phones on Do Not Disturb when they drove? If only she followed her own advice. In the second she'd looked away from the road, traffic came to a standstill. She slammed on the brakes and screeched to a stop with the front bumper of her car mere inches from the truck trailer in front of her, just as the radio station began playing "King of the Road," a song she hadn't heard in years. The phone number for King of the Road trucking filled her line of vision.

"If this is some kind of sign"—she held a hand over her pounding chest—"you don't need to be so dramatic about it."

You could do it, kid. Hit the road and start over. Her father's voice reverberated in her ear as if he were sitting in the car with her, not dead for the past thirty years. The song on the radio had been one of his favorites, something he whistled every evening as he rambled around the house while she and Marian cleaned up after dinner. Her mind flooded with the usual emotional stew brought on by thoughts of her father— affection, grief, and anger. She reached out and snapped the radio off. "You're a good one to be handing out advice."

chapter

FOUR

DAN MOVED OUT ON SATURDAY. ANOTHER PERFECT October day with crisp air and a sunny blue sky. The type of day that makes any awful thing in your life seem even worse by comparison. Dee sat at the kitchen counter pretending to read a magazine while Dan and the movers he'd hired boxed up what he considered to be his half of their life and loaded it into a truck.

If anyone had asked Dee's opinion, the truck and the moving crew were a little over-the-top, considering he wasn't taking much beyond the guest room furniture and his clothes. Dee supposed he was planning to buy some stylish new furniture to go along with the expensive-looking sports car he had parked out front. A convertible no less. He was unironically following the midlife-crisis checklist.

After the last box had been carried out, Dan walked into the kitchen and stood there for a moment, jangling his keys. "Well, I think that's it. I guess if there's anything I've forgotten I'll come back for it later."

"Sounds good." Dee flipped a page and leaned forward to study the article in front of her as she waited for him to leave.

"And you'll stay on top of the bill paying, right?"

"Yup."

"You remember the banking log-in and how to transfer money from savings?"

Blah, blah, blah. Just leave already. "I'm not a child, Dan. I'm perfectly capable of handling the bills." God. He was so annoying with his pedantic approach to their finances. Double-checking every charge when everything was set up to pay automatically anyway.

"Okay, well, I'll be going, then."

"Mm-hmm." Dee didn't look up. Couldn't he see she was busy reading?

Even after Dan drove away, Dee continued to sit at the counter with her magazine just in case he remembered something and came back.

"He's not coming back," she said, finally. "You know he's not coming back."

She left the magazine lying on the counter and went upstairs. She'd made the bed with extra care that morning, fluffing the decorative pillows and draping a cashmere throw artfully over the comforter. She didn't want to appear sloppy to the moving crew when they packed up Dan's clothes.

Now she stood in the doorway to her carefully curated master bedroom, a tranquil scene of restful ivory and beige, wondering why she cared what perfect strangers thought of her. Why did she care what anyone thought of her? She slammed the door to the half-empty closet, walked across the room, and climbed back into bed fully dressed.

♛

DEE SPENT MOST OF THE NEXT WEEK IN BED. AFTER coming downstairs in the morning and fixing a cup of coffee, she sat on the couch watching Turner Classic Movies. It didn't matter that she'd seen every film. She couldn't follow the plots anyway. If she got tired of sitting up, she went back to bed. She wore pajamas all day long. She ignored all calls and texts, except Katie's. For those, she somehow mustered the energy to respond normally. Everything about her felt weighed down and lethargic. Her legs might have been encased in concrete. A lead apron seemed to compress her chest. She wanted to go to sleep and never wake up.

The one thorn in her side was Susan. That woman just would not give up. She called daily, and if Dee didn't answer, she came to the door. Dee knew better than to lie and say she'd been out running errands or visiting friends. Ms. Neighborhood Watch would see right through her.

On the morning of October 30, Susan made her daily phone call. Dee had been sitting in the kitchen, wearing sweatpants and drinking black coffee for two hours.

"Hi, Susan," Dee spoke in a monotone.

"Do you know what day tomorrow is?" Susan didn't bother saying hello.

Dee studied her cuticles. "I don't know, and I don't care."

"It's Halloween." Susan's voice was even more annoying than usual. "You know, trick-or-treat. Have you stocked up on candy?"

"No. I'll leave my lights out."

Susan snorted. "I can't believe you're going to disappoint the children like that."

"It's not a big a deal. They'll get plenty of candy from everybody else."

"Candy? It's not just the candy. Your house is everyone's favorite stop. All that spooky music you play, and the fog machine and your crazily carved pumpkins. And answering the door in costume! Everyone loves it. I hate to admit it, but I've always been a little bit jealous of your Halloween extravaganza. And to think that this year you are going to just up and skip it."

"Sorry," Dee said. "Maybe next year."

Dee ended the call and stared at her coffee. She'd begun drinking it black when she used the last of the half-and-half two days earlier. She hated black coffee. What was wrong with her? Was she going to stay in her house until she ran out of food completely? Was she going to turn into a recluse with unkempt hair who terrified neighborhood children by screaming at them to stay off her lawn? With an angry shove she pushed herself away from the counter and threw what was left of her coffee in the sink. Then she stormed out the front door and began race-walking down the street.

Returning home an hour later, Dee knew two things: one, bedroom slippers were not an appropriate substitute for athletic shoes; and two, it was time to figure out what she was going to do with the rest of her life. Right now, she wanted to simply run away. As much as she loved her home, she felt smothered by the memories it contained. It would be different if Dan had died. Then all the home improvements they'd completed, the framed snapshots of their family, the vacation mementos—all of it might offer some peace.

Instead, everything her eyes rested on seemed like a lie. Had he loved her when they built the wall of bookshelves and window seat in the living room? How about this photo of them with Katie last summer at the beach—had he been thinking of the other woman then? What about the Tiffany vase he gave her for Christmas with a dozen perfect red roses—did he buy it with someone else in mind?

She picked up her phone and opened the photo app to the last picture she'd taken. The phone number for King of the Road Transport loomed on the screen. After her near-accident she had snapped a photo of the truck and its help-wanted ad. A ridiculous idea, really. What did she know about driving a truck? There were probably height restrictions. Could she even reach the gas pedal in one of those behemoths? Before she could talk herself out of it, Dee placed the call.

ON HALLOWEEN NIGHT, DEE SAT IN THE ROCKER ON her porch, holding a half-full cauldron of candy in her lap. It was getting late. Fifteen minutes had passed since the last child ventured up the foggy steps and pushed through the dollar-store cobwebs she'd strung along the rafters, but she wasn't ready to go inside. Then she heard someone walking up the sidewalk. She readjusted her witch's hat and arranged the strands of the old hag's wig around her shoulders.

"Hello, hello! Are you there Dee?" Susan came up the porch steps, ice rattling in the drinks she was carrying.

Dee gave a cackle from her chair in the darkened corner, just for the heck of it.

Susan cackled back. Or maybe that was her real laugh.

"I'll tell you what, you really outdid yourself this year." She walked over and handed Dee a cocktail. "I believe you deserve a grown-up treat for all that hard work."

"Thanks," Dee said. "And thanks for talking me into doing it."

"Yeah, well, I know how hard it can be when you're on your own." Susan helped herself to a Snickers bar and sat down with a sigh. "I went through a tough time myself when John died. It's tempting to just tell the world to go to hell and hole up in the house, but you know, the longer you do that, the harder it is to dig yourself out."

A wave of regret washed over Dee. John's sudden death from a heart attack a few years earlier had barely registered in the Levari household. Katie had been having trouble with some girls in high school, and Dee was consumed with her daughter's drama. She and Dan attended the funeral, of course, and Dee fixed a tray of baked ziti and visited for a few minutes when she delivered it, but that had been the extent of her condolences.

And really, as far as Dee had noticed, Susan hadn't missed a beat. She'd been back at work within a week, and she always appeared to be pulled together and in control of things. Even when Dee dropped off the ziti, she recalled being struck by the fact that Susan had her hair freshly dyed and styled and a full face of makeup applied. At the time, it occurred to her that her neighbor was like one of those characters on a soap opera—no matter what horrific thing occurs in their lives, they are always beautifully dressed and made up.

"I'm sorry. I don't think I was much help to you back then. I guess I thought you had everything under control."

Susan shook her head. "One thing I've learned after seventy years on this earth is that things aren't always what they seem. But I did okay. I pulled myself together and went to the office. I made a point of staying busy."

"But why? Why did you even care?"

"I don't know." Susan glanced over at her house. "I guess maybe I was doing it for the kids. I didn't want the boys to have to worry about me on top of losing their father."

Dee looked down into her drink and nodded. What a dummy she'd been. She liked to think of herself as a kind person, but apparently she was so self-absorbed she completely overlooked other people's pain.

"You just need to get yourself into a routine. That's the secret," Susan said.

"You make it sound easy."

"No, I wouldn't say that." Susan helped herself to another candy bar. "You're going to be fine. Just put the past behind you and take things one day at a time."

"That sounds like good advice."

"Oh, I'm full of good advice, ask anybody."

Dee laughed at her neighbor's unexpected candor. "I think it probably helped that you had your career to keep you busy. I kind of dropped the ball on that one."

Susan waved her hand dismissively. "You're still young. You have plenty of time to find work you enjoy."

Like everything else, Dee thought, age was relative. She felt positively geriatric after the turmoil of the past couple weeks, but evidently from an older person's vantage point, she was still in her prime.

"Have you ever thought about becoming a real estate agent? You're personable and you have an eye for design. I can just see you taking a young couple around and helping them appreciate the potential in some run-down starter home."

Dee shook her head. "No. I think I might have enjoyed that when I was younger, when I still believed . . ." She almost said, *when I still believed in happily-ever-after*, but that sounded a bit dramatic. "It's just not for me."

"So, what kind of a job sounds good to you?"

"Promise not to laugh?"

Susan held up her hand in the Scout's honor sign.

"I think I might want to drive a truck."

Susan tilted her head to the side. "What kind of truck?"

"A tractor-trailer. The big ones that go all over the country." Dee avoided Susan's gaze and plunged ahead. "Here's the thing—sometimes I feel like if I don't get out of this house, I might explode. I just want to get away."

Susan concentrated on flattening the candy wrapper in her lap and then met Dee's eyes. "Well, it doesn't sound very appealing to me, but I think at this point in your life, you need to trust your instincts."

"Follow my heart, and all that good stuff?"

"Well, you're not getting any younger."

Dee gave a shake of her head. "Wait a minute. You just finished telling me how young I am. That I have plenty of time to find work I enjoy."

"That's true, but I was just trying to make you feel better."

Dee considered chugging the drink she held.

"I'm sorry, hon. I'm so tired I don't make sense anymore." Susan stifled a yawn as she rose from the chair. "I think it's time for me to follow my heart across the street and get to bed."

"Thanks for talking me into this."

Susan patted her shoulder. "Ten-four, good buddy. I think that's how truckers say okay."

Dee laughed. "Wow. You're just a jack-of-all-trades, aren't you?"

"Not really. I just happened to catch *Smokey and the Bandit* on the movie channel last night."

Alone again, Dee took a sip of her cocktail and wrinkled her nose. Gin and tonic. The smell of gin made her think of a floor freshly mopped with pine-scented cleanser. With a quick glance up the street to be sure the coast was clear, she poured the drink into the bushes and set the empty glass on the railing. Then she gathered up her cape and walked around the porch, blowing out candles.

It had been a good night. All the work she'd done to get ready—decorating the porch, dragging the fog machine out of the basement, and carving pumpkins—had left her little time to think. Maybe that was the secret to happiness. More action and less thinking.

chapter

FIVE

KING OF THE ROAD TRANSPORT WAS LOCATED JUST ten miles from Dee's house. She'd never paid much attention before, but two nearby interstates made the area a convenient place for trucking companies to locate their hubs. When she'd called their number, the woman who answered the phone sounded positively giddy at the idea of having a woman driver join the team. In a matter of minutes, she'd been added to the orientation class roster.

Now, she chewed at her lip as she drove and tried to ignore the bowling ball of dread in her stomach. *You're not nervous, you're excited.* She'd read this bit of self-help advice in some magazine and repeated it to Katie a million times—before high school theater auditions, taking her driver's test, starting college—any nerve-racking event in her daughter's life was met with the same pep talk. Purportedly, the physical signs of anxiety and excitement were identical, so just relabeling your emotions made you feel better. Clearly, she was much better at dispensing advice than taking it.

Pulling into the lot, Dee met her first obstacle—all the parking spaces in front of the dispatch office were full. She made her own spot across the lot near a garbage dumpster and forced herself to get out of the car. *Excited, you're so excited!*

She walked toward the office, noting the gleaming truck cabs lined up along the back of the paved lot next to a sparkling new Morton Building. It appeared cleanliness was important. A phrase floated up from her subconscious: *Cleanliness is next to godliness.* She rolled her eyes. Her Methodist upbringing raised its head at the oddest times.

In front of her stood a one-story brick office building attached to another large warehouse with three oversize garage doors. As she crossed the yard, an ancient Subaru pulled up and a dark-haired young man jumped out of the passenger side. A pretty girl about Katie's age rolled down the window.

"Good luck, baby," she called. He grinned and waved, then seemed to notice Dee.

He inclined his head toward the car. "She's really excited about this." He seemed full of nervous energy himself, bouncing lightly on his sneaker-clad feet while pulling the door open for Dee to walk in ahead of him. His tattoo-covered arms and tight T-shirt accentuated every muscle, which would have intimidated her if not for his angelic face. He looked like a choirboy with a five o'clock shadow.

"Are you here for orientation?" Dee said. *Where is your coat?* She managed to keep that to herself.

"Yeah. Do you work here? I'm not late, am I?" He rolled his shoulders and cracked his neck to the side as he spoke.

Dee shook her head. She was tempted to share her relabeling-your-feelings advice but thought better of it. She didn't come here to be anyone's mother. "I'm here for orientation too."

"Really?" He glanced down at her with raised eyebrows but recovered quickly. "That's cool." Another boyish grin lit up his face. "That's really cool."

Together they walked into an office space filled with desks and computers.

The woman at the first desk glanced up from the three monitors in front of her as she spoke to them. "If you all are here for the new driver's class, it's in the conference room, through that door back there. Otherwise, just hold on a minute while I finish this up."

The young man tossed the hair back out of his eyes. "I think we're good." He began walking and then looked back at Dee.

"I'm Rico," he said.

"Nice to meet you, Rico. I'm Dee." *Rico, Rico, Rico.* She chanted the name silently to herself. In her new life, Dee hoped to become one of those people who remembered names effortlessly. Starting with this nice kid.

Halfway across the room, another woman seated in front of an array of monitors waved at Dee and gave her a thumbs-up. "Good luck in there," she stage-whispered.

"Thanks," Dee whispered back. She wondered if this was the woman she'd spoken to on the phone. She also wondered if being wished good luck meant she'd need it. Maybe the instructor was a creep. Or maybe getting the license was more difficult than she anticipated. Or maybe, and this was her truest fear, she looked like she couldn't cut it.

Walking into a room full of men seated at conference tables gave Dee a queasy feeling she hadn't experienced since her years leading PTA meetings. Her new friend was waved over to a table with shouts of "Yo, man, you made it" and "Sit here, dude." She took a seat at the one empty table and studied her fellow students.

The table next to hers held two heavy-set middle-aged men who seemed to be striking up an immediate friendship. Another table at the front of the room held two men about Rico's age who were talking to a man with steel-gray hair combed and lacquered across his balding head. He stood in front of a whiteboard holding a marker, and the black polo shirt he wore had a King of the Road logo, so Dee supposed he was the instructor. Rico and his two friends sat at yet another table, all of them simultaneously looking at their cell phones and carrying on a low-voiced conversation.

Dee turned at the sound of the door opening again, hoping it might be another woman joining the class. Instead, she met the eyes of a short scowling man with a shaved head whose expression seemed to grow even darker as he looked at her. He crossed the room and squeezed in at the next table, forcing the men already sitting there to slide over and make room for him. He slouched in his chair with his legs spread wide, like a bantam rooster trying to take up as much space as possible.

The instructor looked at his watch and cleared his throat. "Looks like everybody's here now, so let's get started." His voice sounded like whiskey and cigarettes. "I'm Frank Allenwood, the owner of this outfit. My granddad founded King of the Road back in 1940, and now my son's running most of the operation, but I like to keep an eye on the nuts and bolts of the business, and that's what you'll be if you make it through the program. Our drivers are the reason we're the number one trucking company in the region. They're the best-trained, most responsible people on the road. If that doesn't sound like you, there's the door."

He paused for a beat, as if waiting for someone to take him up on his offer.

For some reason, he then segued into telling them about his experience in Vietnam. "You can look at this like basic training. When I was a young fellow, the army trained me up and then sent me overseas. We were tethered inside those big birds that deliver payloads onto the battlefield, jumping around inside there and dropping those chutes while taking enemy fire, and let me tell you, that ain't nothing compared to what you all are going to go through." He paused and then broke into a loud guffaw that ended in a hacking cough. "Just kidding."

After his quirky introduction, Frank started a video extolling the virtues of the company-sponsored training program. They were told to expect to earn incomes of $47,000 a year, with average salaries reaching $80,000 within just a few years.

When the film ended, Dee noticed Rico and his friends nodding their heads and looking pleased, but the angry-looking guy at the next table crossed his arms and slid further down in his chair. Since Dee hadn't earned a paycheck in twenty years, it sounded fine to her.

Frank circled the room, distributing study guides, the stub of an unlit cigar in the corner of his mouth. His teeth were the same yellow shade as his tinted aviator glasses. Dee stared at them in sick fascination, thinking a paint that color might be called Nicotine Gold. She wondered who came up with the names for paint. *Now, there's a job I could excel at*, she thought, and envisioned herself sitting in a high-rise office building christening tints for a paint supplier. How fun would that be? When she shopped for paint, she often found herself attracted to shades that conjured up something pleasant. Choosing between two similar shades of blue for the office, she'd of course chosen Bluebell over Sky Fall. Because, really, who wanted to think of the sky falling every time they walked into a room?

"Levari!" Frank stood right next to her. Dee snapped back to the present and yelped in alarm. She heard a smattering of muffled laughter from her classmates.

Frank knit his eyebrows together and blinked at her. "You ever think about switching to decaf?"

Dee felt a blush rising from her neck. If it were possible to die of embarrassment, she would have been dead a long time ago.

"Here's your training material." He slapped a packet of papers on her desk.

Dee glanced up at him as he moved to the next table. His eyes might have been crinkled up with the hint of a smile, but it was hard to tell with the tinted glass. "Jensen!" he barked.

Once everyone had a packet, Frank moved back to the front of the room. "You need to know everything in here for the written test, which you'll take at the DMV. You gotta pass and get a permit before you start training in the truck. That's when the real work'll start. You'll spend three weeks learning to drive these rigs here at the facility and out on a few highways, then you'll head back to the DMV for your road test. Any guesses what comes next?"

"Yeah," said a man at the next table. "I get the hell out of Dodge."

Applause and a few whistles met this statement, but Frank shook his head. "Not so quick. After you earn your CDL, you'll be going cross-country with a driver trainer in one of our double sleepers. That's how we make sure all of you meet the standards of a King of the Road trucker." He leaned forward with his hands on the table and looked around the room. "Any questions?"

Dee had questions. Lots of questions. Was she really going to have to spend weeks in a truck cab with a strange man? Sleeping near him? Was there any chance they had a female trainer? She swallowed her panic. No need to get ahead of herself. She'd cross that bridge, no—she'd *drive* across that bridge when she got to it. She smiled at her little joke.

"You have a question, ma'am?" Frank regarded her with an expression she couldn't read. She gave a quick shake of her head.

"All right, then. You all must be a smart bunch."

Frank headed toward the door, and the class began scraping chairs back and gathering their things. Dee grabbed her purse and packet and trailed after him. Another question had occurred to her. One she wasn't too embarrassed to ask.

"Excuse me? Frank . . . er . . . Mr. Allenwood?"

He stopped next to the break table and turned to her. "Frank'll do."

"Okay, Frank. So, I'm really excited about the program, but I have a vacation scheduled in March. Will I be able to take a week, unpaid of course, that soon after starting the job?"

"Pretty confident, are you?"

Dee felt another blush creeping up her neck. "Well . . . I mean if. *If* I make it through."

Frank poured himself a cup of coffee and shrugged. "If you manage to stick with us, sure. Take your vacation."

"Okay, thanks. I'm looking forward to it."

Frank raised his eyebrows.

"The training, I mean. I'm looking forward to the training. Not, you know, the vacation. Although I'm looking forward to that too, of course." Oh my God, why was she rambling like this? "So, I'll just get going now. Thank you."

She turned on her heel and began speed-walking toward the door.

"Psst." The woman who'd given her the thumbs-up on her way in motioned again, waving Dee over to her desk. "Don't pay any attention to Mr. Grumpy there," she said, in a loud voice directed at Frank. "It's about time this outfit got some female drivers."

Calling the boss names seemed like a bad way to start off, but she also didn't want to alienate this woman who was being so friendly toward her. She gave her a half smile. "Okay, thanks."

"I'm Angie, 'the wife,' as he likes to call me." She made air quotes. *Ah.* That's why she could get away with calling him Mr. Grumpy. Angie had a matter-of-fact look about her—a short sensible haircut, no makeup, and a gray polyester pant-suit. She gestured around the room with her arm. "Look at this place. Besides me and Vicky over there, it's nothing but men. I'm sick of this patriarchy shit."

"Patriarchy?" Dee repeated, glancing toward the door. Wife or not, this didn't seem like a particularly good conversation to be having in a room full of men she was hoping to work with.

"Yeah. That's what my daughter-in-law calls it. The idea that only men should do certain jobs and get paid more and run the dang world . . . Oh, don't get me started. Anyway, I rode with Frank lots of times after our kids were grown and there's nothing about that job you or I couldn't do." She pulled a business card out of a container on her desk. "Here, this is my direct number. Just call me if you have any questions."

"Thanks, Angie. I really appreciate it." The boss's wife was in her corner. That had to count for something.

SIX

ONCE HOME, DEE MADE A POT OF COFFEE AND SAT down at the kitchen counter with her training materials. She flipped open one of the practice tests and read over some of the questions: *How does "bleeding tar" affect the road surface and driving conditions? How many red reflective triangles should you carry? When cargo can shift, how many tie-downs should it have?*

Everything seemed straightforward enough.

She slid the papers back and picked up her phone. She had plenty of time to study. Right now, she needed to schedule a few distractions for the upcoming holidays. First, she called Katie to see if she wanted to plan a trip over Thanksgiving or Christmas. Jancee had suggested the idea when Dee griped to her about spending Thanksgiving with Marian's family.

After a few minutes chatting about Katie's course load, which she insisted was going to kill her, Dee proposed her plan. "So, what do you think? We could do a cruise or maybe fly to an island."

"Huh," Katie said.

"Or we could do something else, maybe go skiing? We could find one of those picturesque lodges out in Colorado . . . of course I don't ski, but you could bring a friend and I'd just hang out by the fireplace and read all day." Dee's right eyelid began to twitch. This was not the response she'd been expecting. "I just thought it might be nice to do something different this year."

"Well, yeah. I mean, we have to, right?"

"We can do whatever you want. If you want to come home and catch up with all your high school friends, that's perfectly fine. But do you mind if it's just the two of us? I don't feel up to spending the day with Aunt Marian and the rest of the family, but I can make us a little turkey and—"

Katie cut her off. "No, I didn't mean I wanted to come home. It's just that, well, Dad already asked me about going to his girlfriend's condo in Florida for Thanksgiving."

"Oh." Dee gripped the edge of the counter as if she might literally fall out of the chair. Blindsided again.

"But there's no way I'm spending time with her, so I told him I had other plans, and then I didn't want to lie so I went ahead and did it, made some plans, that is." Katie sighed. "Please don't be upset, Mom. I just thought it would be good to be around other people. I mean, I'd like to be with you, but I don't want Dad mad at me either, so—"

"No, that's all right. I understand. We all need to make some adjustments this year, I guess." Except for Dan, going off with his trophy girlfriend.

"But how about if we go away for Christmas?" Katie said. "A cruise or an island, whatever. That would be fun. You can give me a tan for a Christmas present."

"So, where are you going for Thanksgiving?" Dee did her best to carry on a normal conversation.

"New York. I think somewhere on Long Island. Remember Cal? He helped us carry the mattress up when I moved in. He lives next door. Anyway, I'm going to his house. They have a farm, and they have, like, a ton of people that come for dinner out in this old barn. He showed me pictures from last year, and it's really beautiful."

"Well, that does sound like fun." Dee tried for a cheerful lilt, but it sounded hollow. She wanted to get off the phone. She didn't even have the energy to pump Katie for information about this new boyfriend, if that's what he was.

"I'm sorry, Mom," Katie said. "I know I'm being selfish here, but I just can't deal with everything right now."

"It's okay, honey. I want you to go and have fun. And take pictures. I'd love to see what Thanksgiving in a barn looks like."

"Why don't you see what Aunt Jancee has planned. Hanging out with her is always a good time, right?"

"Sure." Dee nodded as if Katie were standing in front of her and would be convinced of her positivity. "Sure, that's a great idea."

She ended the call with Katie and called Jancee, who, of course, had some fabulous plan to spend the holiday in New York City with the new man in her life. The potential for heartbreak never seemed to dull her friend's interest in romantic relationships. She was the queen of living in the moment.

"So, did Katie love the idea of the cruise?"

"Oh, yeah. She's thrilled!" Dee couldn't bring herself to tell Jancee the truth. She might insist that Dee join her in New York. Or not. And while the thought of being the third wheel was depressing, the alternative was worse. She didn't want to risk finding out how truly unlovable and friendless she'd become.

Dee set the phone down and slumped over the counter. Thanksgiving Day spent with Marian and Allen loomed in her future. In addition to her other quirks, Marian had always been oddly stingy when she entertained, carefully meting out each individual portion to her guests. Good luck getting second helpings of anything you happened to enjoy. Almost every time they'd eaten there, Dan had come home and fixed himself a sandwich. "I can't understand why your sister has us over for dinner and then refuses to feed us," he'd say.

Time to focus on something positive: planning a Christmas cruise with Katie. Dee retrieved her laptop from the office and began searching cruise lines for availability, but the vast number of options and itineraries was overwhelming. She decided to make it easy on herself and call the travel agent Dan used for conferences.

"Hi there, stranger!" The woman greeted Dee warmly. "So, you and Dr. Levari are planning a little holiday getaway?"

"Hi, Beth. Actually, it's just Katie and me this time. Dan will be on call for the practice for the holiday, so . . ." Dee decided not to embellish her lie any further.

"Oh, that's too bad," the agent said. "But what a stand-up guy your husband is sending you two off to have fun!"

Dee rolled her eyes. "Yep. He's really something."

Twenty minutes later, Dee and Katie were booked for a week in the Caribbean on Princess Cruises' newest ship. Against Beth's advice, she made sure to once again book non-refundable rates. She felt a moment of guilt at the amount of money her multiple vacations were costing, but she shook it off. Soon enough, she'd have to figure out how to live on a truck driver's salary and whatever the courts decided she was entitled to after she and Dan divorced. If they divorced.

Dee filled her time by studying for the commercial driver's license (CDL) permit and watching YouTube videos posted by truckers. Thanks to people with lots of time on their hands and evidently no concerns about privacy, Dee became quite familiar with the interiors of sleeper cabs. She was happy to see that most of them contained microwave ovens and mini refrigerators. Some featured disheveled bunks and overflowing trash bins, while others had coordinated bedding and neatly folded clothes tucked into organized cubbies.

One trucker went on and on about the relative merits of various air fresheners to impart a homey atmosphere in his home away from home. Others complained about big-box stores that made them wait until the following morning to drop late deliveries and excessive downtime waiting for their next loads.

Then there was the raspy-voiced woman with her dog, Karma, who claimed that becoming a trucker helped her leave an abusive relationship and basically saved her life. She'd posted a series of videos with advice for women who might want to follow in her footsteps. Dee watched with a notebook in her lap, jotting down tips.

But the best videos, by far, were uploaded by someone calling himself Long Strange Trip. His roadside panoramas from a truck's cab were shot with evident cinematographic skill and narrated with his mellow voice. Watching his montages of rolling hills, fields of wildflowers, snaking rivers, sunsets, and iconic Americana backed by Grateful Dead tunes made her eager to get on the road herself.

The night before the test, Dee made a meal she thought of as brain food—wild salmon with a side of sautéed mushrooms and quinoa. Then she ran to the store for gum. Somewhere, she'd read a study that chewing gum before taking an exam dramatically improved test scores. With the attitude that it couldn't hurt and might help, she went through a pack of Wrigley's spearmint on the way to the Department of Motor Vehicles.

The actual exam was anticlimactic. Sitting at one of the computer monitors arrayed against the wall, she methodically worked her way through one question after another and two hours later, she had the permit in her hand. She stood for a moment, staring at the flimsy card. It didn't look like much, but maybe, despite appearances, she was holding a *Charlie and the Chocolate Factory* golden ticket that would turn her life from dull and depressing to exciting and adventurous. She tucked the card in her wallet with a smile.

Heading out the door, she nearly collided with a man standing outside. He looked familiar, but it took her a few seconds to place him.

"Oh, hey! I remember you from King of the Road! Are you here to take the test? It really wasn't that bad." Her relief at having passed made her abnormally gregarious. Too late, she remembered his face. He was the angry guy who'd come in late.

He scowled at her. "Yeah, I'm here to take the test, and if you passed, I sure as hell will."

"Right. Well, I guess I'll see you when we start training." Why did she feel compelled to continue being polite when he was so rude?

"Look, Miss Sunshine, I don't need any woman messing up another job for me. Just stay out of my way."

Dee stood mute as the door slammed behind him. His un-provoked verbal attack left her feeling physically assaulted. What if they ended up in the same training group? How could she spend three weeks in a truck with that jerk? All the way home she berated herself for not calling him out for being a creep.

She walked into the house still grumbling. "Leave me alone, you nasty, jerk-face creep." *Nasty jerk-face creep?* She needed to develop a tougher persona. She glared at herself in the foyer mirror.

"Fuck off, asshole."

"Mom?" Katie stepped out of the kitchen, holding a can of La Croix. She wore a loose Happy Valley T-shirt with ripped jeans, and her waist-length dark hair was piled on top of her head in a messy bun. The sight of her instantly righted Dee's world. "Is everything okay?"

"Yes! Everything is fine." Dee grabbed her daughter in a hug. "Especially now. What are you doing home?"

Katie shrugged and took a sip of her drink. "I thought I'd surprise you. I feel bad that I'm not going to be here next week for Thanksgiving. So, when Soph told me she was com-ing home this weekend, I caught a ride with her."

"I don't remember Soph." Dee had prided herself on re-membering all of Katie's friends during high school and wel-coming them into her house. She'd always had plenty of chips and soda on hand and made herself somewhat scarce so they would feel comfortable, treating them like small woodland creatures that might run off if they noticed her. She'd enjoyed the hubbub, happily putting up with extra loads of dishes and crumbs all over the floor because if Katie was under her roof, Dee knew she was safe.

"She was a year ahead of me in high school, but we have a stats class together and she said she was coming home for her dad's birthday. Who were you yelling at when you came in?"

Dee grimaced. "Nobody. I was thinking of things I should have said to this jerky guy at the DMV."

Katie raised her eyebrows. "Isn't everybody at the DMV a jerk?"

"Yeah, I guess so." Dee didn't feel like going into detail about what had happened, so she let Katie think it was just the usual aggravation of dealing with a government agency. She walked into the kitchen and opened the refrigerator. A bag of lettuce, some eggs, assorted cheeses, and random condiments greeted her. Nothing that sounded appealing for dinner. "I would have gone to the store if I'd known you were coming home. How about if we go to Cucina Rosa tonight and celebrate me getting my permit?"

"Oh my God, yes! I've been dreaming about their gnocchi with vodka sauce. But why'd you need a new permit? You've been driving forever."

"It's a commercial permit. For trucking school. I need the permit before I can start training."

"Wait. You were serious about that?"

Dee nodded. She had mentioned her plans to Katie at least weekly. Did no one listen to her when she spoke?

"I thought you were just, I don't know, brainstorming."

"Nope."

"My mama, the trucker." Katie grinned at her mother. "I love it."

"It's the new me." Dee gave a half-hearted jazz-hands salute.

OVER DINNER, KATIE CAUGHT DEE UP ON ALL HER news from school. Even though they spoke on the phone nearly every day, the calls were usually just a quick check-in. But the relaxed surroundings of their favorite restaurant's back dining room encouraged deeper conversations.

Cucina Rosa had a split personality of sorts. The front room was a bright and noisy pizza joint, but through the back door and across a private garden courtyard stood a separate building that housed what Dee thought of as the winter dining room—a two-room dimly lit space with a crackling fireplace, leather banquet seating, and vintage Italian movies playing on the television above the bar.

"I can't eat another bite." Katie set her knife and fork on her dish and looked up at the movie playing silently across the room. "Is that the Trevi Fountain?"

Dee followed her daughter's gaze to the television.

"I think it is. That's *Three Coins in the Fountain*. They all make wishes after tossing coins in it, and I think one of the women ends up staying in Rome and one marries a prince or something."

"Thanks for the synopsis," Katie said dryly. Then she rearranged her knife and fork. "Is that how you're supposed to put them to show you're done eating?"

"No idea. I don't think anybody knows that anymore, including our waiter."

"So, anyway." Katie paused and took a sip of water. "I might apply for study abroad next spring semester. What do you think about that?"

Dee's mind began to race. So many things could happen in a foreign country. Katie took Spanish in high school, but she certainly couldn't be considered fluent. What if she ended up in a hospital and couldn't communicate?

"Where were you thinking of going?" Dee congratulated herself for sounding completely unfazed by the idea.

"I haven't really made up my mind, but Cal suggested Italy. Apparently, there are some decent engineering classes. And it would be so cool to see things like the Parthenon and the Colosseum and, well, just a lot of ancient feats of construction. And the Trevi Fountain." She inclined her head toward the television.

Italy. Wasn't that where a college student was murdered by her study-abroad roommate? She managed to keep the thought to herself. "That does sound interesting."

"You don't want me to go?"

"What? I didn't say that."

"No. But you don't sound happy about it."

Their server's well-timed stop to clear the plates and in-quire whether they wanted dessert gave Dee a chance to rein in her anxiety. She didn't want Katie making the same mis-takes she'd made, always taking the easy route, never venturing too far from what was familiar and safe. "We'll take two of the pistachio chocolate cannoli and one tiramisu, please."

"Mom! I seriously cannot eat another bite."

"Neither can I right now, but later tonight I'm going to want something sweet." She handed the dessert menu to the waiter. "Can you make them to go, please?"

Dee folded her hands on the table. "Okay, back to study abroad. You're right, my knee-jerk reaction is to try to talk you out of it because I would worry about you being so far away, but that's not fair. And trying to avoid every type of risk is no way to live your life. So, I think you should go."

"Well, I need to apply. I'm not even sure I'd get accepted."

"Of course you'll get accepted. You're doing so well in all your classes. Any program would be lucky to have you."

"Not that you're biased or anything." Katie threw an indulgent smile her way, then looked down at the phone in her lap and began rapidly texting someone. Seconds later, she was done. The speed with which Katie and her peers communicated via a text fascinated Dee. "Cal says his mom is going to go over with him to help him get settled the first week or so. Do you think you could do that? I mean, if I end up going?"

Dee had traveled to Europe exactly once in her life, with her high school French club. She had vague memories of traipsing through damp castles and riding an elevator up the Eiffel Tower. She was due for another trip. One without the awkward teenage cliques, boring tours, and a bus driver who made inappropriate overtures whenever the chaperone was out of sight.

"I'd love to."

"Cool. I'll show you the program I like on my laptop when we get home."

They gathered up their purses and dessert containers and headed for the door. Dee glanced up at the television, which now showed a small convertible racing along a cliffside roadway—maybe the Amalfi Coast? She didn't recognize the movie. If Katie studied in Italy, maybe she really would visit. Maybe she'd even drive along that terrifying roadway. She refused to let fear run her life anymore. She could handle anything!

"Dad?"

Dee followed Katie's gaze to a couple seated near the fireplace. Dan stood and began to walk their way, while the blonde next to him turned her back and spoke into her phone.

Dee's stomach dropped. What was he doing here?

"Hi, sweetheart." Dan took Katie's hand and gave her a peck on the cheek, then leaned toward Dee as if to do the same.

She quickly sidestepped him and waved like a beauty pageant contestant. *Argh*. How were you supposed to act when you ran into your almost-ex and his new girlfriend?

"What are you two doing here? Aren't you in the middle of finals?"

"Not on the weekend." Katie spoke in a clipped tone. Apparently, she hadn't yet forgiven him.

Dee felt a frisson of satisfaction at the thought and then immediately felt guilty. She shouldn't want Katie to have a screwed-up relationship with her father. Even if it was all his fault. She noticed he'd gained a few pounds. Maybe the girlfriend refused to stick to his strict carbohydrate rules. She slid her eyes across the room, but all she could see was the back of the woman's head.

"Oh. Well, good. Still on track for dean's list?"

Katie shrugged. "I guess."

Dan fiddled with his watchband, then cleared his throat.

"So, when would you like to get together with me and—" He paused and seemed to reconsider his words. "I know you're busy for Thanksgiving, but when would you like to celebrate the holidays? You never answered my texts about that."

Katie lifted her shoulder in another dismissive shrug. "Mom and I are going on a cruise at Christmas, so I guess after we get back."

"Cruise?" He smiled, but it didn't reach his eyes. "I don't seem to recall us discussing this, Dee."

"Beth didn't mention it to you? She made all the arrangements for me."

"You know damn well Beth didn't mention it!" Dan's voice reverberated in the normally quiet room. Remembering himself, he spoke in a furious whisper. "Just because we're separated doesn't mean our money rules don't apply. We discuss big purchases, remember?"

"Does that rule apply to your new Mercedes? Because I don't remember discussing that."

He looked at her incredulously. "It's my money!"

He still knew how to get to her. She'd always felt like the lesser half of their partnership, despite his platitudes about how taking care of Katie and their home was worth the financial sacrifice. It was just her sacrifice.

Katie was having none of it. "God, Dad, you're being so rude. Mom can pay you back for the stupid cruise. We're here celebrating her new job. Thanks for ruining it." She spun on her heel and flounced out the door.

A pained expression crossed Dan's face.

"What job?" he said.

What job? What job, indeed. Reimbursing him would probably take half her yearly salary. And that was *if* she even made it through training and passed all the tests.

"I have something in the works, something I might do." She turned to leave. "It really doesn't concern you."

"I hope it pays well," he said under his breath.

She heard his parting shot as she walked out the door and had to bite her lip to keep from laughing hysterically. She was going to be in debt for the rest of her life.

chapter

SEVEN

THE FIRST DAY OF TRAINING, DEE LEFT HER HOUSE half an hour earlier than necessary so the possibility of being late wouldn't add to her stress level. A sign on the office door directed trainees to the adjacent garage. Taking a deep breath, Dee squared her shoulders and entered a cavernous space containing a few truck cabs, stacks of tires and other truck parts, and pneumatic tools hanging from cables overhead. The air had an unfamiliar odor, maybe tool grease and testosterone. After a moment's hesitation, she walked over to the small group of men milling around one of the semi cabs.

The young man she'd met at orientation flashed a smile at her. "Dee, right?"

"Yes." Dee smiled back, touched that he remembered her. "And you're Rico?"

He nodded. The first day of her maybe-new-career and already she was on time and remembering names. Dee 2.0 was off to a promising start.

Rico inclined his head toward the open door. "Frank just took the other guys across the lot."

Dee looked at the two remaining men in their group, and her stomach dropped. Next to one of Rico's buddies stood the skinhead she'd run into at the DMV. Just as she feared, she was going to be stuck training with this creep. He didn't look up from his phone, seemingly mesmerized by the photos he was scrolling through. *Wait.* Were those naked women? Seriously? The guy was looking at porn.

Frank entered the building and the pervert put the phone in his pocket.

"Good morning, Ms. Levari. Glad to see you've joined us," Frank said.

Dee's eyes flew to her watch. She'd left so early. How could she have gotten here late? Did she misread the start time?

"I'm sorry. I thought class began at eight."

Frank nodded. "Yeah, it does. I just want to make sure you feel welcome. The wife's real excited about us having a woman joining the team."

The porn watcher snorted.

"Angie? Yes, she was, um, very encouraging when I came in for orientation," Dee said.

Taking the cigar out of his mouth, Frank looked her up and down. "How tall are you?"

Shit. She should have asked about a height requirement. Had she come this far for nothing? "I'm five one."

Frank nodded. "We might have to get a pedal extender in the truck for you."

"Oh. Okay. Thank you," Dee said. She heard a muttered curse.

"You got a problem with that, Jensen?" Frank said. "'Cause fact of the matter is you might need the same."

Dee glanced over at the porn guy, Jensen apparently, who responded to Frank with a quick shake of his head. His face had gone nearly purple.

"All right, then." Frank shoved the cigar back in his mouth. "Let's get you all started learning your way around the truck. First, we're going to get a look under the hood here." He reached in and pulled a lever in the cab and then walked around to the front and pulled down the full front end of the truck.

Within an hour Dee had the worst headache in her memory. The sheer number of things she needed to know about trucks overwhelmed her, but it was compounded by the malevolent presence of Jensen. She could feel the hatred rolling off him like a dark fog. From their one interaction at the DMV, it was clear he had issues with women, but why would he have anything against her personally? She hadn't done anything to antagonize him.

She tried telling herself she was imagining things. He was a miserable guy, and maybe his anger was directed at everyone in the group. She had to stop being so sensitive.

They had moved into the classroom to watch a video about backing into loading docks. Dee, Rico, and his friend Josh were at one table, and Jensen sat by himself behind them. When the video concluded, Frank turned up the lights and asked if there were any questions.

Dee half raised her hand and then thought better of it. This wasn't elementary school. "Will there be people to help direct us back into the dock?"

Behind her, she heard Jensen mumble, "Stupid bitch," under his breath.

"Sometimes yes, sometimes no. But in any case, you need to get out and look yourself. If some dumbass screws up and sends you into the wall, he's not going to have to pay for it, you will." Frank took a marker and scrawled across the white-board: *G. O. A. L.* "You'll notice this word on decals on all our trucks' side mirrors. Stands for *Get out and look.* That's the only way to be sure you've got a clear path."

Dee nodded, but she hadn't been focusing on his answer. She'd been blinking back angry tears and fighting the urge to get up and leave. Did no one else hear him? Or maybe they heard and felt the same way. He was just the only one awful enough to voice it.

ON THE AFTERNOON OF THE SECOND DAY, WHEN they were outside learning how to inspect a truck before driving it, Dee bent under the wheel well to take a closer look at a mud flap connection Frank was describing. She didn't hear what Jensen said, but the next thing she knew, he was sitting on the ground holding a bloody lip, with Rico standing over him.

"I told you to lay off her," he said. Josh stood to the side with his fists clenched, clearly ready to jump in if his friend needed help.

Jensen scrambled to his feet and jabbed a finger toward Rico. "Listen, punk, you're lucky I don't call the cops and have you charged with assault." He turned toward Frank. "Are you going to let him get away with that?"

Frank scratched the back of his head. "Well, you know, I was busy under the truck here and missed the whole thing. You better go get some ice on that lip."

Jensen shot a venomous look at Dee and then stalked off toward the office.

There were a few moments of charged silence. Rico stared at his feet and rubbed his knuckles. "I, uh, I'm sorry for losing it like that," he said.

"Yeah, well, generally speaking we try to discourage violence around here." Frank cleared his throat. "But truth be told, I was about ready to pop him myself." He looked at his watch. "That's enough for today. Go home and cool off. Get in here tomorrow ready to do the inspections individually."

Dee made a beeline for her car. She didn't know how to feel. Rico and Frank coming to her defense like that had both surprised and gratified her. They liked her. Or, at least, they didn't loathe her like Jensen. But how many more men might she run into on the road who would be enraged at the sight of her? Maybe there was a reason there weren't more women truckers. Angie might think dismantling the patriarchy was a great idea, but Dee was no trailblazer.

The following morning, she reported to the training center with knots in her stomach. Frank was already outside by the truck, chewing on his ever-present cigar.

"Ms. Levari!" he called. "You're up first."

Dee glanced toward the training center entrance. Rico and his friend Josh stood talking by the overhead door, but there was no sign of Jensen.

"Here's the situation," Frank said. "Hypothetically, you're about to leave the distribution center with a delivery. I want you to take a walk around this rig and tell me everything you're checking before you get on the road."

She started at the cab, trying to recall all the checkpoints. She looked under the hood, inspected the belts for wear, glanced at the cars in the lot, then moved on to make sure the windows were operable. Now was she supposed to check the mirrors or the position lights? After another nervous look around to see if Jensen had arrived, she gave up on trying to do things in order and began calling them out randomly.

"Whoa there, speed demon," Frank said. "Everything you need to look at is on this here rig, not over there in the parking lot. You missed three key areas already." He tapped his pen against three points on the clipboard.

Dee bit her lip. "I'm sorry. What happened yesterday threw me off."

"Yeah, well . . ." Frank cleared his throat. "If you're going to be driving a truck, you're going to have to man up. There's no room in this profession for sissies."

Her eyes welled up with tears. He had called her a sissy, and now she was going to break down and cry and prove him right. She turned her head and wiped at her eyes with the sleeve of her jacket.

"There's also no room for assholes, and that's what that Jensen fellow was. He's not coming back." He paused to hitch up his pants. "So how 'bout you start over with this inspection and keep your mind on the job."

"He quit?"

"More or less." Frank wouldn't meet her eyes. "Come on now and get this inspection done. I don't want to be standing out here in the cold all the damn day."

"Right. So, I'll just start at the beginning?"

Frank nodded. "That's usually the best place to start."

Dee straightened her jacket and walked back to the front of the truck. Her second pass at the inspection went smoothly.

"Good job, Ms. Levari," Frank said. "Keep this up when we get behind the wheel, and you're going to make a real fine trucker."

Dee crossed her arms. "As long as I don't run into any more like Jensen."

"Ah, there's jerks everywhere. You just got to toughen up. Remember: 'What doesn't kill us makes us stronger.'"

Somehow, Dee had never found that phrase helpful. "Maybe it just makes us bitter and angry."

Frank shrugged. "Same thing, right?"

After Josh and Rico took their turns completing the pre-trip inspection, Frank led them to the classroom to watch a video detailing the reasons for each part of the inspection and what could go wrong if they failed to notice a problem. Dee had no trouble embellishing each of the cautionary tales: If she neglected to check the air brakes, not only would she fail to stop but it would happen on a mountain and send her over a cliff. If she missed a problem with the coupler? She wouldn't just drive off without her trailer, it would disconnect and careen into a school bus full of children. Neglect a problem with the driving lights? An innocent motorist would drive into the back of her darkened vehicle. Even as she entertained these thoughts, she knew she was being ridiculous. Why did her mind go immediately to the worst-case scenario?

Frank pointed the remote at the screen and turned it off. "Okay, people, now that we know the truck is road-safe, we're going to get each of you behind the wheel for a bit. If you need to use the john, do it now."

As the group of them walked toward the truck, Rico broke off and ran to the driver's side. Frank ambled up, chewing his cigar. "I guess you're up, eh, Rico? Nice to see a little enthusiasm on the job."

"I'll go next," Josh said, as he and Dee climbed into the back.

Frank heaved himself up into the passenger seat. "This ain't a democracy, Josh. Ms. Levari is gonna drive next. She scored highest on the written test. By rights, she should be first, but I don't feel like arguing with Johnny-on-the-spot here."

The relief she felt at not having to go first almost made her ignore being called Ms. Levari. Why was everyone else on a first-name basis? It made her feel so old.

"Please, just call me Dee."

Frank turned in his seat and regarded her with a half smile. "Okay, *Dee*, pay attention to what I tell Rico here, so I don't have to repeat myself like a dang parrot." He turned back and slapped his hand on the dashboard. "First off, this here's a 378 Peterbilt tri-axle heavy hauler. Under the hood, we got a big cat—six and a quarter. She's got small stacks for such a big engine, but she runs like a champ. Okay, Rico, fire it up. And buckle your damn seat belt."

The engine growled to life, and Dee leaned forward to see better.

"You got eighteen speeds in this here rig. I'll do a little bit of explanation before we head out. You're probably thinking, *There's eighteen gears in there? How in the world can you keep track of everything?* It's really not as hard as you think. It's like shootin' pool, easy to understand but hard to get good at." He glanced over at Rico. "Know what I mean?"

Rico shrugged. "Sure."

"I know what you mean," Josh volunteered. "Like playing *Call of Duty*. Like, it's easy to get off a shot, but not to get a kill."

With his eyebrows knit together, Frank swiveled around to stare at Josh.

Josh tucked a blond dreadlock behind his ear and began bouncing his knee under the scrutiny. "It's a video game."

Dee suspected Frank was as in the dark about *Call of Duty* as she was about the inner workings of a Peterbilt engine.

"Humph." The seat springs squeaked as he turned back. "Anyway, what we have here is an eighteen-speed Eaton Fuller transmission. That's the biggest transmission they make now. There's eighteen, fifteen, thirteen, a ten-speed, and a nine-speed. I think they used to make an eight and a seven, but that was before my time." Frank paused to clear his throat. "This is basically a nine-speed, just doubled. Now let me explain that: You have your typical H shift pattern, just like in a Ford Mustang. Push in the clutch, and show us how you'd shift a five-speed transmission, Rico."

Rico shifted as Frank spoke. "Reverse, first, second, third, fourth, and fifth. Make sense? That's low range. Now on here, on the front of the gear shift, we got a switch." He pointed to the front of the stick shift. "This here's a high-load selector switch . . ." Frank droned on. Attempting to focus, Dee bit the inside of her lip and concentrated on watching Rico follow Frank's instructions. She hoped she was more of a visual learner, because everything he said sounded like gibberish.

After another ten minutes of instruction Dee couldn't follow, Frank finally wrapped it up. "Let's try that out on the road, because it won't go in very smooth unless you're rolling. Okay, Rico. Let's see what you got."

Rico rolled his shoulders and cracked his neck, then put the truck in gear and drove around the lot, staying between the traffic cones and shifting with ease. Frank nodded his approval. "Okay, hotshot. Let's take it out on the highway and see how you do."

Rico merged into the heavy morning traffic on the interstate and drove as if he'd been doing it for years. Frank sat in stunned silence for a while and then pointed to the upcoming exit.

"Pull off here and take her in for a fill-up."

As soon as the rig rolled to a stop in front of the pumps, the interrogation started.

"Where'd you learn to drive like that?"

"I used to ride with my uncle, and he showed me a few things."

"He let you drive without a license?" Frank's voice bounced around the confines of the cab.

Rico shook his head vigorously. "No. I mean, not on real roads. Like on crappy farm roads in the middle of nowhere."

Frank chewed at his cigar. "He show you how to refuel?"

"Uh, no."

"Humph. Glad to know there's something I can teach you. Okay. We're all going to learn how to top off the tank, and then we'll head back to the shop and let Dee here take over driving."

They all piled out of the truck and stood looking at the diesel fuel pumps.

"You're all gonna be issued a fuel card before—" Frank stopped talking and stared as Rico pulled a pair of black latex gloves from his pocket and put them on.

"What the hell are you doing? You some kind of germophobe?"

"No. I just don't want to get my hands all grease-stained."

"That another tip from your uncle?"

Rico looked down at his gloved hands. "They're my girl's idea."

"Jesus." Frank closed his eyes and appeared to be praying for patience. With a heavy sigh, he finished showing them the refueling routine and had Rico drive them back to the lot for Dee's turn behind the wheel.

It quickly became apparent that Dee had no uncle in the trucking business. She didn't completely stall the engine, but her progress involved lots of grinding gears and jerky movements staying between the cones on the lot. There was no highway driving for her. Oddly, Frank seemed more comfortable with her typical newbie mistakes than he had been with Rico's skills. Maybe he liked being needed. She finished her shift behind the wheel and was relieved when Josh had as much trouble starting out as she had. Incompetence, like misery, loves company.

A chill wind blew dry leaves across the lot as they stood near the truck. Dee shivered and tucked her hands in the pockets of her fleece jacket. The part of autumn she loved was giving way to shorter days and icy temperatures. Frank squinted into the sun setting behind them. "Okay, folks, not bad for our first outing," he said. "On Monday, we're going to tackle backing up, so review your notes and watch the videos. Have a good Thanksgiving."

chapter

EIGHT

DEE DROVE HOME IN THE DARK, WISHING SHE COULD crawl right into bed. But first she had to make a pie to take to Marian's. She could have picked one up at the supermarket, but that would have been admitting defeat. In the rarely acknowledged but ever-present competition of sisterhood, Dee had always been the better cook. She couldn't walk into her sister's house with some generic store-bought pastry.

She opened the pantry and began pulling out cans and boxes that she hardly remembered putting in there. Finally, she found a can of pumpkin puree. It was a little dusty, but the expiration date checked out. Then she searched the freezer for the convenience packs of piecrust she usually had on hand. No luck. She was going to have to make it from scratch. Reaching behind her collection of muffin tins and baking pans, she retrieved the rolling pin and her mother's file box of recipes. She bit her lip as she ran her fingers across the banged-up metal lid with its once-trendy Harvest Gold design.

She could still remember her mother teaching her to make pancakes, holding the bowl while Dee stirred the eggs and milk into the flour. She'd felt so grown-up standing on the step stool, flipping the cakes on the griddle. She didn't realize that the cooking lesson was a goodbye. Her sister clued her in a few months after their mother died. Their dad had returned to work and left teenage Marian in charge of cooking. One night, after they'd been eating the same few meals over and over, Dee asked her to make meat loaf for dinner. "I don't know how to make it," she'd said. Dee continued to whine for meat loaf until Marian stopped stirring the pot on the stove and slammed the spoon on the counter. Campbell's tomato soup splattered like blood on the yellow Formica.

"I can only make what Mom taught me to make! She knew she was sick, Deirdre. She knew she was going to die, so she taught me to make five dinners, and that's all I can make!" Then she'd run from the room crying.

Dee studied the faded curlicued script of the piecrust recipe. Her mother had had such beautiful handwriting. She gazed off into the middle distance and tried to conjure up her mother's face but couldn't do it. The memory of her mother had faded even more dramatically than the recipe card.

The funeral, though, *that* she could remember as if it happened yesterday. The cloying scent of the lilies piled around the casket; her father slumped on a metal folding chair at the grave site, twisting his handkerchief in knots; Marian in the limousine, refusing to get out. And then there was her mother's sister, crushing Dee to her chest and sobbing about her being a poor motherless child. Aunt June had dementia now and could be forgiven for stating the obvious, but she could have used a filter that day.

Dee felt her throat closing and her eyes filling with tears. Everyone left her. Her mother and father by dying, her sister by shriveling into an unfeeling shell, her daughter by growing up, and Dan by turning into an asshole. She felt herself standing on the edge of a deep black grief. One that she might never be able to escape.

"No!" She screamed and swung her arm across all the baking supplies, sending measuring cups, bowls, flour, and the recipe box crashing to the floor. A cloud of flour filled the air. She would be finding remnants of the dust for months. But she didn't care. She knocked the paper towel holder into the sink and slammed the dishwasher closed. Then she stood panting, gripping the granite counter, looking for something else to destroy. Her eyes fell on the Tiffany vase. She grabbed it from the kitchen table and turned to smash it against the granite.

Just before she swung it down, her cell phone began ringing. Katie. Probably calling to say she'd made it to New York. Dee answered the phone, dropping the vase and chipping the bottom edge as she set it down.

"Hi, sweetie!" She tried with little success to control her breathing.

"Hi! We got to Cal's house," Katie said. "Why are you so out of breath?"

"Oh, um, I just ran up from the basement."

"Huh. Okay. Well, anyway, I was just calling to let you know I'm here. And I miss you."

"I miss you too."

"I can't wait for our cruise!"

"Me too."

By the end of the call, Dee's anger had dissipated. Her baby still loved her. She picked up the damaged vase and dropped it into the garbage. Then she took a deep breath, set her jaw, and mechanically cleaned up the mess she'd made.

New dents marred the surface of the old recipe box. While returning it to the pantry, a surprising thought occurred to Dee. Had her mother ever thrown it in a fit of anger? It didn't match the saintlike image in her memory, but in some twisted way the notion made her feel closer to a woman she could barely remember.

BEFORE THE SUN WAS UP THE NEXT MORNING, DEE slipped outside and put her car in the garage. Thanksgiving at Marian's was out. The thought of spending the day with her extended family filled her with dread instead of joy—and she was through doing things out of a sense of obligation. But she wanted Susan to believe she'd gone. If her neighbor looked over and saw the car in the driveway, she would not rest until she'd dragged Dee across the street to celebrate with her houseful of sons and daughters-in-law and grandchildren.

After lying to her sister about a stomach bug, she whipped up a tray of brownies—the extra-gooey ones with chocolate chips and walnuts. She ate them in front of the television with multiple glasses of milk, watching first the Macy's parade, then the Hallmark Channel's twenty-four-hour Christmas movie marathon. The blandly repetitive storylines used to irritate her, but today she craved predictable happy endings. Despite everything, she still believed they were possible. Gas fireplace on low, knit blanket on her lap, and a Christmas Cookie–scented jar candle burning beside her, Dee was drifting into a sugar-fueled slumber when her cell phone rang.

"Hey! You answered!" It sounded like Jancee had something stronger than milk with her dinner. "I wanted to call and wish you a happy Thanksgiving, but Richard said your phone wouldn't work on the ship—*see, I told you it would work*—but anyway, he was wrong and here you are. So, how is the cruise? Did they serve turkey and stuffing?"

Dee tried to come up with a convincing fib, but her mind was too fuzzy to do anything but tell the truth. "I didn't end up going on a cruise."

"What? Wait. So, where are you?"

"I just, um, had a quiet day at home. I made brownies."

"Oh, Dee," Jancee groaned. "Where's Katie?"

"She had plans with friends."

"You're there all by yourself? That is just not okay. I'm coming over there right now. *Richard, you need to go get the car.* Listen, honey, I am on my way. My best friend is not going to be sitting in a house all by herself on Thanksgiving, no way."

Dee heard a low voice protesting in the background. *Poor Richard.*

"Jancee, listen, I appreciate the offer, but technically it's not even Thanksgiving anymore. It's after midnight. So, you know, it's okay."

"Well, tomorrow then, or today, whatever. Richard will send a car for you in the morning—*won't you, Richard*—and you can come up here and spend the rest of the weekend. We'll go shopping. I'm not taking no for an answer."

Shopping in New York on Black Friday would be a blast with Jancee. But not with Jancee and Richard.

"What does Richard think of this plan?"

"Oh, he's all for it," Jancee said. "He has to go back to Philly for a meeting anyway."

"In that case, count me in," Dee said.

She ended the call and stared at her phone. Had she just agreed to leave for a weekend trip in less than nine hours? If she were the heroine of a Hallmark movie, this would lead to a meet-cute with some New York City bigwig who she would at first find obnoxious and then grow to love. She caught sight of herself in the foyer mirror as she headed to bed. Could a buttoned-up midlife suburban mom get the Hallmark treatment? She pulled the pins from her French twist and shook her hair out around her shoulders, imagining herself as a leading lady with sexy, tousled tresses. Her reflection didn't support the fantasy—a smear of chocolate on her chin, the imprint of the sofa pillow on her cheek, and a tangled cloud of hair revealed the truth. She was a mess. With a sigh, she dragged herself up the stairs. Bingeing on chocolate and rom-coms might have been a bad idea.

chapter

NINE

EARLY THE NEXT MORNING, DEE FOUND HERSELF IN the back of an Uber Lux Mercedes, her overnight bag stowed next to her. Scenery flew by as they cruised along Route 73 toward New York City, a straight shot across northern New Jersey from her little town on the Pennsylvania border. Farmland and rolling hills made up the bulk of it, which would probably surprise people whose only reference for the state was an old reality show about badly behaved young adults. She glanced at her driver. Somewhere in his thirties, she guessed, dark hair in a man-bun, reflective aviators, and a sharp dark suit. He didn't have much to say, which suited Dee just fine. She looked out the window at a formation of geese flying overhead.

Her cell phone pinged and she fished it out of her purse. Marian. She considered dropping it back unread. Knowing her sister, it was probably some passive-aggressive message meant to make her feel bad for not showing up with a pie. She sighed and opened the text.

Hope you're feeling better.

Dee stared at the message like it was a hieroglyph. Taken at face value, it seemed nice enough, but why a period? Why not an exclamation point or a smiley face? Her sister could simply be clueless about texting norms, but no. This was Marian. She probably suspected Dee of lying and was trying to make her feel guilty. "I don't feel guilty at all," she hissed.

"What's that, ma'am?" The driver cocked his head toward her.

"Oh, nothing," Dee said. "I was just, um, reading something."

"COME ON UP," JANCEE SAID WHEN DEE CALLED HER from the hotel lobby. "You can help me pick out an outfit."

Jancee opened the door and waved her into a suite filled with cream-colored furniture, marble floors, a fireplace, paneled doors that appeared to be bedrooms, a dining table, and a baby grand piano. It was larger than the entire first floor of Dee's house.

"Wow," Dee said. "How many people are living here?"

"Richard is into conspicuous consumption." She lifted her shoulders and glanced around the room. "Which works for me, actually."

"Of course it does."

Jancee linked her arm with Dee's and led her over to a pile of shoes in front of the sofa.

"What do you think, the ballet flats"—a small frown appeared in Jancee's eyebrows—"or these awesome boots?" A large grin replaced the frown.

"Well," Dee said, "I know I'm supposed to say the boots, which *are* awesome by the way, but how in the world will you walk around in them all day? I mean, the heel looks like it's three inches high."

"Four," Jancee said, "but they have a platform, so it's not so bad. And I don't plan to walk much, silly. We'll take a cab."

"In that case, you should definitely wear the boots."

Jancee put them on and smiled down at Dee. "I knew you'd agree with me."

"Now I just need a pair of stilts so I can look you in the eye."

"No. What you need is a great pair of boots. That should be our first order of business. A shoe store." Jancee strode across the room to grab her purse.

"So you can sit down," Dee said, under her breath.

"I heard that."

Everything with Jancee turned into an adventure. But shopping in New York City took it to a whole other level. She visited the city frequently on business and knew the best places to shop for everything. "Whatever you need, you can find it here. We can hit Uniqlo for basics, Tiffany's for jewelry, Bergdorf's and Saks for quality fashion, or if you want something a little edgier, we can head to Bleecker Street or Nolita and hit some boutiques." Jancee kept her eyes on the approaching cabs as she spoke, then stepped off the curb and hailed one. Pulling the door open, she turned to Dee, "Where do you want to go first?"

"I haven't the faintest idea. You choose."

"Let's start on Fifth Avenue—it's iconic."

They stopped first at a shoe store with an Italian name that made Dee hungry for a plate of pasta, but it was the boots in the window that drew her in. Turquoise and black, I-will-kick-your-ass cowboy boots. Dee could just picture herself hopping out of a truck cab wearing them, dust rising as her feet hit the ground.

Jancee, oddly enough, seemed pleased with the purchase. "You are really on the cutting edge, girlfriend."

Dee looked up from tucking the receipt in her purse. "Huh?"

"The western wear! That's going to be the next big thing. All the buzz is that fashion week in February will look like a rodeo!"

Dee couldn't detect any sarcasm, so she supposed it was true. "You know me. Always on trend."

Over lunch Jancee sprung a surprise on Dee. "Okay, now don't get mad, but while you were trying on the boots, I made some appointments for you."

Dee couldn't imagine where this was going. "Appointments? What kind of appointments?"

Jancee chewed at her lip. "Well, I don't know how to put this, but I think you could use a makeover. You know, new hairstyle, a rockin' new wardrobe, the whole nine yards. You need a new look to go with your new life."

"But I hate my new life."

"Exactly. If you had a different look, you might start to like it better. You know what they say, 'When you look good, you feel good.'"

"And I'm about to feel marvelous, is that it?"

Jancee nodded and beamed.

What did she have to lose? If she didn't like the new look, she'd simply change it back. "Whatever you want, Jancee. I'm putty in your hands."

Dee loved the place they'd stopped at for lunch. It reminded her of the grand Crystal Tea Room she used to go to in Wanamaker's with her mother when she was very young. Aside from the fact that Marian had been in school and she'd had her mother's undivided attention, she'd felt like a princess sitting in the room with its high ceilings, crystal chandeliers, and real linen napkins.

"Do you ever wish you were born in an earlier time?" Dee blotted her lips with the linen napkin currently in her lap.

Jancee shook her head. "Absolutely not. Quite the opposite, as a matter of fact. Why would you want to be older?"

"It's not that I want to be older, it's just that the past seems a lot more romantic."

"Like how far back are we talking?"

"I don't know. The forties I guess." Dee buttered a piece of roll. "Yeah, I think it would have been exciting to live in the forties. I mean, the clothes were amazing, everybody wore hats, and I love hats, and I like the music and the movies—"

"How about the fact that you would have been living through World War II and your husband or boyfriend would likely have been overseas getting shot?"

Dee pursed her lips. "So, it wouldn't have been perfect. It just seems like it was a simpler time. Everybody knew what they were supposed to be doing."

"Sure, they knew what they were supposed to be doing because gender roles were set in stone; they had no choice in the matter. It doesn't mean they were happy. And there was rampant discrimination. What if you were Black, or gay . . . I mean, my God, they sent Japanese Americans to prison camps."

"Fine. You win. I would have been miserable back then too." Reality was such a bitch.

"That's not what I was trying to say." Jancee paused. "Listen, life is going to get better for you, you'll see. Don't take this the wrong way, but Dan's leaving could be a good thing. You can make a whole new life for yourself."

"But I don't want a new life. I liked my old life." She was being obstinate. If Dee was honest with herself, she knew she'd been bored. She and Dan had been going through the motions for years. There'd been no spontaneity, no unexpected delight between them. They were like two oxen yoked together, pulling forward through life, not questioning where they were headed. Well, Dee hadn't questioned. Dan obviously had.

"You sure about that?"

Dee shrugged. "I guess things could have been better."

"And now they can be. You can do anything. You could move into the city, or take a trip around the world, or go back to school, or hike the Appalachian Trail."

Dee cut her off. "Do you even know me? Hike two thousand miles? Sleep in the woods? No thank you."

"Okay, fine. It was just an example. Who knows, maybe if you tried it, you'd discover you love it."

"That's sushi. You got me to try raw fish, and I like it. But camping in the dirt I won't like. Ever."

This conversation presented the perfect opportunity to talk about her plans to become a driver for King of the Road, but for some reason, Dee hesitated. Jancee might currently be trying to convince her to go get lost in the woods, but she had a feeling long-haul trucking wouldn't get the same level of support.

After lunch, Jancee hustled Dee down the street to Slay Salon. The sleek, ultramodern space with its profusion of stainless steel, glass, and mirrors seemed designed to show lesser mortals how hideous they looked next to the perfectly coifed and styled people who belonged there. Just walking through the door made Dee feel as if she were going to hyperventilate.

"I really don't think this is for me."

"Don't be absurd." Jancee took Dee's coat out of her hands and handed it to the receptionist. "Slay has the best stylists in the city. And when you're going for a new look, you need a good stylist."

"But I like my hair. I think it suits me."

Jancee steered Dee across the room to one of the full-length mirrors. "What do you see?"

"I see a middle-aged woman in jeans and a sweater, nice and normal."

"Okay, nice and normal, but why settle for just normal? You should be wearing clothes that show off your figure and makeup to play up your eyes. And your hair, well, to be perfectly frank, you are way overdue touching up the roots and your updo went out with Cindy McCain."

"Jeez, Jancee, don't hold back or anything." Dee leaned in toward her reflection and grimaced. Her hair did look terrible. And her bulky olive-green sweater washed out her skin and made her look twenty pounds heavier. "How did you manage to get me an appointment so quickly?"

"I have a standing appointment with Sergio every six weeks when I'm in the city, but I can just clean it up myself with some clippers when I get back to Philly." She raked her fingers through her pixie, making it stand up in spikes on top of her head. "I'm sacrificing for the greater good. You should go platinum blonde like me. Trust me, blondes do have more fun."

"Me as a blonde? I'd look ridiculous!"

"Come on, putty in my hands, remember?"

"Oh my God. Sure. Whatever."

By appointment's end, Dee's hair ended up quite a few shades lighter than platinum. Sergio raved over Dee's roots and talked her into bleaching her whole head to match. According to him, silver hair was now *a thing*.

While her hair processed, Jancee tweaked Dee's makeup and convinced the stylist to keep her turned away from the mirror.

"This is a little over-the-top, you have to admit," Dee said.

Jancee and the stylist exchanged a grin and spun her around.

Dee blinked at her reflection. She didn't look younger, but she didn't look any older. With the sleek precision cut and less makeup, she just looked better. Striking, even.

The stylist made Dee pose for a photo in his sample book and half the salon came by the chair to exclaim over the transformation.

"It's unbelievable," said one. "You don't look like the same woman who walked in the door."

"Beautiful," said another. *"Bellissima!"*

"So, what do you think?" Jancee stood off to the side grinning.

"I think I like it," Dee said. "Actually . . ." She paused to swing her head back and forth. "I think I might love it."

"Me too. I never thought I'd like gray hair, but you are rockin' it!"

After paying a bill that seemed more like a mortgage payment, they headed back uptown for another mysterious appointment.

A horrifying thought occurred to Dee as they sailed down the street in the cab. She reached over and gripped her friend by the arm. "You're not taking me to a plastic surgeon, are you?"

Jancee burst out laughing. "What kind of a crazy person would do that to a friend? If you must spoil the surprise, I'll tell you—I got you an appointment with a personal shopper in Saks. She's going to help you put together a whole new wardrobe."

Dee sipped at the champagne cocktail Jancee had smuggled into the dressing room and brushed her fingers across the items of clothing hanging on hooks. She took a closer look at some of the price tags and rolled her eyes. Then she took another sip of wine. The old adage was true—revenge literally tasted sweet. She'd been afraid Dan might freeze the credit card after he found out about the cruise, but so far he hadn't. She was going to take full advantage of his guilty conscience.

Jancee and the stylist walked back in with more armloads of clothing. What was her name? Griselda? Esmerelda? Something exotic. Dee really had to get better about remembering names.

"Here you go, my dear," Griselda/Esmerelda said, in what Dee guessed was an eastern European accent. Her thin frame towered over Dee and Jancee. Maybe she'd been a runway model. "We must get you out of those"—she turned to Jancee—"what did you call them?"

"Mom jeans," she said.

"Yes." The stylist forced a smile. "Mom jeans. They are not flattering. You need something with a fit that will boost you up."

She grabbed the waistband of Dee's jeans and tugged them up in the back. Dee had never been given a wedgie as a kid, but now she figured she knew what one felt like.

"You want the jeans to touch your buttocks, not slouch down like that." The woman let the waistband go and Dee's jeans once again sagged in the seat. Her underwear, however, remained jammed. Jancee snickered from her seat in the corner.

Dee shot her a dirty look.

"That's why you need to wear thongs," Jancee said.

"Oh sure, then I'd be used to feeling like something was stuck up my butt."

The stylist looked from one to the other of them with an imperious frown on her over-filled lips. "While you try these jeans, I will grab you some Hanky Panky thongs. Everyone loves them."

"No," Dee said. "That is where I draw the line. I'll go along with whatever you two want on the outside, but I am not changing my underwear."

"But, darling, surely you don't want to have visible panty lines?" The stylist sniffed and looked at Dee with arched eyebrows.

Dee crossed her arms. "Yes, actually I do. I do want panty lines. I don't care if people know I'm wearing underwear. As a matter of fact, I want to make it very clear that I am not running around without any panties. God!"

The stylist backed toward the dressing room door. "Of course, of course, Madam. Whatever you say. I apologize for the suggestion."

The dressing room door closed, and Jancee hooted with laughter.

By the end of the day, Dee had an entirely new wardrobe. Lots of jeans that made her butt look perky (according to Jancee and her accomplice), little fitted jackets and tops, and a seafoam-green tankini with a matching cover-up from the resort wear collection for her Christmas cruise. In the end, she'd even agreed to new lingerie. She didn't cave on the thong issue, but she did agree to the purchase of some supposed miracle underwear with a disappearing edge and a black lace bra and panty set destined to live forever in her bedroom dresser.

Darkness fell as their taxi crawled through the city streets. Dee gazed out the window at the crowds of people hurrying along the sidewalk and wondered where they were all going. Maybe to visit the tree at Rockefeller Center, or to catch a show on Broadway, or to see a lawyer about a divorce. She sighed.

"Long day, huh?" Jancee attempted to stretch her back in the confines of the cab.

"Mm-hmm." She'd had such a good time all day, but now her upbeat mood had evaporated. Maybe her blood sugar was low. It had been a long time since lunch.

"What should we do for dinner?"

"Would you mind if we just got room service?" Jancee said.

"Not at all. I know shopping with me is exhausting."

"No, that was fun. It's my feet. You might have been right about the boots."

Dee suppressed the urge to say, *I told you so.*

Abandoning Dee's shopping bags and Jancee's boots in the foyer of the hotel suite, the two old friends settled on the couch and studied the hotel menu as if it were a best-selling novel.

Ordering takeout at home always seemed lazy, but for some reason, fancy-hotel-style room service felt indulgent. Dee considered carefully. Did she want the beef Wellington with mashed potatoes on the side and a glass of cabernet? Or maybe the roast free-range chicken with an apricot glaze and wild rice. And dessert. Oh, dessert was easy. A triple-layer chocolate cake with raspberries. She couldn't wait for the cart to appear at the door with the pressed white linens and silver warmers covering all her choices.

During her days as a drug rep, she had sometimes been sent to conferences in New York. Her room service meals had been the highlight of every trip. Dee realized how sad that sounded. She hardly remembered the meetings themselves, except for the one where they took the Myers-Briggs personality test. That had been interesting. She still had her results filed away somewhere in the office. Every once in a while she'd get it out and study it, imagining all the things she might have done if she'd lived up to her potential.

An honest-to-goodness dining table in the suite made the room service meal even better. Instead of balancing plates on their laps while seated on a couch, they sat at the table and watched the lights of the city twinkling through floor-to-ceiling windows. When they finished their meals, they lingered at the table, picking at cake and drinking wine.

"I feel like I've been away for a week," Dee said.

Jancee smiled. "I think we packed enough shopping in for a week."

"At least. That was more shopping than I do in a year."

"Yeah. You were due."

They fell silent for a few minutes, and then Jancee began tapping her fingernails on the tabletop. "Listen, I don't want to bring you down from your retail high or anything, but have you given any thought to what you might want to do for a job?"

"Sort of." Dee shifted in her seat.

"Anything I can help with? I could give you some pointers on updating your résumé or maybe put you in touch with my neighbor. I think she has something to do with Human Resources at Johnson & Johnson. I mean, pharmaceutical sales aren't what they used to be, but you could probably get back into it with some connections. Or if you want to try something different, maybe Richard could help."

Dee set her wineglass down. "I've decided to give long-haul trucking a try."

Jancee rolled her eyes. "Come on, Dee. I'm serious."

Dee bit her lip and looked at her glass.

"A truck driver? Are you serious? You want to drive, like, one of those giant trucks on the interstate?" Jancee refilled her wineglass. "I think I need something stronger than cabernet."

"That's a little dramatic, don't you think? I didn't just confess to a murder. It's a job. A nontraditional job. I thought you, of all people, would be kind of excited about it."

"Excited? Why would I be excited? It sounds dangerous. And lonely. Won't you be lonely out on the road by yourself?"

"I'm already lonely with Katie away at school and Dan . . ." Dee exhaled. "I don't really mind being by myself that much. I think it could be a fresh start for me. Besides, you're the one who suggested a road trip when we met for lunch, remember? So I could find myself?"

"Since when do you listen to the stupid shit I say?" Jancee raked her fingers through her hair. "Besides, I was suggesting a week or two driving to vacation spots and staying in nice hotels, not this"—she waved her hand around vaguely—"whatever this is."

Dee crossed her arms and looked out over the city. She should have just kept her mouth shut like she'd planned. Wait until she finished training and had her license, and then let people know what she was doing. When it was too late for them to talk her out of it.

"Come on, Dee. Be reasonable. You're a homebody. You'd be miserable living in a truck. Where did you even come up with this?"

"On my way home from lunch last month. I had sort of a revelation."

"A revelation?"

Dee ignored the scoffing tone in Jancee's voice.

"I was just driving along, obsessing over what I'm going to do with my life, and the oddest thing happened. This big black truck with a King of the Road banner painted across it stopped dead in front of me, and I just missed crashing into it. And at that exact second, the song 'King of the Road' began playing on the radio."

Jancee held up her hand. "You lost me already. What the hell is 'King of the Road'?"

"It's a song my dad used to whistle all the time. You know it." Dee began singing. "'Trailers for sale or rent, rooms to let, fifty cents—'"

"Okay, okay. Got it. Though I have to say, if you heard that on the radio, I think you were traveling through some other dimension, like a *Twilight Zone* episode."

"Don't you see? It was a sign! King of the Road truck, 'King of the Road' song. At the same time. The truck even had an advertisement on the back door saying they were hiring new drivers. It felt like my father was sending me a message." Dee paused. When she said it aloud, it sounded crazy, even to her.

Jancee reached over and gave Dee's hand a squeeze. "I get it, girlfriend. I'm just worried you might not know what you're getting yourself into. Have you even spoken to anyone at a trucking company?"

"As a matter of fact"—Dee emptied the wine bottle between their two glasses—"I've already started training."

"Wait. You're in truck-driving school? Why didn't you tell me?"

Dee pursed her lips and directed an *Are you kidding me* look at her oldest friend.

Jancee shrugged. "Okay. I guess I could have reacted a little better, but it just seems so radical. Like, what even sounds appealing about driving a truck?"

"I don't know, all sorts of things." Up to this point, Dee had never clearly defined even to herself why she was drawn to the job, but now the reasons poured forth. "I enjoy driving, for one thing. When I was a drug rep, being on the road was my favorite part of the job. And I've always wanted to travel cross-country. I thought Dan and I might buy an RV and do that when he retired, but . . . well, this way I can get paid to do it driving an eighteen-wheeler. And mostly, just because I need to get away. Being cooped up in that house, I don't know, it's like I'm trapped with these memories, and it just makes me sad all the time."

Jancee sipped her wine and nodded. "I guess I get it, on some level, but I worry . . . Listen, just promise me if you don't like it, you won't be a hardhead and stick with it just to prove you're not a quitter."

"Me? Be stubborn about something?" Dee sat back in mock offense.

"Oh no, not you."

"But you love me anyway."

Jancee leaned out of her chair to give Dee a fierce and awkward hug. "Yes, I do. So please be careful."

chapter

TEN

RICO AND JOSH RODE IN THE BACK SEAT WHILE DEE drove. They were in their last week of training and Dee felt confident behind the wheel, but Frank was still micromanaging her every move. "Don't get too close to the car up in front. Keep an eye on your rearview mirrors in case some yahoo sneaks into your blind spot. Don't grip the wheel so tight." A steady stream of instruction poured from the man. Dee had the urge to borrow teenage Katie's attitude when she had her learner's permit and snap, *"I know what I'm doing, okay!? You don't have to tell me every freaking thing."*

"We're going to stop at this next rest stop and use the facilities, Silver Queen. Get ready to downshift as you pull off the exit."

Dee rolled her eyes. The constant driving tips were bad enough, but she had mixed feelings about the new nickname. Frank thought he was a regular comedian. When she'd walked into the dispatch office after her trip to New York, he did a double take and bellowed, "Will you look at this! Our Queen of the Road turned into a Silver Queen." Even Angie laughed, although she quickly recovered and told Frank he was being inappropriate. It didn't matter. The die was cast. Now everyone called her either Silver Queen, like something you'd pick up at a roadside stand, or Queenie.

Instead of wilting from embarrassment, which was her first reaction, Dee decided to lean into it. With her new fitted jackets, jeans, and cowboy boots, she looked like a cross between ladies-who-lunch and Rosie the Riveter. Her days of fading into the background were long gone. Even the way she carried herself had changed thanks to the boots: she found it impossible to walk in them without a bit of swagger.

She strode across the parking lot humming "Jingle Bells." The Christmas cruise was coming up, and she'd finished her allotted hours behind the wheel for the day. She couldn't pinpoint the reason for her good mood, but she didn't want to overthink it. Another reason to be happy—these service plazas on the Pennsylvania Turnpike. They were clean and well lit and almost always had a Starbucks on-site. She loved walking into Starbucks, or any coffee shop, just for the aroma. Most times that had to be enough because Frank rarely gave them enough break time to wait for the barista to make a drink. There was no line today, so she hurried over and ordered a nonfat latte with extra espresso.

Spotting Rico by the exit, she stopped to wait with him. He raised his eyebrows at her Venti coffee cup. "You sure you want to drink that?"

"Why wouldn't I?"

"Lotta caffeine. I thought you might be shook after all Frank's coaching on the road. Good thing he's on top of things or we'd probably be in a ditch back there somewhere, am I right?" He motioned to a spot on the giant wall map of the turnpike with his can of energy drink.

Dee gave him a death stare. "You're hilarious." She paused to take a sip of foam. "But seriously, why do you think he does that? I mean, obviously he doesn't need to tell you anything, but I think I drive at least as well as Josh and he barely says anything to him."

Rico shrugged and took a swig of his drink. "Looks like you know what you're doing to me. But Frank's old-school. Probably not used to having a woman behind the wheel."

"But that's not right. That's sexist, that's what it is."

"I hate to break it to you, but there's a lot of guys out here with"—he paused as Josh joined them—"screwed-up attitudes."

"Hey, taco head, are you driving next, or am I?" Josh said.

Rico smirked at Dee. "See what I mean? And this asshole is supposed to be my friend."

"Ah shit, Rico. You know I'm just messing with you." Josh smacked a pack of cigarettes against the heel of his hand and offered one to Rico. "Peace offering, man."

"No thanks. I quit, remember?"

"Yeah. Whatever." Josh lit up and headed for the door. "See you two losers back at the truck."

Dee watched him walk away, fighting back the urge to chase him down and lecture him about his casual racism and the dangers of tobacco use.

"I'm glad you quit smoking," she said to Rico.

"Yeah. So's my mom."

"So, you think I should just put up with Frank nagging at me whenever I'm driving?"

Rico lifted a shoulder. "You could say something, but it'd probably make things weird. Did you schedule your driver's test yet?"

Dee nodded. "I go Monday morning."

"Same. So just hang in a few more days and you'll be on the road with a trainer, seeing the country." A shadow crossed Rico's face. "If he's sus, though, say something."

Dee shook her head in confusion. "What?"

"If you get a bad vibe when you meet the dude who's training you, speak up. Frank's a pain in the ass, but he's got your back."

Dee's stomach lurched. She was a little bit terrified about these next steps, and Rico had just voiced her biggest fear—what if she had to spend three weeks cohabiting in a truck cab with a man who was demeaning or abusive? She couldn't think about that now. "How about you and Josh? Are you going to say something to him?"

Rico looked off toward the parking lot. "Nah. He's dating my cousin Selena now. She'll set him straight."

Frank came out of the men's room, and the three of them headed back to the truck.

"Yo, boss, are there any women trainers?"

"Why Rico? You think a female would go easy on you 'cause you're good-looking?" Frank shook his head. "You millennials sure work all the angles, don't you."

"Not for me. For Queenie here," Rico said.

"Oh." Frank grunted something unintelligible and chewed on his cigar.

"I don't need any special treatment, Frank. Don't worry about it." She made bug eyes at Rico and mouthed, *"Stop it!"*

That evening as she ate takeout pad thai on the couch, half watching a Hallmark movie, her cell phone rang with an unfamiliar number. Normally, she let those go to voicemail, but something made her answer this time. It was Frank's wife, Angie.

"Hey, Dee. Sorry to bother you at home, but I have a proposition and I wanted to see what you thought."

"You're not bothering me at all. What's up?"

"Okay, so Frank's been lining up trainers for this class after you all get your CDLs and, as you can imagine, there aren't many female leads available. If you want to wait on that, it may be two or three months before you get on the road."

"Oh." Dee snapped the lid on her leftovers. "What do you think I should do?"

"Well, I spoke to Frank about him doing it."

"Frank? Frank would co-drive with me?"

"You're comfortable with him, aren't you? I mean, I know he can be a little gruff, but he likes you. We both do. He'll make sure you know what you're doing."

"That would be—" Dee's voice broke, and she swallowed a sob. They liked her. "I would really appreciate that."

"Great. It's all settled then. You get your license and be ready to go out on the road January 2."

"Thanks so much, Angie. I can't tell you how much this means to me."

chapter

ELEVEN

CHRISTMAS EVE FOUND DEE AND KATIE STRETCHED out on deck chairs by one of the cruise ship's multiple pools. They'd come straight to the dock from the Fort Lauderdale airport and were one of the first groups to board. It seemed like a small miracle, leaving behind the steely-gray skies of Philadelphia and in a few short hours finding yourself blinded by the bright glare of a Florida afternoon.

Dee was heading into the new year focusing on the positive. She'd finished her training at King of the Road, and she'd earned her commercial driver's license. She hadn't hit a curb, or rolled through a stop sign, or forgotten to signal while changing lanes during the driving exam, all automatic failures. Had she ground the gears a few times while shifting and driven a bit too slowly and maybe teared up when the examiner reprimanded her? Yes. But her embarrassment had faded, and she now had a week in the sun with her daughter to celebrate her success.

"This is the best, Mom." Katie rubbed more tanning oil onto her leg. "I swear, I think I'm getting darker already."

QUEEN OF THE ROAD

"Mm-hmm." Dee felt like the heat had penetrated all the way to her backbone, finally chasing away the chill she felt constantly in the winter.

Katie put the cap on her bottle of Sun Bum and looked at Dee. "But the hat you're wearing is ridiculous. I don't know if I can sit by you all week with that thing on your head."

Dee touched the brim of the enormous canvas hat she'd ordered from a sun protection catalog. It was a little annoying when she tried to look up from her book—she had to fold it up to see anything not directly under her nose—but if it prevented age spots as promised, it would be totally worth it. She lifted the hat to look at Katie in her tiny black bikini. She was slathered with tanning oil, her chair positioned far from Dee's umbrella to maximize sun exposure. Her hair was swirled into a top knot, and the Gucci sunglasses she'd cajoled Dan into buying her last summer sat discarded on a side table with her melting nonalcoholic strawberry daquiri.

"You might want to think about protecting your skin too. The sun's a lot stronger down here by the equator."

Katie yawned and lay back in her chair. "I never burn."

It was true. Katie had olive skin like Dan and never once had a sunburn.

"You're still damaging your skin. You don't want to be all leathery and spotty when you're my age, do you?"

Katie didn't even bother to turn her face Dee's way. "By the time I'm your age, they'll have some miracle treatment for it. Besides, I've got your genes, so I'll look great, just like you."

Dee shook her head at her daughter's flawed logic and offhand flattery. Was she ever that young and optimistic? She'd certainly never been that tan. She glanced at the watch on her freckled arm. "I'm going to check to see if our bags are in the room yet."

Katie smiled up at Dee with closed eyes. "Okay," she said. "I'll come down in a little bit too. I want to get a shower before dinner."

Entering the stateroom, Dee was happy to see their suitcases had been delivered and were positioned on luggage racks near the bureau. Folded towels fashioned into sea creatures perched on the beds, an octopus on one and a starfish on the other. Except for the towel menagerie, the room had a sleek Danish look. It was large by cruise ship standards, and the private balcony's room-width atrium doors made it feel even more spacious.

Grabbing a bottle of sparkling water from the mini fridge, she drifted out to the balcony to watch the dockworkers load the ship. Soon enough, Katie returned to the room and plopped her beach bag in the middle of the floor. Vacation-mode Dee didn't get annoyed. Someone would be coming in to clean every day, so she wasn't going to bother nagging Katie to keep the room neat. She would remember to give the stateroom attendant a hefty tip.

"This place is seriously cute," Katie said, joining Dee on the balcony.

"It's amazing how they make use of the space, isn't it? Our house is going to look huge when we get back."

"Our house *is* huge. From an environmental standpoint, it doesn't make a lot of sense for just one person to live there."

"Okay, Greta. Maybe I'll take in boarders."

"I'm serious, Mom. Why do you want to stay in that big drafty house all by yourself?" Katie plopped into the chaise lounge across from Dee.

"It's not drafty." Dee took all criticism of her home personally. "You think it's drafty?"

QUEEN OF THE ROAD

Katie shrugged. "Not really, but it is a lot of house."

"Well, to be honest, I have been thinking about selling it, but I thought it might upset you. It's the only home you've ever known. Wouldn't you be sad to lose all the memories it holds?"

Katie tapped the side of her head with a forefinger. "All my memories are here. I don't need a house to remember my childhood."

Dee smiled. "Good to know. Maybe I'll just stay here on the ship."

Katie rolled her eyes. "What do you want to do tonight?"

"I don't know. Let's see what our options are."

Katie brought the cruise itinerary out on the balcony and the two of them looked it over.

"Wow, there certainly are a lot of options," Dee said.

"Yeah. There's even a teen lounge, but it will probably just be a bunch of high schoolers. I wonder if there are any people my age on board?"

"You'll have to check it out and see." Dee flipped to the last page. "Oh, here's something I'd like to do. Christmas caroling on the lido deck."

"Hmm. Maybe." Katie didn't sound enthused.

"Come on. It'll be fun. Remember when we went caroling with the church youth group? And the last house we visited made hot chocolate for everybody?"

"Yeah. They gave us candy canes to stir it. Ooh, remember how someone kept ringing jingle bells while we were going between houses and the little kids thought Santa was coming? And it was snowing, wasn't it? Or did I make that part up in my head?"

"No, that's exactly how I remember it too." It had been a perfect night. One of those times you recall and then wonder if it really happened or if you were mixing reality up with a movie you'd seen or book you'd read. Dee took a breath and rose from the chair. "So, what do you think. Will you come Christmas caroling with me?"

"Sure. Maybe they'll give out candy canes."

CAROLING WAS NOT QUITE AS FESTIVE AS THEY'D hoped. Aside from Dee and Katie, only four families took part. Instead of a live musician or band, they sang along to a prerecorded soundtrack as the words of the familiar tunes scrolled across a screen on the stage.

"This is lame," Katie whispered.

Dee had to agree. Only one group appeared to be having much fun. The eight of them, all adults, appeared to have hit the eggnog hard beforehand. But their raucous laughter and off-key renditions of the songs somehow saved the event. Fifteen minutes in, everyone in the room reached an unspoken agreement to sing as loudly and obnoxiously as possible. The sing-along ended when the karaoke machine went haywire in the midst of everyone bellowing "Jingle Bells." For a while, the crowd repeated *dashing* along with the faulty recorder, and then it quit.

An inebriated woman two seats down applauded and whistled. She looked especially festive in her Santa Claus sweater and tinsel-strewn headband. "Merry Christmas, everybody!" she shouted. Then she turned to Dee. "Thank God that's over with. I need a drink."

Dee laughed and turned to see Katie talking with an athletic-looking blond kid in a Duke sweatshirt. Her holiday cheer began to deflate. If she were a better person, she would simply be happy that her daughter found someone her age to socialize with on the ship, but she didn't want to give up the cozy mother-daughter trip she'd envisioned.

"I'm going to check out the teen lounge with Trevor, okay? I'll be back in time for Santa." Katie winked.

Dee buried her self-pity and smiled. "LOL. Sure, go have fun."

Katie leaned over and whispered, "You don't say 'LOL,' Mom. You text it."

Dee rolled her eyes. "I know that." Did she know that? She waved her daughter off and looked around the now-empty auditorium. On a ship the size of a small city, she suddenly felt completely alone.

She pasted a smile on her face and began exploring the ship, nodding and smiling at the people she passed in the corridors. *Look at me! I'm happy and outgoing and not even a little bit sad to be spending Christmas Eve all by myself.* After a second group she passed doubled back to ask her for directions, she let her face fall back into its neutral position. Her weirdly friendly demeanor had people mistaking her for one of the cruise directors.

She strolled around each of the decks, taking in the huge variety of available entertainment—an onboard version of the game show *Deal or No Deal*, a half-finished performance of *A Christmas Carol* (she'd catch that another night), a nightclub, and a glittering casino that filled an entire level—but nothing appealed to her.

On her way back to the stateroom, she heard music. Not the ear-splitting techno tunes that shook the nightclub, but someone playing songs she recognized on a piano. Stepping around the bow of the ship, she discovered an enchanting little lounge. Forest-green velvet drapes hung at the windows, a large mahogany bar lined the back wall, and brown leather club chairs circled low tables in the dimly lit space.

Taking a seat at the bar, she ordered a glass of New Zealand sauvignon blanc with an unsophisticated side of ice cubes. She loved the little tang of grapefruit she smelled when she brought the glass to her lips. Just like her morning coffee, the first sip was always the best.

She grabbed a handful of pretzels from the oversized goblet by her elbow and glanced around the room, taking in the dinner jacket–clad pianist in the corner and a smattering of couples seated at the tables. No one seemed to be judging her for being alone. No creepy men hit on her. Of course, no attractive men hit on her either. Did she want a man to hit on her? No. Absolutely not. At least, not yet.

Before she could order another glass of wine, Katie called.

"Hey! How's the teen room?" Dee said.

"Meh," Katie said.

Dee could picture her daughter's dismissive shrug. "Not fun, huh?"

"Not so much. I knew it would be a bunch of high schoolers. That kid from caroling is only sixteen. Don't tell anybody. It's too embarrassing."

"Who on earth would I tell?"

"Good point. So, where are you now?"

"Just hanging out in a bar."

"You go, girl!"

Dee laughed. "It's a piano bar. Very low-key. Come on up and I'll buy you a Coke."

"Really, Mom? Come on, I'm twenty. How about if you buy me a beer."

"I don't know . . ."

"You're aware that I drink at school, right? And I'm responsible about it. Besides, we're in international waters. I'm legal out here."

Dee knew Katie was manipulating her, but what the hell. Playing by the rules had never gotten her very far. And for that matter, she'd always thought the drinking age should be eighteen. It made no sense to her that a person could legally vote, go to war, and be charged as an adult criminally, but not buy alcohol.

THE REST OF THE WEEK, THE TWO OF THEM WERE INseparable. Dee couldn't remember the last time they had spent this much time together. They had long conversations by the pool and at port-of-call beaches during the day, and in the stateroom at night. They talked about Katie's sort-of boyfriend, Cal, and her plans to study abroad. And Katie showed genuine interest in Dee's life.

"Didn't you have a career in pharmaceuticals before you had me? Maybe you could do that again instead of driving a truck." Katie blew a wayward strand of hair from her face. "Dad used to tell me you were the only drug rep he ever met with because you were so . . . persistent."

They were sitting outside their stateroom on the last evening of the cruise.

"'Persistent,' huh? What did he really say?"

Katie rolled her eyes. "He said you brought treats for the receptionists until they made him meet with you."

Dee gazed out at the starlit sky. Time was such a funny thing. In a way, it felt like that meeting occurred yesterday.

She remembered seeing him for the first time, the little shock of surprise when he walked into the conference room. She'd expected someone old and gruff, and instead this guy who looked like he stepped out of *Goodfellas* appeared. He must have found her attractive too, or maybe it was the double-fudge brownies she'd baked after the office staff let her know he had a sweet tooth. With other accounts, Dee shipped in delicacies from around the country—Joe's stone crabs from Miami, lobster from Maine, cases of wine from Napa—but none of that worked on Dr. Dan. In those days, he stayed trim no matter what he ate and chocolate was his weakness.

After eating two huge brownies and listening to her pitch the newest children's asthma medication, he'd asked her to dinner. What followed was not so much a courtship as an immediate relationship. Dee had been so infatuated (and a little intimidated—Dan was five years older and a doctor, after all), she'd begun assuming the same preferences as him—meat and potatoes over pasta, Bob Dylan over Bruce Springsteen, preppy clothes over the bohemian styles she once wore. Now she wondered if the last twenty-five years happened simply because she'd intentionally adapted herself to Dan's oh-so-structured life.

"That was a long time ago." Dee fingered the wedding rings she still wore. "Drug companies don't hire nearly as many people now, and honestly, I'd like to try something different."

"Sorry for telling Dad you'd pay him back for the cruise."

Dee snorted. "Yeah, that was a good one. Don't worry about it. I ran up a lot of other charges too, but he'll probably let it go out of guilt."

"Do you think he'll ever, like, come to his senses?"

"I don't think so, sweetie."

Katie's face crumpled. "I just don't see how I'll ever get married and be happy. Everybody gets divorced now. I used to think I'd be different, like you and Dad, but . . ." She paused and blew her nose on a cocktail napkin. "It's not like you guys argued or had fights like some of my friends' parents. Like the Sullivans, I mean, of course they got divorced. They hated one another. But you and Dad always seemed happy enough to me."

"I guess we were happy enough," Dee said. "But, you know, I'm beginning to think maybe 'happy enough' *isn't* enough."

Katie raised her tear-streaked face and frowned at her mother. "You mean you *want* to get divorced?"

Dee shook her head. "No. I'm just saying that there are a lot of truly happy marriages out there. Your grandparents, for instance." Dan's parents doted on one another. "And Mr. and Mrs. Taylor, remember? They're adorable together."

"And you and Dad weren't that happy?"

"I don't know. Sometimes I wonder if we rushed into things. Maybe we would have been happier with other people."

"Great. Then I wouldn't even exist."

Dee sprung up and threw her arms around her daughter. "You know that's not what I meant. You're the best thing that ever happened to me. Or your father."

"I know." She sniffed into Dee's shoulder. "I'm just being dramatic."

"You know, some people say that when things fall apart it's so that something better can grow. We need to have faith that everything is going to work out for the best for all of us."

Katie extricated herself from Dee's embrace. "Do you really believe that?"

Did she? She sometimes said things just to make Katie feel better. "I'm trying to believe it."

Katie nodded and looked at her mother for a few moments. "So, you think you're going to be happy driving all around in a truck forever?"

"Not forever, no. But I think it will give me time to think about what I want to do with the rest of my life. Kind of like you doing study abroad in Italy—not quite that glamorous—but I think getting away will give me a fresh perspective. It's an adventure."

"Oh! I almost forgot!" Katie jumped up and went into the stateroom, returning with a chilled bottle of Moët & Chandon and two flutes. "I was right about being able to buy alcohol on the ship, so I got us this to celebrate early New Year's Eve and your first road trip."

Katie popped the cork and poured them each a glass. It had been the perfect mother-daughter trip. An experience Dee planned to hold in her memory and look back on when life swerved to the left, as it inevitably would. Neither the good times nor the bad lasted forever. One perk of growing older was understanding that truth.

Dee sipped her champagne and reached over to give Katie's hand a squeeze.

"I love you, Mom," Katie said.

"I love you too, baby."

They gazed out over the balcony at the endless sea and sky surrounding them. An undulating reflection of the rising moon extended to the horizon and countless stars twinkled above. Everything vast and unknowable—as was the future. Dee could choose to be terrified or amazed at the possibilities.

chapter

TWELVE

PREPARING FOR HER THREE-WEEK ROAD TRIP RE-
minded Dee of getting ready for summer camp when she was
a child. She had to pare down to just the essentials. Like the
Girl Scouts, King of the Road supplied a packing list to follow
when going out with a driver trainer—sleeping bag, pillow,
one medium duffel bag and suggestions for the types of clothing to pack, a shower kit with toiletries, and shower shoes. She
didn't need to iron on name labels in her clothing, but other
than that the similarities were uncanny.

On the day of departure, she met Frank at the King of
the Road terminal, and they walked over to a spotless black
Peterbilt 579.

"Isn't she a beauty?" Frank said. "We just added her to the
fleet. I figure if I'm going to be back on the road, I'm going to
ride in style."

"I can't believe I'm saying this, but yes, this really is a beautiful truck," Dee said, running her hand along the gleaming
chrome trim.

She climbed in and stowed her sleeping bag and duffle on the top bunk. "It even has that new car smell." She stepped aside to let Frank put his things on the lower bunk.

"Yeah, well, don't get too used to it," Frank said. "My son's got dibs on her once we finish the trip." He looked at his watch. "Okay, it's about time for us to head out. What's the first thing you need to do?"

Use the restroom was on the tip of her tongue, but she decided not to test Frank's patience. "Pre-trip inspection."

"Correct."

Dee grabbed a pair of black disposable gloves from her tote bag and pulled them on, then she walked around the truck and trailer, checking the connections, tires, and lights. Frank walked beside her but gave no instructions. And he made no mocking comments about her choosing to wear gloves like Rico.

"I think everything looks good," Dee said.

"Did you take a close look at the lockjaw on the kingpin to make sure it's fastened on there securely?" Frank shone his flashlight on the pin that coupled the trailer to the truck.

"Yes. It's closed around the shank."

"All right, then, Queenie. You sound like a pro. Let's hit the highway."

The bulk of King of the Road's business was known as drop-and-hook, meaning they were crisscrossing the country, dropping a loaded trailer at a warehouse and then hooking up to an empty trailer to take to another location. As Frank explained it, this newer method of transporting goods was a lot more efficient. Rather than having drivers waiting around for trailer contents to be unloaded, they were able to get back on the road immediately. They covered four hundred to five hundred miles a day and soon got into a routine. Frank told Dee about the apps she could download on her phone—Trucker Path, TruckSmart, RoadBreakers, and MyDAT Trucker Services—and showed her how to use them to find the cleanest truck stops, best prices on fuel, and open spots to park at the end of a shift.

Spending the night with a man in the confined space of the truck cab had been Dee's biggest concern about the three weeks, but Frank made the situation more than tolerable. He told her from the outset that he wanted both of them to have some time to themselves each day. So each evening, after they had dinner together, he stayed in the restaurant FaceTiming Angie and his kids and grandchildren and watching videos on his laptop. This allowed Dee to have her privacy getting ready for bed and her own alone time in the truck. Lucky for Dee, she'd never had trouble sleeping, and she was almost always sound asleep in her bunk when Frank returned.

Another pleasant surprise was the fact that Frank made few comments about her driving. He sat in the passenger seat with his cigar clamped in his teeth, alert and scanning the roadway in front of them, but he only offered instruction when there was something new for Dee to learn, like how to use PrePass to bypass the weigh stations at state lines.

"See this transponder here?" He pointed to a small electronic box mounted on the windshield. "When we cross into Ohio, about a mile from the weigh station, this little gadget is going to send a signal to identify and weigh our truck, and then we'll get a green light to let us sail right by. No need to pull in. That used to be a real pain in the ass, waiting around to get weighed, then waiting around to get unloaded once you got to your destination. You're getting into this business at the right time. Things are a lot more efficient."

✠

DAY MELTED INTO NIGHT, CITIES AND MOUNTAINS appeared on the horizon and then disappeared in the rearview, over and over again. They headed west on the northern route, hitting Illinois, Michigan, Wisconsin, then dropping down to Nebraska and Kansas.

Most of the time, they rode in companionable silence with the radio tuned to a country station, or they talked about the weather or the scenery they were passing. Purely small talk. But after a few days on the road, Frank broached a more personal subject.

"So, what does your husband think of you working a job like this?"

"My husband?" Dee glanced at the wedding and engagement rings still on her hand. "Oh. We've separated."

"Sorry to hear that. I know this line of work can be tough on a marriage."

"It didn't have anything to do with this. He left me for someone else."

Frank made a grumbling noise under his breath. "Doesn't say a lot for his judgment."

Dee smiled. "Thanks for that. How about you and Angie. How did you work it out when you were on the road?"

"Ah, Ange is the salt of the earth. We've been together since high school, best friends and all that, you know. So we always trusted one another. We talked on the phone every day. And she's an independent woman, so I don't think she minded being on her own too much."

"My husband and I didn't have that kind of marriage. I guess we didn't communicate very well. Here's how clueless I was—I always wanted to get an RV and travel the country together. I clipped all these articles of places we could visit. For like, years. And when I finally mentioned it to him, I found out he hated the idea." Dee sniffed. "Anyway, that's one of the reasons I wanted to become a trucker. I'm hoping I get a chance to sightsee a little bit on my downtime. Do people do that?"

"Sure they do. Where'd you want to go the most?"

Dee thought about it. "There are so many places. I don't know, I guess the Grand Canyon. I feel like pictures of that probably don't do it justice. Yeah. I definitely want to get there someday."

Frank pulled out the trip plan. "Well, I tell you what, Queenie, we're going to be heading through Arizona on our way home, and I think we'll have time for a little detour."

Dee turned her head to look at him. "Really?"

"Really," he said and pointed his finger to the windshield. "Eyes on the road."

A silver minivan came up alongside them in the passing lane with a *Minions* movie playing on screens behind the headrests. Dee understood the appeal of entertaining kids with videos on long car trips—it had to cut down on the *Are we there yet?* complaints—but she wondered if they were shortchanged by missing the scenery flying by them. She herself had fond memories of hours spent playing twenty questions and license-plate bingo when her family traveled.

"Hey, Frank," Dee said. "Do kids still make that hand signal to get us to honk the horn?"

"Not as much as they used to, but yeah, you'll probably see a few kids do it." Frank scratched the back of his head. "I always got a kick out of that. At the end of my driving career, I was running night line-haul. My first load every night, I'd make a left turn in this little town right by an ice-cream shop.

All the kids there would see me at the stop sign and run to the curb doing the arm pump. I'd always give them three good blasts as I drove past." He chuckled. "Honestly, that's one of the things I miss most."

After they'd crossed the Continental Divide on Route 70—a harrowing roller coaster of a road that took them eleven thousand feet above sea level and then back down—Dee thought she'd conquered the worst of her fears. They'd double-checked the brakes before starting the climb, but the biggest takeaway for Dee was learning how to master driving downhill in the lowest gear. She'd had nightmares about needing to pull off on a runaway truck ramp—clearly, they weren't on the roadsides as a joke. Frank congratulated her on mastering the roadway and then immediately pulled out his phone and began scrolling through it like a teenager.

"What the hell's up with this weather?" he said. "Not a bit of precipitation in the forecast anywhere."

Dee glanced over at him. "Isn't that a good thing?"

"Ordinarily, yes. But when we're out here training, I'd like you to experience everything Mother Nature can throw at you." He tapped a bit more on the phone. "That's more like it. Looks like we're going to catch a rainstorm and some wind tomorrow on our way through Oregon. I can't find any snow, but when we stop for the night I'm going to have you practice putting snow chains on and off."

"Oh, goodie," Dee said.

THE SKIES WERE OVERCAST AND GRAY WHEN THEY started out the next morning headed for Northern California.

"Okay, Queenie. Today you're going to learn how to handle a rig when you've got windy conditions. We've got a full trailer, so we shouldn't have too much trouble. They're forecasting winds of thirty miles per hour, which will give you a good feel for handling the truck, but no real risk of flipping."

"Flipping?" Dee's voice rose a few octaves.

Frank shrugged. "It happens, but mostly to dummies who don't know what they're doing. You never want to drive with an empty trailer in the wind, and if you're dealing with crosswinds, you want to get off the road when it hits forty. Don't worry, I'll keep an eye on things."

The weather held off until they neared the California border, when a light rain began to fall.

"This may not look like much, but it can be tricky. Stay in the right lane and drop your speed to thirty-five," Frank said. "The first ten minutes of rain like this is the most likely time to hydroplane. Water mixes with the oil on the road's surface and can turn it into a skating rink."

Dee nodded. She'd seen the results of hydroplaning a few times when she'd done all that driving as a drug rep. Somehow, she'd thought having eighteen wheels and thirty thousand pounds of weight would prevent it from happening to a tractor trailer.

In minutes, the gentle rain morphed into a deluge and wind appeared out of nowhere. Sheets of water blew against the passenger side.

"There's the wind. You feel that?" Frank said. "You're doing fine. Just keep a firm grip on the steering wheel and drop your speed a bit more."

Dee struggled to keep the truck in her lane. She could feel the wind like a malevolent force trying to push them across the highway. Soon leaves and small twigs were hitting the side of the truck along with the downpour.

"Okay, Queenie, this is a little more than we bargained for. There's a rest stop coming up on the right in a mile. We're going to pull in there and face the truck into the wind, understand?" Frank spoke in an unhurried and calm manner, but Dee heard the tension in his voice.

Dee nodded, lips pressed together. She didn't trust herself to speak.

It seemed like the longest mile of the trip, but eventually Dee pulled off the highway and Frank directed her to a spot facing the wind. It still buffeted the truck but didn't rock it. Before either of them could sigh in relief, the sound of a freight train rumbled in the distance. Dee clapped her hand over her mouth and looked wide-eyed at Frank. There was no train. A funnel cloud had dropped from the sky, and they were directly in its path.

"Check your seat belt, Dee. And start praying." Frank's face was grim as he tightened his own seat belt and stared out at the tornado bearing down on them. He seemed to be trying to hold it off with the sheer force of his will.

A trash can sailed across the parking lot, and garbage and tree branches blew against the truck as the monster cloud spun nearer and nearer. Dee stopped breathing.

Just before the tornado reached the visitor's center, it veered off into the trees. Shingles from the building's roof settled on the roadway in front of them. The downpour let up and reverted to a gentle rain. Dee let out her breath and peeled her hands off the steering wheel.

Frank cleared his throat. "Well, that wasn't exactly what I was hoping to show you. Count on the goddamn weather service to get it wrong every time." He looked at his watch. "What say we drop this load in Crescent City and go have a drink. I sure could use one."

Dee held her shaking hands in front of her. "I don't think I can drive."

Frank nodded. "You earned yourself a break. I'm going to go in and use the facilities and then we'll get back on the road. You can ride shotgun."

By the time they sat down in Ristorante Enoteca, an Italian restaurant with a parking lot that could accommodate the truck, Dee's nerves had settled enough to hold a wineglass without sloshing it all over herself.

Frank took a long draw of his draft beer. "Well, that was more excitement than I've had in a few years."

Dee dipped a piece of focaccia in the saucer of olive oil. "The only time I ever saw a tornado before this was on the Weather Channel. Does that sort of thing happen often?"

Frank shook his head. "I never saw one that close before. And I was on the road for thirty years."

They ordered their meals, chicken parmigiana for Frank and lasagna for Dee, and Frank asked the server for another round of drinks. "Not to set a bad example, but cheating death makes me thirsty," he said. "And there's plenty of time to burn it off before we need to get back on the road tomorrow."

"Sounds good to me, Frank."

Frank pulled the trip planner from the utility bag alongside his chair. "The last leg of our trip should be smooth sailing. We've got a couple stops down in Southern California, and then we'll jump over here to Arizona and fit in a visit to the Grand Canyon."

"Really? You think we'll have time?"

"Absolutely," Frank said. "We're right on schedule. We'll spend a few hours there and then hopscotch our way back home."

A talented cover band in the next room played renditions of country tunes while Dee and Frank ate their meals. As they finished up, the band segued into Carrie Underwood's angry ballad, "Before He Cheats." Dee saluted the band with her wineglass. "I love this song," she said.

Frank raised his eyebrows. "Sort of violent, isn't it?"

"A little fantasy revenge doesn't hurt anybody. And my husband did buy himself a shiny new convertible." Dee threw back the rest of her wine. "It's kind of fun to think about trashing it."

"Hoo, boy." Frank waved for the check. "I think it's time to cut you off."

chapter

THIRTEEN

BEFORE LEAVING FOR HER TRIP, DEE HAD PUT A COU-
ple of lights on timers so her house would look occupied. But
when she pulled into her driveway, everything was dark. She
must have set them up the wrong way. Fumbling with her keys
in front of the darkened front door, it occurred to her that
the porch lights should have been working even if the timers
were faulty. The light sensor brought them on every evening
automatically.

She entered the house and flicked the light switch. Nothing
happened. The security system panel by the kitchen door was
chirping, so the battery backup had engaged. She looked up
and down the street. A homey glow illuminated every house
but hers. She felt her way down the hall and into the kitchen
to get the flashlight and matches out of the junk drawer. After
turning off the alarm, she lit a few candles and made a quick
inspection of the house. It was eerie walking around in the
dark. And it was so cold. She tried a few more light switches,
hoping something would flare to life.

Her earlier feelings of accomplishment vanished. She didn't want to take care of herself anymore. She wanted someone else to go down in the basement and check the circuit breakers and call whoever you were supposed to call when things like this happened. Then she poured herself a glass of Kim Crawford and picked up the phone to call the electric company.

Dee remembered the days when you could call a company of any size and get an actual person on the other end. Now you got a creepy robot weirdly interacting with you and misunderstanding your answers.

"I'm calling to report an outage." Dee enunciated carefully.

"The area that you are calling from has no reported outages," the mechanical voice came back.

"But my electricity is out."

"The area that you are calling from has no reported outages," the voice repeated.

How did you get a live person on the phone? She remembered seeing a television commercial where a man kept yelling "Representative!" into a phone. She didn't have a clue what the commercial was selling, but in frustration she began yelling herself.

"Representative!"

"Representative!"

"Representative!"

At great length, someone picked up.

"Hmm," the rep said. "I'm not seeing any outage reports for your neighborhood. Are you the account holder?"

"Account holder?" Dee repeated. "I don't know. I mean, I live in the house. I think my name is on the account. The last name is Levari."

She felt like an idiot. How could she not know if her name was on the account? Was her name even on the house? Dee had no idea. She'd always let Dan handle all of that.

Dee waited for a few more moments while this information was entered.

"Well, Ms. Levari, there is no outage. Your account was terminated last week."

"What? But I'm living here. I need the power turned back on."

"I'm sorry, ma'am. You'll have to call our billing department during business hours."

This was unbelievable. Did Dan call them and have the account closed? How could the man she'd spent twenty-five years of her life with be so mean? So spiteful. Why would he do something like this to her? Was he getting back at her for all the money she'd spent in New York and on her cruise with Katie? She dialed his number and listened to it ring. He didn't answer.

She sat in the dark with her coat on, watching the candles cast their flickering demons on the walls, and stewed for a while. Then she lit the gas fireplace and called Jancee for the name of an attorney.

THE LAWYER IN QUESTION HAD REPRESENTED JANCEE in two complicated divorce proceedings and went on to become a close friend, so he agreed to see Dee immediately. After giving the utility company a credit card number to get the power restored, she drove to Philadelphia singing "Before He Cheats" and daydreaming about whaling away at Dan's car with a Louisville Slugger.

The attorney's office space was not what Dee expected. Not that she had much experience with such things, but she'd seen a few courtroom dramas. The office building itself fed into her preconceptions. Comcast Technology Center was a new-ish addition to the Philadelphia skyline, and it had that sort of *Star Wars* futuristic vibe going. In fact, if one were inclined to flights of fancy, the building looked like an enormous silver rocket about to be launched into space.

Then she walked into the office of Adrian Rummel and crashed back to earth. She always tried to use the trick of matching a person's physical attributes to their name to help her remember them, but it usually didn't work very well. She would remember the mnemonic device Tiny Eyes, while the real name—Theresa? Tammy?—escaped her. But this guy made it too easy. He looked as if he had gotten dressed in clothes that had been languishing in the bottom of a laundry hamper for a week. His tie was askew, and his hair seemed to be trying to escape from his head—overgrown tufts sprouted in every direction. Dee's optimism began to evaporate at the sight of him. Mr. Rumpled didn't look like he could get her off on a traffic violation, let alone go up against any hotshot barrister Dan might hire.

Rummel was speaking on the phone as the receptionist es-corted her into the office. He gave Dee a distracted smile and motioned for her to sit down. There were two black leather chairs across from his desk, but both were stacked high with files. She considered moving one of the piles, but there didn't appear to be an open space to relocate them. She just stood there. Finally, he realized her predicament and came around the side of the desk to clear a seat. With the phone cradled against his shoulder, he gathered the files into a precarious stack and dumped them on the pile in the next chair. The Leaning Tower of Pisa, rendered in paper.

Dee glanced around the room while she waited for his call to end. More piles of paper littered the desk and a credenza across the room. It wasn't clear to Dee how anyone might reach the credenza because the floor in front of it was two-deep in file boxes. Could he be preparing to move to another office? Dee wanted to move to another office. Any office. The sight of all the clutter made her want to jump up and start tossing things in a garbage bag. She tried to concentrate her attention on the walls, which were covered with diplomas and plaques of commendation, along with an assortment of framed photos featuring the attorney in chummy poses with Very Important People.

Finally, the call came to an end, and he gave Dee his full attention. He leaned across the desk and extended his hand. "Adrian Rummel," he said. "Jancee tells me you need some help with divorce proceedings."

Dee shook his hand and debated whether she should introduce herself, then decided it would be stupid since he obviously knew who she was. But wait. Divorce? She just wanted the lights turned back on, didn't she? Was she rushing things? Maybe Susan was right, and Dan would come to his senses and return home. "Um, I don't know." She glanced down at her hands and twirled her wedding band and engagement ring to line them up. "I think I might be making a mistake. Maybe I should just go."

"I'm sorry?"

Dee stood to leave. "I'll pay for the session, appointment, whatever you call it, but I need to leave now. I shouldn't have come."

"Hold on. Let's just talk for a minute, off the clock, and you tell me what's going on." He buzzed his receptionist. "Helen, bring us a couple of coffees, would you?"

Dee took a breath and nodded. She would just talk to him. It didn't mean she had to go ahead and do anything.

Rummel leaned forward and gave her his full attention. "Okay, so what's going on?" He uncapped his pen and waited for Dee to start.

She relayed the whole sorry tale while he took notes on a yellow legal pad with a chewed-up BIC pen. Where was his laptop? Even her gynecologist and dentist had switched to computer note-taking. And the way he sent the receptionist to get them coffee. Who did that anymore?

When she finished, he straightened up and flicked his eyes over his notes. "So, you think this is some kind of midlife crisis and you're willing to wait for him to come to his senses?"

"I don't know. That's what my friend said."

"Jancee?" His disbelief was palpable.

"No, another friend."

He tapped the tablet with his pen. "And what do you think?"

"I think we're through." Dee blurted this out without even being aware of what she was about to say. Some alternate personality had taken over her voice. She burst into tears.

"Okay." He handed her a travel-size pack of tissues from a carton on the desk. "Here's what I think we should do. We hire an investigator to get a handle on your husband's finances and legal dealings, determine how long this liaison with the other woman has been going on and go from there."

Rummel went on to detail all the steps to begin divorce proceedings and what she could expect if she went ahead and filed. In contrast to his sloppy appearance and old-school work habits, his recommendations were organized and decisive.

"Why don't you think it over and give me a call if you want to proceed."

Dee wiped her nose. "Okay. Thank you. I'll do that."

chapter

FOURTEEN

ON HER WAY HOME, DEE SWUNG BY THE HOSPITAL. She still had one of Dan's parking passes on her dashboard, so the attendant waved her through with barely a glance. She pulled up alongside Dan's gleaming black convertible. Thanks to the unseasonably warm and sunny day, he'd left the top down. She now reconsidered Rummel's behavior. How thoughtful of him to send Helen out to get her coffee. Too bad it had grown cold. She grabbed the cup from the console and walked around the Volvo to Dan's *What was it?* Oh right, a Mercedes. With a deliberate turn of the wrist, she poured what remained of her coffee onto the burnished leather seat. She heard the parking attendant yell something at her, but she was past the point of caring. She tossed the empty cup in after the coffee and drove away. Dan should count himself lucky she didn't have a baseball bat in the trunk.

Later that afternoon, as she took the first load of laundry from the now-functional dryer, she heard Dan's car squeal into the drive. She threw the jeans she was folding back in the basket and marched upstairs to meet him in the foyer. The fact that he let himself in without bothering to knock fanned the flames of her fury.

But the moment she saw him, she was overcome with sadness. The solid reality of having Dan standing before her, in their house where he belonged, strangled the angry words before she could speak.

"Do you have something you want to say to me?" he said.

"Why did you do it?" Her voice shook with tears she refused to cry. "Why did you have the electricity turned off?"

Dan frowned at her. "I don't know what you're talking about."

"The electricity? The power to the house? I came home from three weeks on the road and you had it turned off."

"Dee," he spoke carefully, as if he were addressing a spooked animal . . . or a mental patient. "I have no idea what you're talking about."

"Well, then, why did they cut it off?"

"Have you been paying the bills?"

"Of course, I've been paying the bills. They're set up to pay automatically."

"Most of them, yes. Have you been transferring money to the checking account?"

Dee had a sinking feeling in her stomach. "Isn't that automatic?"

Dan sighed and closed his eyes. "No, Dee, it's not automatic. I showed you all this. You have to log in to the bank and transfer money from our savings."

"But . . . but I did log in. Everything said, 'Pending,' so I thought the bank would just take care of it."

"They can't very well take care of it if there's no money in the account!"

Why, oh why, was she such a moron? She wished she could seep into the floorboards the way the cup of coffee she'd dumped sunk into the perforated leather of the convertible's seats. "Oh no," Dee said in a sudden panic, "the mortgage." Was she going to lose the house to a sheriff's sale?

"There is no mortgage." Dan stared at her with his eyebrows knit together. "We own the house outright. We just pay property taxes. You did pay the tax bill, didn't you?"

Tax bill, tax bill. She was sure, yes, she'd written one big check last month. That must have been the taxes. She rushed to the basket of paperwork on the office desk for the checkbook and flipped open the register.

"Yes, here it is. I paid it."

But her moment of triumph was short-lived. Dan went to the computer and signed into their account. He sat there, shaking his head. "All of these are past due. What have you been doing?"

Dee jutted her chin forward. "I've been learning to drive a truck."

Dan sighed again. "Right." He started tapping at the keyboard and then paused. He signed out of the account and motioned Dee over. "Pull up a chair and log in. You need to learn how to do this yourself from start to finish."

For the next hour, Dan went over finances with her, displaying more patience than he ever had when they'd been together.

"I, um, I'm sorry about the coffee."

Dan glanced at her and then looked out the window.

"I know you're angry, Dee. And I guess I deserve some of it." He looked back at her. "But you have to move on and learn to take care of yourself."

"I am taking care of myself," Dee said, her voice rising. "I just drove a truck around the country for three weeks, so I think that proves something."

"Yeah, well that's another thing. What are you doing driving a truck? Why couldn't you just take a job in retail or go back to pharmaceutical sales?"

How dare he? "Because this is what I want to do. I'm going to see the country and get out of this stupid life that you ruined for me." *Shit.* She sounded like an eight-year-old. She cleared her throat and tried to get rid of the whiny tone in her voice. "And besides, I'm good at it."

"You're good at a lot of things."

Was he being condescending? It was the old chicken-and-egg argument—did she behave like a juvenile around Dan because of the way he treated her, or did he treat her this way because she had always been so dependent? The realization shed a whole new light on their marriage.

"No. I'm not. I'm not good at a lot of things. I was a good mom. I thought I was a good wife, but apparently . . ." Dee stopped speaking and waved a hand in front of her to deflect any attempt he might make to humor her. She didn't want his pity. And she didn't need to explain herself to him anymore. "Driving a truck is what I want to do right now, Dan. That's all. It's my decision."

He rose from his chair and jangled the keys in his pocket. "You're right. What you do with your life is none of my business. I just don't want you getting hurt, that's all."

A few weeks earlier, that statement would have hit her with the force of a sucker punch, but now it just made her tired. "It's a little late for that."

He seemed to flinch at her words.

"Thanks for helping me straighten out the banking. I think, at some point, we need to separate, well, everything. I spoke to a lawyer." She still held a flicker of hope that he might contradict her on this.

"Now that you bring it up, I've been wanting to talk to you about . . . um, divorce"—he paused—"and, well, some other things." Dan looked at his watch. "How about if we have a drink?"

Dee braced herself for more bad news while pouring two glasses of scotch. She had a feeling sauvignon blanc wasn't going to cut it today.

"Your hair's different," Dan said.

"Yup." Dee had wondered if he'd mention the change in her appearance. But she found she didn't care one way or another what he thought of it.

"I can't believe how big that maple tree got," he said.

She followed his gaze to its naked branches as she worked furiously to pry her wedding rings off her finger under the table. Wearing them now made her feel foolish. Why had she kept them on all this time?

"Remember when we planted it?" he said. "It wasn't much more than a twig."

"I remember. You don't have to . . ." No, she wasn't going to be adversarial. "Why don't you just tell me whatever it is that I need a drink to hear?"

Dan took a swig of his scotch. "Okay. I'm getting married."

Dee blinked. She waited for the wave of pain to engulf her, but felt nothing. Not even numb.

"To the Berger woman?" she said in, to her ears at least, a strangely calm voice. "How is her little boy, by the way?"

Dan frowned at her. "What are you talking about?"

"The day you left, you asked if I remembered Adam Berger. You said you were dating his mother."

"I said no such thing. I was about to tell you about meeting Barbara, the consulting doctor on the case, and then you went apeshit and didn't listen to another word I said."

Dee blinked. All this time she'd thought she'd been replaced by a woman half her age. "So, who is she?"

"Barbara Geist. She consults on some of our more complicated cases, like the Berger case . . . Anyway, we just kind of hit it off. She graduated from Drexel around the same time I did. She has a condo in Boca near my parents . . ." Dan's voice trailed off. Maybe he realized how callous he sounded gushing about his new love to his old wife. "We just have a lot in common."

What could she say? She took a long swallow of her scotch, not to calm her nerves or drown her sorrows but simply to have something to do. They sat there in silence, and it felt familiar, in a way. How many evenings had she spent trying to come up with something to talk about with this man? The dryer signaling the end of its cycle broke the stillness.

"My lawyer's Adrian Rummel. In Philadelphia." Dee stood and pushed her chair back. "Let's just get it over with as quickly as possible."

Dan remained seated. "Have you thought about what you want to do with the house?"

Dee bit her lip. Naturally it wasn't going to be as easy as that. *Call my lawyer.* This was real life, not a melodrama. The messy details would have to be dealt with.

"Katie thinks I should downsize."

Dan nodded. "Yeah, this is a lot of house for one person."

"Are you . . . I mean, do you want to buy me out?" The thought of him living here with Dr. Wonderful made her want to vomit, but she needed to be practical.

He gave a cursory look around the room and then shook his head. "Nah. Barb would like the kitchen, but the rest of the house isn't really her style. I think we should sell it and split the proceeds."

Dee agreed. That's what she wanted too. So why did she feel personally insulted? *It's not really her style.* Who the hell cared what Barb's style was? She swallowed her anger and gave him a stiff smile. "That sounds like a good idea. I'd like to list it with Susan, if that's okay with you."

He drained his glass and set it on the table. "Sure. Have her send a copy of the comps to me. I want to be sure we get top dollar."

At the door, Dan paused. "Promise me you'll be careful out there."

The nerve of this guy, acting like her well-being meant something to him when he'd been the one to blow her life to pieces. If she were a cat, she would have flattened her ears and raised her back.

"I'm done being careful. I'm focusing on being happy now." She enjoyed the puzzled look on Dan's face as she closed the door. Then she returned to the kitchen and dropped her rings in the junk drawer.

chapter

FIFTEEN

"SO, MY LIFE IS NOT A CLICHÉ, AFTER ALL. DAN ISN'T leaving me for a younger woman. It's even more pathetic than that." Dee was pacing around the house with her tumbler full of ice and scotch in one hand and the phone in the other. She had topped off the drink, envisioning herself as a broken-hearted heroine in one of those films from the 1940s that she loved. Trouble was, she didn't really feel brokenhearted. She felt ridiculous. So she'd called Jancee.

"Are you saying what I think you're saying? He left for a dude?"

"Wait. What?" That hadn't even occurred to Dee. Leave it to Jancee to come up with an even more complicated scenario than the one that existed. "No, it's not a guy, it's just that she's not young. She's even older than me, judging by her picture. And he's planning to marry her."

After Dan left, she'd googled Dr. Geist and found a photo of her on the Children's Hospital of Philadelphia's website. She had the taut jaw and oddly full lips and cheeks that modern dermatology can deliver, making her look not young so much as belonging to some strange new subset of women that all resemble one another in later life.

"So, how do you feel about this?" Jancee slipped into therapist mode, her years as a patient making her somewhat of an expert by osmosis.

"Honestly? It's like I have this confusing mix of emotions. I mean, clearly, it's not just some midlife thing he's going through; he really was bored with me. Which is kind of insulting, but then I realized I find him kind of boring too. He's moving on with his life, and maybe I'm ready to move on with mine."

"So, why did he have the electricity shut off?"

"Oh." Dee had forgotten about that. "It was just a misunderstanding. He didn't do anything." This was so embarrassing. "I, um, didn't pay the bill."

Jancee had the good grace not to laugh in her ear. Although free-spirited in most respects, her friend had never approved of Dee's willful ignorance when it came to finances. She made it her business to know, down to the penny, how much money she had in her checking account, what her investments were doing, and when every bill was due.

"How can you stand not knowing this stuff?" she used to ask. But Dee had been more than happy to let Dan handle it.

"You could probably use a system, to stay on top of the bills," Jancee said. "Do you want me to help you get things in order?"

"No. I'm good now." Dee looked in the office at the neat stack of billing statements ready to be shredded. "Dan helped me with it."

"He came over to tell you he's getting married and then helped you do the banking?"

"Not exactly. He came over to yell at me for dumping coffee in his car." Dee told her about the detour by the hospital. "He took it pretty well, all things considered."

"Good for you, girlfriend," Jancee said, after a burst of laughter. "He deserved a helping of crazy."

"Maybe," Dee said. But the initial thrill she'd felt at her act of criminal mischief had evaporated. Instead, she felt a flush of embarrassment rising from her chest as she recalled the parking attendant running after her car when she drove away from the scene of the crime.

"So, what are you planning to do now?"

"I guess just let the lawyers handle it. I gave him Adrian's name." Dee swirled the ice in her scotch and dumped the contents in the sink. "And we're going to list the house. I want to make a fresh start somewhere."

"You should move down here near me," Jancee said. "There are some great condos right on the river. You'd love the view."

Dee assured her friend she'd think about it and then got off the phone to wander aimlessly through the darkening house. This place she'd once loved seemed as foreign to her now as Dan did. Everywhere she looked she saw some ghost from her past, a now-distorted vision of the life she had lived here. It was time to get back on the road.

THE NEXT DAY, DEE WHIPPED UP A BATCH OF BANANA nut muffins—not keto, in fact, loaded with granola and chocolate chips—then took them across the street to Susan before she left for the office. There was a guy with a caulk gun balanced on a ladder alongside the front entry. Rather than take a chance on having latex dripped on her head, she headed around to the side yard, pausing to look at her own house on the way. Did anything need attention before listing it? She'd ask Susan. She stayed on top of home maintenance. And she knew how to stage a home.

She tapped on the kitchen door window, startling the older woman as she scooped coffee grounds into a filter. She sometimes forgot Susan was in her seventies. Maybe she should have called first. What if she had a heart condition like her late husband?

Susan recovered quickly and came to the door with a big smile. "Hey, stranger! It's good to have you back in town. How did everything go?"

"Better than I expected, actually," Dee said.

"Well, that is good news. How about some coffee? I don't have to be in the office until ten today, so I have time to hear all about your travels."

"Coffee sounds wonderful. And here"—Dee handed over the basket of still-warm muffins—"I missed baking, so I whipped these up for you."

"Ooh! I was wishing I had something sweet for breakfast and thought I'd have to settle for jelly on toast. Thanks, hon."

Dee pulled out a chair at the counter while Susan finished setting up the coffee maker and then bustled about putting place mats and napkins down and pouring half-and-half into a ceramic creamer instead of just putting the carton on the table. Dee liked to do the same thing herself when she had company. Set a nice table and make guests feel welcome.

Once done, Susan settled into the chair next to Dee with a sigh. "I'll tell you, the older I get, the harder it is to get moving in the morning. It's probably time for me to think about retiring."

"Can you hold on just a bit longer? I have a house I'd like to list with you." Dee pointed her thumb toward her house.

Susan nodded slowly. "Of course. But I'd be lying if I said I was completely happy about this. I'm going to miss having you across the street."

"I'm going to miss you too, but I'll keep in touch." Even as she spoke the words, she wondered if they were true. Over the past few months, she'd come to think of Susan as a real friend rather than just a neighbor, but if she left the area, she didn't think she'd get back much. Sometimes it felt like life was just one painful goodbye after another.

"Where are you planning to go?"

"Maybe Philly. Or maybe . . ." Dee stirred her coffee. "I really don't know. I'll probably just get a short-term rental while I figure things out. Do you handle rentals?"

"Not really, but Shelly in our office is a peach. I'll put you in touch with her."

Dee nodded and tried to shake the feeling of melancholy. Moving forward was her only option. "I noticed your repair guy out there. What are you having done?"

Susan chuckled. "He's here to paint the living room and foyer, but I talked him into fixing the insulation on my bedroom window. I thought I felt a draft up there, and sure enough, half the caulk seems to have cracked and fallen off."

"Do you think there's anything I need to take care of before we put the house on the market?"

"Probably just the basics, you know—pack away the family photos, clear out closets to make them seem roomier. But from what I've seen, your color scheme is pretty neutral, which is good. Unless you have a bedroom painted some crazy color." Susan grimaced. "I had a client once whose teenager was into that goth stuff; she'd painted her bedroom and the attached bath black. Terrible. It took four coats of paint to cover it." Susan took a muffin from the basket. "If you want, I'll come over and take a closer look as soon as I finish this."

"I'd appreciate that." Dee took a muffin herself and bit into the crunchy granola topping.

"So, tell me about your trip," Susan said.

"Well, other than a tornado in Oregon, it was pretty uneventful."

"A tornado?" Susan set down her muffin. "You saw a tornado?"

"Yeah, it was terrifying. It came within a hundred yards of us before it changed direction."

Susan shuddered. "That sounds like a nightmare."

"I don't think I've ever been so scared in my life," Dee said. "I know Frank was afraid too, but he kept his cool and that kept me from completely losing it. And you know how they say tornadoes sound like trains? Well, in my head I thought that meant like a train whistle, but really it's this steady over-whelming rumble, like a freight train with a hundred cars."

"And going through this didn't scare you away from truck-ing?" Susan said.

"No, not really. Frank said in all his years on the road he'd never seen a twister that close. And the rest of the trip was good. You know, I've always wanted to travel across the coun-try and sightsee. I mean, I didn't really get a chance to visit many places, but just seeing all the different states was pretty cool. And Frank built a visit to the Grand Canyon into our itinerary."

"He sounds like a nice guy, this Frank."

Dee nodded. Expanding her circle had her realizing that most people were kinder than she expected.

Susan balled up her muffin liner and put it on the plate. "Ready to give me a tour?"

"Absolutely. I want to make sure it's perfectly staged to sell, so don't hold back."

Susan tilted her head and put her hands on her hips. "Oh, honey, when have I ever held back?"

"Good point." Dee laughed and lowered her plate and cup into the gleaming stainless-steel sink. Susan's house always looked like it was ready for a showing.

They walked across the street, Susan shading her eyes with her hand and squinting up at the house. Dee no longer wanted to live there, but she still loved the look of it. It was a brick modern colonial with a front porch and four dormer windows in the roof. They'd enlarged the front porch early on, and it was still one of her favorite renovations. Many summer evenings had been spent there with friends enjoying cocktails and appetizers before moving indoors for the main course. And on rainy days, she and Katie used to curl up on the porch swing in the corner, reading in companionable silence. She would miss the porch.

"Roof looks good. How long ago did you replace that?"

"Not long, maybe five years?"

They circled around the outside of the house, Susan nodding her head to some internal checklist.

"I don't see anything that needs work out here. Let's take a look inside."

In the foyer, Susan lifted one of the frames on the gallery wall of family pictures. "Okay if I head upstairs?"

Dee swooped her arm toward the staircase. "Be my guest."

Susan made little admiring comments as they walked through the house. "Oh, I love this room . . . so bright . . . so cozy . . . fabulous bathroom."

Finally, they made their way back to the foyer.

"The only bit of work I might suggest is repainting in here. The color's faded around the picture frames, and you don't want to leave a wall full of nail holes anyway. You could just leave the photos up, but I advise against it. You want prospective buyers to picture themselves living here."

Dee nodded. She'd been actively avoiding looking at the gallery wall ever since Dan left anyway. It was long past time to take it down. "Do you think your painter can fit me in when he's done at your house? I usually paint myself, but I'm back on the road the day after tomorrow and I'd like to get this moving."

"Sure thing. I'll send him over to give you an estimate as soon as he's through." Susan opened the front door. "Do you want him to start while you're away, if he's available?"

"Yes, if you don't mind letting him in."

"I'm happy to do it. And I'll keep an eye on things."

"Thanks, Susan." Dee cleared her throat. "And could you send Dan a copy of the comps and, well, everything, I guess. I'll send you his email." It gave her a queer tightness in her chest, bringing him up in conversation. She wondered if it would always feel that way, or if eventually it would be like talking about anyone else from her past—just someone she used to know.

chapter

SIXTEEN

HER NEW WHEELS STOOD ACROSS THE LOT—A LOOM-
ing mass of red steel and chrome. Frank was his usual gruff self
when he pointed it out to her. "She may not be as pretty as the
579, but she runs like a top."

He opened the driver side door, and the smell of stale cigarette smoke and body odor wafted out. Her new home away
from home smelled like the inside of a dive bar after a busy
night. Frank coughed and fanned at the air with one of the
discarded magazines littering the seat.

"You might want to spray a little disinfectant in here.
Miller took care of engine maintenance, but he's a hell of a
slob."

Stifling a sneeze, Dee climbed into the back of the cab to
check out the sleeping accommodations. A single bunk with a
thin mattress and a refrigerator-microwave combination greeted her. It reminded her of Katie's freshman dorm room, but
smaller and gloomier. Flicking the light switch above the bed
on and off, she squinted up into the dim light. The limited
amount of space meant paring down to the necessities, but

she could already picture it transformed into a bright and cozy little haven.

She made a quick stop at HomeGoods, where she found a lime-green down comforter on clearance along with a hot-pink corduroy armrest pillow, a foam mattress pad, a feather bed, and an assortment of coordinated bright throw pillows. She usually gravitated toward neutrals, but she felt the need to brighten up her on-the-road accommodations. Also into the cart went a superbright battery-powered lantern, a large lavender-scented jar candle, and a thick, fluffy bedside rug.

She headed back to the truck with all her purchases and a supply of cleaning products. After sprinkling two boxes of baking soda on the upholstery, she sprayed disinfectant and scrubbed the dashboard, microwave, and refrigerator. Then she vacuumed up the baking soda and went at the seat cushions with extra-strength upholstery cleaner.

Frank ambled over after she'd been at it for an hour. He leaned his head in the open passenger door and coughed. "Smells like a chemical plant exploded in here."

Dee brushed damp hair out of her eyes and sniffed a couple of times. "I think I've lost my sense of smell."

"You planning on taking care of the engine like this?"

Dee almost laughed in his face, but she wasn't so sure he was joking. "I'll do my best."

"All righty, then, I'll see you bright and early tomorrow." He gave the side of the cab a slap with his meaty hand and turned to walk back to the office.

Half an hour later, Dee was finally done. She'd made up the bed, arranged the pillows, and put the rug in place. Her bright and cheery bunk looked like an illustration from *The Princess and the Pea*.

EARLY THE NEXT MORNING, SHE PULLED INTO THE lot at the same time as Rico. He slung a black backpack over his shoulder, slammed the door to his rust-tinged Subaru, and ambled over to where Dee stood, unloading the back of the Volvo. "You sure got a lot of stuff there," he said.

Dee straightened up and looked at him. "Is that backpack all you're taking?"

Rico patted his pack. "Yeah, I travel light."

"Not me." Dee waved toward the bins.

"You didn't have all that stuff on Frank's truck, did you?"

Dee laughed. "No, I followed the packing list. But now I'm going to settle in like I own the place."

"So, how did you and Frank get along?"

"Great, actually. He's a good trainer and a really nice guy under that tough act he puts on."

"Yeah. I had that impression."

"How about you? How'd your training go?"

"It was chill. They paired me up with this dude around my age, and he was totally cool. I mean, he was serious about the job, but it felt like hanging with a bud."

"Sounds like we both got lucky. I saw some awful videos on YouTube from people who had real jerks as trainers."

"Facts," Rico said. Dee didn't always follow Rico's slang, but using context clues, she got the gist of it. He agreed with her.

"Well, I guess I better get started putting stuff away."

"I'll give you a hand." Rico grabbed the largest bin and headed to her truck before Dee could refuse.

"You really don't need to do this," she said, all but running to keep up with him.

Rico set the bin down next to the passenger side and then pulled his phone from his pocket. "You want to trade digits? So we can check in, you know?"

"Oh, sure," Dee said, handing him her phone. Either he was the world's biggest Boy Scout or there was something about her that brought out this kid's protective instincts.

"Okay, then." Rico handed her phone back and tossed the hair out of his eyes. "See you on the flip side."

After eight hours of driving, Dee decided to combine refueling with her mandatory thirty-minute break. She'd prepared some chicken Caesar salad wraps and tuna fish with crackers and stocked them in her mini fridge along with a bag of clementines—her meals might be monotonous, but at least they would be somewhat healthy. Pulling up to the diesel pumps, she grabbed her latex gloves from the center console and slipped them on. Frank may have mocked Rico for wanting to keep his hands clean, but Dee thought it was genius. And the black ones were kind of sophisticated-looking. Like something Audrey Hepburn wore in *Breakfast at Tiffany's*. She held her hand out with a limp wrist. All she needed were a cigarette holder and some pearls.

Once the fuel started running, she decided to kill time by double-checking the truck's connections and tires. She smiled with satisfaction as she jiggled the trailer harness. Anyone watching her would think she'd been doing this for years.

Reaching the back of the trailer, she froze at the sound of a familiar voice. Across the lot at a second set of diesel pumps, the awful guy Frank booted from training stood next to a fuel truck yelling into a cell phone. Her body recoiled as if she'd received an electric shock. He must have found a company that put up with his miserable attitude. She scurried to the other side of the trailer, hoping he hadn't noticed her.

She stayed rooted to the spot, afraid to return to the cab and finish refueling. Staying out of sight until she saw his truck pull out seemed like the best option, even if it ate into her break time. What a way to start her first solo trip. As she glanced at her phone to check the time, she felt the hair on the back of her neck stand up.

"Boo!"

Spinning on her heel, she found herself standing face-to-face with Jensen.

"Whatcha doing back here? Hiding from the bogeyman?" Tobacco spittle sprayed from his mouth.

"Get away from me." She tried to sound angry instead of frightened but didn't succeed. Jensen's hand rested on the bowie knife strapped to his leg. "Not so tough without your bodyguard, eh?" He took another menacing step toward her.

Dee backed away and glanced about the truck stop. There were people everywhere. If she screamed, surely someone would come running.

"Go. Away."

"Go away? I'll go away when I'm good and ready. Thanks to you and that goddamn spic, I'm stuck working for a bunch of assholes who don't pay shit." Jensen spat on the ground at her feet. "You're lucky we're not alone."

Dee finally found her courage. "Go to hell, you racist jackass." She turned her back on him and forced herself to walk, not run, back to the cab. Slowly and deliberately, she put the fuel nozzle back in its cradle and closed the tank. Out of the corner of her eye, she saw Jensen approaching. Could he be crazy enough to attack her here in broad daylight? She looked toward the windshield squeegee near the pumps. Not a very effective weapon, but it was something. She lunged for it just as a different male voice shouted.

"Hey!" The man jogged across the median and stopped in front of Dee. He pointed at Jensen, who had reversed course and was now heading toward the mini-mart. "That guy giving you trouble?"

"Yeah." Hands on her knees, she tried to catch her breath.

"Somebody you know?"

"Not really." Dee rose to a stand and replaced the dripping squeegee. "We were in the same trucking school, and he got thrown out. I guess he blames me."

The stranger nodded. He had eyes that looked like they'd seen too much of the ugly side of life.

"Thanks for stepping in like that," Dee said.

"Sure thing." The man stuck his hands in his jacket pockets. "Mind if I ask you a strange question?"

She shook her head. *What now?*

"So, I was kind of watching you. Not in a creepy way," he hurried to add, "but that's why I overheard that jerk. Anyway, I notice you drive for King of the Road. You're not by any chance the one they call Queenie, are you?"

Could she be dreaming? This whole episode was beginning to feel like one of those weirdly lifelike nightmares. Maybe she should try pinching herself.

"Um, I don't know. Some of the guys I work with call me that."

Sad Eyes nodded. "Well, I'm glad to know you. I'll just stick around until"—he paused and jerked his head toward the mini-mart—"he's out of here."

She smiled at him. For every Jensen, she was pretty sure there were ten good guys like this. "I'll be okay. Thanks for chasing him away."

chapter

SEVENTEEN

THE ENCOUNTER WITH JENSEN REPLAYED IN HER mind until she stopped for the evening. What if she had been alone when he confronted her? Or what if he ran into Rico? As threatening as the man had been with her, she could only imagine what he might do to someone who had punched him in the mouth. She scrolled through her phone for the number Rico entered.

"Hey, Rico, it's Dee. How did you make out today?"

"Who? I don't know anybody named Dee. You sound like my dude, Queenie."

Dee sighed.

"Just kidding," Rico said. "Everything was smooth. How 'bout you?"

"I had a pretty good day," Dee said. "I was just wondering if you've run into that guy from training, Jensen."

"No, why?"

"I saw him today. Outside of Winston-Salem when I stopped to fill up. Looks like he's driving for an oil company."

"Did he bother you?"

"Not for long. Another trucker chased him off."

"Humph." Rico's voice sounded tight.

"It's no big deal. He's just really a jerk, so if you see him around, keep your distance, okay?"

"Me? He's the one that needs to keep his distance. I hate guys like that."

"Yeah, I know. But he carries a knife now, and he definitely holds a grudge. I don't want you getting into any trouble because of me."

"Don't worry about it. I run into enough guys like him, and they're mostly full of shit. He didn't even come back at me when I hit him."

"I never thanked you for that."

Rico barked a laugh. "No problem, for real."

"It's kind of discouraging, needing men to step in and defend me. I feel like Blanche DuBois depending on the kindness of strangers."

"Okay, well, I've got no idea who this Blanche chick is, but you're not exactly big enough to beat up somebody yourself."

"She's this helpless character in the movie *A Streetcar Named Desire*. It's before your time . . . before my time too, actually. I just like old movies." She paused to bite her cuticle. "Do you think I could get a Taser?"

Rico made a sound like he was choking and then coughed for a while. "Wow. I did not see that coming." He coughed again. "I've got Red Bull all over me. And no. My buddy got caught with one and almost ended up doing time."

"Oh. How about pepper spray. Do you think that's okay?"

"You should get a dog. That's what I want to do, just for the company."

"I don't know." Dee balled up her sandwich wrapper and dropped it in the trash. "I never had a dog. I wouldn't know the first thing to do with it."

"You seemed to get along okay with that old man's shepherd. Remember him?"

"Ha! He scared me half to death."

"Yeah, that's my point. People don't like to mess with strange dogs."

"I don't know. I think pepper spray would be easier."

"Whatever, Queenie. Dogs are awesome."

Dee brushed at nonexistent fur on her jeans, remembering the dog Rico mentioned. On one of their final training days, Frank had treated them to lunch at a Flying J, the ubiquitous nationwide rest stop that caters especially to truckers. After pausing to check a text message from Katie, Dee had been hurrying to catch up to the group when a huge German shepherd jumped out barking from between two idling truck cabs. Just behind the dog, an old trucker came jogging up, the keys on his belt loop jingling wildly.

"Whoa there, King." He'd snapped a leash on the dog and patted its enormous head. "Sorry about that. He won't hurt you. He just wants to say hello."

Dee had shrunk back without taking her eyes off the dog. To her, it looked like he wanted to say, "Come over here and let me rip your arm off." She'd taken another step backward and bumped into the truck cab behind her. The old trucker had laughed.

"There's nothing to be afraid of; this is my buddy here." He'd yanked back on the dog's collar. "Sit, King." King sat.

"Come on," the trucker urged. "He likes you."

By that point, Frank and the others had paused to wait for her, and she could feel them watching her. She'd moved closer to the dog and hesitantly held out her hand. King stuck his slimy snout up into her palm and wagged his tail. He was a little gross, what with all the saliva coating her hand, but he wasn't mean.

"Oh, he really is nice." Dee had felt a rush of affection for the dog as he leaned against her while she pet him. Dog hair covered her jeans. "Does he ride in the truck with you?"

"Yup, he sure does." The trucker scratched behind the dog's ear. "Best company in the world, especially on those long hauls."

"I didn't know you could do that."

The old man had chuckled. "You can do anything you want out here on the road, little lady, just as long as the smokeys don't catch you." He winked. "Well, I got to get moving on. Thanks for saying hello to my friend here." And with that, the old trucker and his dog had walked off across the blacktop.

DEE LOOKED AROUND THE DARKENING CAB AND OUT across the parking lot at the line of trucks under the streetlights. It was a lonely view. Maybe it would be nice to have a dog for company. She set her phone on the console and then picked it up again. She'd call Jancee; Jancee had opinions on everything.

"What do you think about me getting a dog?"

"Who is this?" Jancee said.

"Very funny," Dee said. "I'm serious."

"How about all of those times I wanted to get a dog for Katie, and you wouldn't let me? You said they were too much work, and you didn't want the mess, remember?"

"Yeah, okay, so I was a mean mom. But now I'm reconsidering."

"What brought this on?"

"I ran into that creep from my first week of training when I was refueling earlier today. He kind of threatened me, and Rico suggested I get a dog for protection."

Jancee scoffed. "A dog? No. What you need is a gun. A gun and a concealed carry permit and some lessons on a shooting range."

"Oh my God, Jancee! I am not going to start carrying a gun."

"Don't be so quick to say no. You should at least think about it. You're out there by yourself, and you have no idea what sorts of people you'll run into. You should have some way of defending yourself if you ever get in a bad situation. I never go anywhere without my little Glock."

"Ha-ha. You're hilarious." Dee reached over to check the door lock.

"I'm serious. I've been carrying for about five years now."

"You're telling me you've got a gun tucked in your purse along with your breath mints and cell phone?"

"Oh, God no. I'd never find it in there. I wear a holster."

Dee pinched the bridge of her nose as her friend continued to speak.

"I used to go to the shooting range with Howard . . . Remember Howard? He worked for the Securities and Exchange Commission? Kind of a dull guy, but he sure could handle a gun. Anyway, he pointed out that making jewelry deliveries the way I do is like an invitation to criminals, so he got me a gun and some lessons, and I've gotta say, I'm a pretty good shot. I was sure I told you all about it."

"No, Jancee, I forget a lot of things, but that I'd remember."

"So, what do you say? I could take you to the range next time you're home."

DEE WAS ASLEEP IN HER CAB FOR THE NIGHT WHEN her cell phone pinged with a message from Rico.

> Watched ur Streetcar movie on Hulu. That dude was seriously f'ed up. Blanche also pretty cray. You seem more like a Princess Leia to me.

What?

A second ping. Later on, when she's a general.

Okay, so not the bikini-clad version. That would have been weird.

> I'll take it. She was pretty tough, Dee texted back.

> Yeah. Ur not that tuff. Get a dog.

HER FLORIDA DELIVERIES WENT OFF WITHOUT A hitch. In spite of horrible traffic on I-75 making her an hour late, she didn't have to wait to drop her load in Orlando. She congratulated herself on backing the truck up to connect to trailers like she'd been born doing it. Then she breezed into the port in Jacksonville for her return load of paper pulp with enough time left over to fit in a quick walk on the beach. And everywhere she stopped, she found herself noticing dogs. Dogs in the passenger side of the trucks that passed her, dogs playing fetch with their owners in roadside dog parks, dogs frolicking on the beach in Jacksonville. She spent her downtime in the truck scrolling through the Petfinder app on her phone. It felt as if some weird virus had infected her and made her desire something she had never before even considered.

The day after she completed her trip, Dee made an appointment at Almost Heaven Animal Rescue. She wondered where they'd come up with the name. The squatty cinderblock building surrounded by knee-high weeds and a rutted dirt parking area looked nothing like paradise. Grabbing her keys, she forced herself to get out of the car and wade through the weeds to the sorry-looking shelter in front of her.

She glanced around the gloomy front room. Off to the side was an old bathtub on a metal stand. The steadily dripping sprayer hose suspended above had left an impressive rust stain. Alongside the tub was a faded pink washer and dryer, mostly obscured by a mountain of dirty towels, blankets, and rags. A girl with lank black hair hanging in her face sat hunched behind a battleship-gray desk.

Dee cleared her throat. "Hi," she said. The girl didn't respond, but Dee forged ahead. "I'm looking for a good guard dog. One that doesn't get carsick."

The girl didn't look up from her phone. Her thumbs flew across the screen as she chewed her lip in concentration.

"They're all in the back," she said, waving her arm toward the rear of the building. "Just come tell me if you find one you want."

So this was a self-service animal shelter. Dee began walking back to the kennels.

"Don't stick your hand in any of their cages," the girl called in a bored voice.

Dee pulled her scarf up over her nose as she walked between the rows of barking dogs. It looked like texting girl couldn't be bothered to clean up after the animals either. The smell was nauseating. Dee looked at each dog in turn, trying to imagine it sitting in the cab next to her.

Someone, surely not the girl at the desk, had carefully stenciled and laminated signs identifying the breed of each dog and posted one above every cage. Dee stopped in front of the cage that held a Yorkshire terrier mix.

"Aren't you sweet," she crooned. The little dog wiggled happily.

Dee was about ready to scoop him up when she remembered her original purpose in getting a dog. She wanted protection. Who on earth would be afraid of a squirt like him? "Sorry little fellow, I can't take you with me."

Further down the aisle were the more-appropriate breeds. A rottweiler, a jumble of German shepherd mixes, and something that looked like a bear. Maybe it was a bear. Judging from the absence of a label above the cage, even the stencil-happy sign maker had been stumped. Unfortunately, these dogs who looked the part were also acting the part, snarling and snapping at their chain-link enclosures.

Dee continued walking. At the very end of the kennel, curled up on the concrete floor of her cage, was a medium-sized black-and-white dog. The dog followed Dee with her eyes but made no attempt to get up. The sign over the cage said, "Pointer / Pit bull."

She'd always thought of pit bulls as aggressive and mean, but this dog didn't look scary at all. If anything, the poor animal seemed frightened of all the other dogs barking and howling around her. Dee stooped down in front of the cage.

"Hey, puppy," she said in a high-pitched, singsong voice.

The dog didn't move except for her tail, which thumped against the floor.

"Come here, girl." Dee reached her hand into the cage, ignoring the instructions of the sulky teenager out front. The dog rose and walked over to Dee, then sniffed and licked her hand. A blotch of white stood out on her otherwise black back.

"Hey, you have a spot on you, girl." The dog's wagging tail sped up. "I think I'll call you Spot."

"WHAT KIND OF A NAME IS SPOT?" KATIE SAID, WHEN Dee called her later that evening. The dog lay curled up in her new beanbag bed next to the couch. She'd wasted no time settling into her new home. In a strange way, Dee felt as though she had been meant to adopt this particular animal. Like they were cross-species soulmates.

"It was the name of the dog in those vintage *Dick and Jane* reading primers," Dee said. "I'm being ironic."

"Huh." Katie didn't sound impressed.

"Okay, then. What do you think of the name Bone-O?"

"Bone-O?"

"Yeah, like the singer from U2."

Katie snorted. "Do you mean Bono, Mom?"

"Have I been pronouncing it wrong all these years?"

"Sure sounds like it." Katie giggled into her ear. "How often are you discussing U2, anyway?"

"Never, really. That's just how I heard it in my head."

"Maybe Spot isn't such a bad name after all. At least you know how to say it."

"Okay, Miss Smarty-Pants. I didn't call you to get abused."

"Sure you did. That's what daughters are for. Anyway, I'm glad you got yourself a guard dog. Does she look like she'll scare away the bad guys?"

Dee looked down at Spot, who was staring up at her in seeming adoration. No one in their right mind would be afraid of this dog. "Yeah. She looks fierce."

"It's going to be okay, girl," Dee said, after ending the call. "You and I will learn to be brave together."

chapter

EIGHTEEN

TWO DAYS LATER, DEE WAS ON THE ROAD WITH HER new traveling partner. She was glad for the company because this would be her longest solo trip yet, three weeks cross-country. She glanced over at Spot and gave her a pat as she waited for a traffic light to change. "We're a pretty good team, aren't we, pup?" The dog responded with a Chewbacca-like whine, something she'd begun doing almost any time Dee spoke to her. She had a job and a talking dog. What more did she need?

An enormous sprawling complex of corrugated metal buildings just outside Chicago appeared in the distance a good mile before she arrived. Angie had warned her about this distribution center, and the minute Dee pulled onto the property, she was proven right. A line of trucks circled the block waiting to get in.

She pulled in behind them and prepared herself for a long afternoon of killing time. She'd packed her Kindle, but had forgotten to load new books on it and there was no WI-FI signal.

As the truck idled, Dee walked Spot to the far side of the warehouse to explore a patch of scraggly-looking weeds.

Another unforeseen perk of owning a dog—the multiple walks she required forced Dee to get some exercise. She pulled a waste bag from the dispenser attached to the leash and picked up Spot's mess, then headed back, trying to keep the bag from swinging. She'd always thought it comical to see her neighbors with dogs walking by the house jauntily carrying a bag of pet waste like it was a doughnut from the bakery, but now she found it was impossible to carry it any other way.

When she reached her truck, she noticed the driver in front of her sitting in a folding chair, knitting. With his Carhartt coveralls and black knit hat, a band saw or a log splitter would have looked more natural in his hands, but he wielded the bamboo needles with finesse. The project filled his lap. She couldn't tell just what it was, but it was intricately patterned and full of bright primary colors.

He looked up from his knitting and nodded at Spot. "Nice to see somebody pick up after their pet like that," he said. "It drives me crazy when people just leave it."

"Yeah," Dee said. "That's one of my pet peeves too."

"Pun intended?"

"What? Oh, pet peeve. Ha."

Dee watched him knit for a few moments, fascinated. Her church group had knit hats and scarves for a homeless shelter, but she'd never attempted anything beyond a simple stockinette stitch.

"What are you knitting?" Dee said.

"It's a sweater." He held out the needles and unfurled an array of cables and ribbing and multiple yarn changes. "Kind of hard to tell when it's all jumbled up like this, huh?"

"I used to knit a little, but never anything that complicated. How long did it take to get so good?" She surprised herself by asking. Usually she simply wondered things about strangers and didn't voice them aloud. But with this job, if she didn't talk to strangers, she would have no one at all to talk to.

He chuckled. "Years. Here, you'll get a kick out of this." He pulled a folded paper from the bag holding his yarn. It was an article from the Oprah magazine about a prolific knitter who covered city tree trunks and parking meters, as well as an entire Mini Cooper, with brightly colored knitwear. Aside from marveling at those creations, Dee found it amazing that this burly guy seemed to enjoy reading women's periodicals.

"My wife saved that for me," he said, as if reading her mind. "She's the one who taught me to knit."

"I wish I had something like that to pass the time. It looks like we're going to be here for a while."

"Oh, yeah. This place is the worst. I used to go a little bit stir-crazy when I had to wait on loads like this, but now I feel like I'm getting something done. And with the sun out like this, it's not too cold to sit outside the truck."

Dee watched him knit a while longer. "Do you ever get teased by the other guys?" She didn't know why she asked him that. What if it made him remember a hurtful comment someone once made?

He didn't seem to mind, though. He looked off to the side, as if trying to recall a particular incident. "Nah, not too often anyway. Besides, it's worth a bit of kidding just to have something to take my mind off all the waiting. And I'm not the only one. There's a couple fellows who knit and crochet. There's even a guy who has a sewing machine in his cab. Makes quilts, I hear."

"That's amazing," Dee said. "I feel like a real slacker—I spend all my time reading."

"No shame in that." He nodded his head toward Spot. "Nice dog you got there."

FROM ILLINOIS, DEE'S ROUTE TOOK HER TO WASHINGTON, California, and Arizona. And while she'd finally gotten a chance to see a few more landmarks on her bucket list—the Seattle Space Needle, Sequoia National Park, and Montezuma Castle—visiting them alone was a bit sad. Having Spot with her eased her loneliness a bit, but the dog had no opinions to share about sightseeing.

Dee had come east from Arizona on Route 40 to pick up her last load—wind turbine parts from a company in Norman, Oklahoma—and she was looking forward to ending the trip. Heading north through Kansas and jumping on Route 70 East looked like the most direct route to Pennsylvania.

The dispatch office sent a text earlier in the day alerting all Midwest drivers to a winter storm warning for that evening, so Dee consulted the BringFido app on her phone and made a hotel reservation in Wichita. A snowstorm was just the excuse she needed to treat herself to a long hot shower and a night's sleep in an actual bed. Before she left Norman, she double-checked the weather and the distance she needed to cover. She had plenty of time to get to the city before the storm hit.

Unfortunately, the forecast was off by a few hours. As soon as Dee crossed the Kansas state line, snow began to fall. Just a few flakes at first, but Dee could tell from the ominous gray clouds it was going to get worse, and fast. Could she outrun the storm? Wichita was less than an hour away and she really wanted that shower. She decided to call Dispatch and get a second opinion.

"How you makin' out, Queenie?" Frank's raspy voice echoed through the phone.

"Hey, Frank! Are you working Dispatch now?"

"Ha. Yeah, I'm a regular jack-of-all-trades around here. Angie left early to see one of the grandkids in a school play. You need help with something?"

"Not really. I'm just hitting a bit of snow right now in Kansas."

Frank sighed. "Yeah. I saw that forecast come through this morning. And we couldn't find a single damn flake when we were training."

"I guess that's Murphy's Law," Dee said. She was trying to make light of the situation, but her shoulders were already tense from gripping the steering wheel too tight.

"Okay. What I'm seeing on the radar right now looks pretty bad, but you can handle it. Get the snow chains on, keep your speed down, and leave plenty of room between you and whatever's in front of you. If it gets too bad, get off the road and find yourself a motel on the company dime. Get yourself a hot shower and take it easy for the night."

"Okay, Frank. I'll do that."

It only took Dee fifteen minutes to get the chains on, but by the time she finished, her gloved hands ached from the cold and her jeans had soaked through at the knees. She climbed into the back of the cab and changed into a dry pair of jeans, then held her hands over the heater vent in an attempt to warm them up. Getting back behind the wheel, she reached a hand over to rub Spot behind her ear. "You ready for this, Spot girl?"

The dog thumped her tail once in response. Seemed like a no.

Twenty minutes later, the storm hit in earnest. The snow fell so thick and fast that Dee could see only a few feet in front of her. She slowed to a crawl and scanned the roadside for a place to pull over. There were very few cars on the road, but every now and then one inched its way past.

At last, Dee approached an exit. Through the swirling snow she could see a faint glow of lights from fast-food restaurants and gas stations. She didn't care if she had to eat a Big Mac from McDonald's and spend another night sleeping in the truck and missing a shower, as long as she could find a place to park and wait out the storm. Just as she flicked on the turn signal, a small black SUV flew in front of her and went into a tailspin. Dee slammed on her brakes.

Out of the corner of her eye, she saw Spot fly into the dashboard and everything that wasn't tied down in the cab tumbled forward. She tried steering to the left to avoid the SUV, but she was skidding to the right and had no control. She lost sight of the SUV. The truck windshield showed nothing but an explosion of headlights reflecting on the falling snow. She held her breath and braced for impact. The truck slid sideways onto the shoulder and then ground to a halt. Dee peered out of the windshield through the snow. She couldn't see where the SUV ended up, but she hadn't run over it.

Then she turned to check on Spot. She lay on the floor, motionless.

"Oh no." Dee threw off the seat belt and knelt on the floor. "Oh no, no, no." She stroked the dog's side and began to cry. "Come on, baby. Wake up." What had she done? This was all her fault. She should have stopped for the night when the snow began.

A sudden pounding sounded on the driver's side door. "Hey! Are you all right in there?"

Dee pulled herself back up on the seat and opened the door. "I think I killed my dog," Dee said, choking on the words. "She hit the dash and she's not moving."

A man in a cowboy hat and a shearling coat stood there. "Let me come around and take a look. Could be she's just stunned."

Dee sat with her fist to her mouth while the stranger ran his hands over the dog, checking for injuries. Midway through his examination, Spot regained consciousness. She rose shakily to her feet and stood quivering. The cowboy continued stroking the dog from head to haunches, talking to her in a low voice, until the shaking stopped.

"There you go—she's good as new," he said.

Spot looked at the open passenger door and whined. "I guess it's a good sign that she wants to go out," Dee said. She grabbed the dog's leash and snapped it on. The cowboy moved out of the way to let them climb down and then waited with Dee as Spot sniffed around.

"Thank you for stopping," Dee said. "I couldn't live with myself if I hurt her." She squatted down to hug the dog and then stood to lift her into the cab.

"How about you? You okay?" the cowboy said, looking down at her with the same calm intensity that had recently been trained on her dog. With a start, Dee realized she was staring at him. Maybe it was all the adrenaline spiking through her, or maybe she had a previously undiscovered thing for midwestern men, but damn he was good-looking.

"Oh! Yeah . . . yes. I'm fine."

"I don't know how you managed to avoid hitting that guy. I saw him fishtailing when he passed me, but it didn't slow him up any."

Dee squinted up the road. She had nearly forgotten the crazy driver that cut her off. What if she had hit him? "Where did he go?"

"He pulled out of it somehow and kept driving like a bat out of hell."

"I could have killed him. If I'd hit that car . . . Oh my God." The full impact of what had happened hit her. "I think I need to sit down." She stumbled back into the truck.

"You sure you're okay?"

Dee closed her eyes briefly and nodded. "I just want to get off the road for the night. I should have stopped before this, but I was trying to get to a hotel in Wichita."

The cowboy adjusted his hat. "Friend of mine owns a restaurant off this exit and there's a motel right next door. Want me to lead the way?"

"You don't have to do that, but thank you."

"No worries. I'm on my way there for dinner anyway. Just follow my taillights."

He slammed the door without waiting for a reply.

Dee followed his pickup truck off the exit and into the packed parking lot of a new-looking Holiday Inn Express. She managed to find room for the truck alongside a chain-link fence at the back of the property.

Instead of waving and continuing on his way, the cowboy pulled in behind her truck and met her as she climbed down from the cab.

"Thought I'd make sure you got in here all right," he said, by way of explanation.

If someone had described this scene to her, she would have been appalled at her response. The thought of him caring enough to make sure she was okay had her ready to throw herself into his arms. She was Blanche DuBois reincarnated.

"Thank you," she said, choking back new tears. "I'm kind of a mess."

Walking toward the entrance, Dee's ankle turned on the icy driveway. Before she could fall, the cowboy's arm shot out to steady her.

"How about if I just see you home, so to speak," he said, offering her his arm to hold. Dee tucked her hand into his elbow. God, she missed the feeling of someone looking out for her.

The front desk manager had good news and bad. They had a room available, and dogs were permitted for an extra fee. The bad news was that only one member of the housekeeping staff showed up to work, so her room wouldn't be ready for at least an hour. Dee then noticed the three families milling around in the lobby with their suitcases.

"That sounds fine." Dee handed over her credit card. "I don't mind waiting."

She turned to thank her cowboy and let him know she was all settled, but he was no longer behind her. For a split second, she wondered if she had imagined him. A guardian angel who came to her aid and then dissolved into thin air. Then she heard his voice and looked across the lobby. There he stood, drawing a map on a napkin for a man in a gray down parka so enormous, he looked as if he'd been swallowed by the Goodyear blimp. Two little girls were hanging on their father's sleeves and staring up at the cowboy in fascination.

He was just a regular Good Samaritan, this one. Dee smiled as if she had some claim on his goodness. He caught her eye and returned her smile. After he finished his direction-giving with some gesturing toward the roadway, he crossed the room to Dee.

"So, how did you make out?"

"Good. They have a room left and I can bring my dog in." She flashed the room key envelope. "Thank you so much for all your help. I really appreciate it."

Dee expected him to leave, but instead he stood there nodding his head.

"Need any help carrying things in?" he said.

"Oh, no but thank you. I, uh, just have a backpack."

He nodded again, but still made no move to leave.

"And I can't get in the room for a while anyway, some problem with housekeeping."

At that, her mysterious cowboy nodded again, still rooted to the same spot.

Dee just stood there too, kind of looking over his left shoulder, because if she looked directly at his face with its square jaw in need of a shave and smiling creases around his eyes and dimples next to his mouth, she started breathing a little too fast.

Then he cleared his throat. "So, listen, would you want to come next door and get some dinner with me?"

"Oh, I guess." Dee felt her cheeks grow hot. Where were her manners? "I mean, yes. I'd like that."

"Great." His smile deepened as he shoved his hands in his pockets. "Name's Grady, by the way."

"I'm Dee." A stupid grin spread across her face.

chapter

NINETEEN

A GLEAMING OAK AND BRASS BAR DOMINATED THE center of the restaurant, surrounded by booths on three sides. Despite the weather, there was a good crowd. As they walked in the door, a bearded thickset guy behind the bar waved and hollered.

"Yo, Grady! About time you got here."

"Yeah, sorry buddy," Grady said. "Had to take care of a few things. Okay if we sit in this booth over here?"

"Sure, sit anywhere you can find a spot."

"That's Dave," Grady said. "He owns the place. We've got a darts competition going on, and he and I are ahead. It doesn't look like the other team showed up tonight, though."

Grady tossed his hat on the seat and hung his coat on a hook on the post between the booths. He took Dee's coat from her and hung it up as well.

Dave came around the bar to take their order, wiping his hands on a red-checkered dish towel. "Who's your new friend?"

"This is Dee," Grady said. "She had some trouble out on the highway."

"Yeah, it's bad out there," Dave said. "You need a tow?"

Grady snorted. "His son has a towing company, and Dave here's always looking to throw a little business his way."

Dee smiled and shook her head. "No. I got off the road okay."

"All right. Let's get your order, then."

Dee glanced around the table for a menu.

"Veggie chili or a burger?" Dave said.

"Um, I guess I'll try the chili," Dee said.

"Good choice," Grady said. "I'll have the same and make mine a double."

"How about drinks?" Dave looked back to Dee.

"What kind of wine do you have?" she said.

Dave scratched his beard and blinked like it was a trick question. "I think we got something red back there."

Grady gave a warning shake of his head. "You'll be safer with the beer. That bottle of wine he's talking about could probably take the paint off your truck."

Dee hadn't had a beer since college. And then she'd only drunk it because it was free. "I guess I'll have a beer, then."

"Bring us two of that cherry lager you have on tap," Grady said.

"You got it."

After Dave left, Dee and Grady sat there in silence for a few moments. Grady turned to look at the television over the bar.

"March Madness," he said over his shoulder.

Dee was momentarily stumped. "Oh! Basketball!"

Grady grinned back at her. "Not much of a sports fan, huh?"

Dee shook her head.

While Grady's attention was on the game, Dee took the opportunity to study him. His graying hair was cropped close to his head. She had a sudden urge to brush her hand over it.

She clasped her hands in her lap. Was she losing her mind? It had to be all the adrenaline still flooding her system.

He was powerful-looking. Like a man who lifted heavy objects for a living, not someone who did reps in a gym. He wore a faded red flannel shirt that had frayed at the collar, and beneath it she could see the neckline of a T-shirt that had probably once been white but was now a strange combination of gray and pink. Grady appeared to adhere to the same school of thought as laundry slackers everywhere—throw everything in the wash together and hope for the best.

She glanced at his hands resting on the table. They were work-hardened, but well groomed. And then she noticed the button missing from his shirtsleeve. A wave of tenderness washed over her. She wanted to fix it. To sit down with a needle and thread, holding Grady's dust-rag soft shirt in her lap and sew on a replacement button, like the girl and her bear in Katie's favorite childhood book, *Corduroy*.

Grady turned his attention from the television. "I'm not in a bracket this year, so it's not all that interesting."

"Oh," Dee said, tearing her eyes away from his wrist.

Then they both started talking at once.

"How did you—"

"What's cherry—"

They both laughed in that embarrassed way strangers do.

"Ladies first," Grady said.

Dee smiled. "I was just wondering what cherry lager is."

"Oh, Dave here is always brewing up something odd. I didn't like the sound of it at first, but it grew on me."

Dee nodded. "It does sound kind of good."

Grady rubbed his hand across his jaw and studied her across the table. "So, I've got to ask you. How is it a nice eastern girl like yourself is out driving a truck through a snow-storm in Kansas?"

"It's a long story," Dee said.

"Don't want to talk about it?"

She didn't want to talk about it, but she liked talking to him, so she gave him an abbreviated version and left out the part in her head where she'd catalogued all of Dan's shortcomings. Dee figured bad-mouthing a man in front of another man was like running down your past employer in a job interview.

Dave set the beers down on the table in the middle of Dee's story without interrupting and disappeared, like a waiter in a fine restaurant.

"So, why not just get a job close to home?"

Dee looked down at her beer. "I don't know. I guess in a way I just wanted to get away from everything. You know? Too many memories."

Grady nodded. He looked for a moment like someone with memories of his own to forget. Then he brightened and motioned toward her beer. "So, how do you like it?"

"It's good. A lot better than the last time I had a beer."

"Which was?"

"At a frat party when I was twenty years old."

Grady laughed. "Boy, you don't give things a second chance, do you?"

Only beer, Dee thought. Mostly, she went through life acting the part of a doormat. If Dan had asked for another chance, she knew she would have taken him back.

Grady didn't seem to mind her sudden silence. Or maybe it was because the chili arrived. He dove into it like he hadn't eaten in a week and finished his double order before Dee was halfway through hers. Then he sat there, drinking his beer while she ate.

She'd never had chili made like this, with big chunks of mushrooms and carrots instead of ground meat. She was thinking she might try making it that way for the next neighborhood chili cook-off and then she remembered. She wouldn't be going to the next one. Dee pushed the bowl away.

"So, how are you at darts?" Grady said.

Dee shrugged and took a sip of her beer. "Probably pretty bad. I've never tried it."

"You want to learn?"

"They're kind of sharp, aren't they?"

Grady looked at her with raised eyebrows. "Yeah. That's about how it works."

"I don't know. I'm afraid I might hurt somebody. I'm not very sporty."

"Good God, woman." He stood and motioned her out of the booth. "Just don't throw them behind you."

They walked across the scuffed wooden plank floor to the opposite side of the room where a dartboard hung on the space of wall between the doors of the men's and women's restrooms. It seemed like a recipe for disaster to Dee.

After setting their beers on the bar, Grady began by demonstrating the correct way to throw a dart. "Got it?"

Dee shrugged. "Seems simple enough."

She picked up one of the feather-adorned missiles and launched it toward the cork disk. The dart embedded itself in the ladies' room door. Thank God no one had been coming out at the time.

Grady retrieved it without a word and set about folding Dee's fingers into the proper grip. "You want to have a light but firm grip on the dart and keep your body as still as possible," he said. Dee liked the way his warm callused hand felt against her cold fingers.

"Okay, let's try this again," he said.

This time, she was sure she had it, but the dart fell to the floor before it reached the far wall.

"Hmm." Grady seemed stumped. Evidently, he'd never come across such a slow learner.

"Try turning a little to the side, like this." He stood close behind Dee, put the dart in her hand, and then drew her wrist back with his hand. Dee fought the impulse to just lean back into his arms. She was paying no attention to his dart-throwing instructions. When he attempted to make the throwing motion, her fingers released the dart too soon and she did just what he had jokingly told her not to do: she threw the dart behind her.

"Hey!" A female voice called from the bar.

"What the hell are you doing over there, Grady!?" Dave picked the dart up off the floor and slapped it down next to their beers.

Grady went to the bar, laughing. "Sorry, Dave. I thought I had a new partner, but it looks like I'm going to have to stick with you."

He tossed the dart and hit the bull's-eye while he walked back to Dee. "How about if we just have another beer?"

"That sounds much safer."

They sat at the bar and ordered another round of cherry lager, and Dee managed to get Grady talking a little bit about himself. It wasn't easy. It reminded her of talking with Katie when she was in high school. To prevent the conversation from screeching to a halt, one had to be vigilant about avoiding questions that could be answered with a simple yes or no.

"So, what's with the hat—are you a real cowboy?"

"I guess you could say that." He picked the hat up off the bar and turned it slowly in his hands. "My family's had a ranch for a lot of years, and I used to ride the rodeo circuit for a bit."

"Wait. You were in the rodeo? Like bucking broncos and all that stuff?"

He set the hat back down and took a swig of his beer. "Yup. All that stuff. I was a bull rider."

"That sounds terrifying."

"Yeah. It was that, sometimes." He turned and grinned at her. "But mostly it was a rush."

"Why did you quit?" Dee regretted asking the question the moment the words left her mouth.

"My father wasn't a fan . . ." He hesitated. "Let's just say it was time for me to grow up. Pull my weight at home." Grady looked off in the distance and was quiet for a bit. "Some people found me a lot more interesting when I was a rodeo man."

For some reason, the words made Dee unaccountably sad.

An old-time jukebox had been playing in the corner all night. Dee hadn't been paying it much attention. But now the restaurant began to empty out and she could hear the beginnings of "Unchained Melody." One of those songs that linked her to some other time, a simpler era. Weary sadness was about to overtake her. Then Grady stood and inclined his head toward the music.

"How about a dance with an old cowboy?" He gazed down at her with a one-dimpled smile. Dee wanted nothing more than to be held in his arms, but she'd never learned to dance properly. At weddings, she and Dan had always just shuffled around to a single slow song and called it a day.

"I'm afraid I'm not much better at dancing than I am at darts."

Grady held his hand out to her. "Just follow my lead."

His gravelly voice traced a warm path from her chest down. Without a word, she took his hand. Good thing she was just passing through because she would be in way over her head with this man.

There was no dance floor to speak of, and Dee really wasn't much of a dancer, but she let herself relax in Grady's arms. With the heat of his hand at the small of her back, her feet followed as if under some kind of spell. She leaned her cheek against his chest and hoped she would be able to remember the feeling of soft flannel on her face and strong arms guiding her.

The song ended, but he didn't let go. They continued to dance to the next tune, Bonnie Raitt's rendition of "Angel from Montgomery." She sang along with part of the chorus, just loud enough for Grady to hear her.

"Make me a poster of an old rodeo / Just give me one thing that I can hold on to / To believe in this livin' is just a hard way to go." His arm grew tighter around her waist.

The song came to an end, and Dave turned up the lights. This always seemed, to Dee, like a cruel way to end an evening. Facing the cold hard truth at the light of day was bad enough. But facing it in the glare of fluorescent bulbs was worse.

Grady stepped back, his one hand still touching her arm. "Guess it's time to go."

They walked out into the swirling snow, Grady with his hat tilted down over his eyes and his hand at her elbow. They stopped at the truck to get her bag and Spot, and then continued into the lobby.

They stood for a few moments looking at each other, Grady with his hat in his hand, Dee with her backpack on her shoulder and Spot leaning against her leg. If she had been a different kind of woman, she would have invited him up. No one would ever know. And for one night, at least, she would have someone to lay down beside her. But she couldn't bring herself to do it.

Grady took a deep breath and let it out. "Well, Dee from King of the Road, I guess I better head on out."

She nodded stupidly. She didn't trust herself to say anything. She might blurt out something ridiculous, like, *I love you*. Dear God, she didn't even know him.

He looked at her face like he might be memorizing it. Then he took a step forward, lifted her chin and kissed her. It was over in seconds. Just a press of his warm lips on hers and his callused fingers holding her chin, but her body reacted like a drought-stricken cornfield hit by a smoldering cigarette butt.

"You take care of yourself now," he said.

"Goodbye," she managed to whisper, as he backed away and set his hat back on his head.

He tipped the brim with a nod, turned, and walked out into the night. Through Dee's swimming eyes, he looked like a mirage.

She forced herself to walk to the elevator. The front desk clerk was staring at her, had probably witnessed the whole thing. She punched the elevator button with a little more force than necessary.

WHEN SHE STOPPED AT THE FRONT DESK THE NEXT morning to return her key, the night clerk greeted her with a big grin. These midwestern people were so friendly.

"Do I need to do anything to check out?"

"No, ma'am, you're all set. But I do have a note for you."

A note? She hadn't told anyone where she was staying. How could anyone have left a message?

"Are you sure it's not for someone else? I don't think anybody knows I'm here."

The clerk's smile deepened. "How about that guy who dropped you off last night?" He slid a piece of hotel stationery across the desk. "He came back in and left this for you."

Dee picked up the note like it might disintegrate in her hands.

Dee—I really enjoyed our time together. If you're ever passing through this way again, give me a call. On second thought, just give me a call. Anytime.
—Grady, 620-625-1102

But she would never call him. She needed one perfect night to remember more than she needed a man who would end up disappointing her. A man she might call and have an awkward conversation with and never speak to again. It was better to hold on to the mythical knight who appeared in a snowstorm and rescued her.

That, of course, was not Jancee's reaction.

chapter

TWENTY

"YOU'RE KIDDING ME, RIGHT?" JANCEE'S INCREDU-
lous voice echoed from the cell phone. "You spend the evening
with some hot cowboy, he walks you into your hotel, and you just
let him leave? Are you simply *determined* to have a boring life?"

"I didn't want to ruin it."

"Ruin it? Oh my God, Dee. The best part was yet to come."

"Let's talk about something else."

"Fine. I did have a reason for calling you, other than to
talk about your nonexistent sex life. Do you want to stay at
my place before we leave for Florida? Then we can just Uber
to the airport together."

JANCEE WAS STRETCHED OUT ON A TOWEL IN A RED
bikini, which naturally still looked great on her. Dee sat on a
beach chair under a rented umbrella, wearing her enormous
canvas hat along with huge black sunglasses and her sarong
wrapped around her shoulders.

"I swear to God, Dee. Do you have some weird aversion to sunlight?" Jancee rose up on her elbows and lifted her sunglasses to squint at Dee. "Come on, get out here and get a little color. Show off that smokin' body of yours."

Dee looked up from her book. "I don't want to get burnt. You know I never tan, so what's the point?"

"I just don't know how you can stand being covered up like that. I love soaking up the sun. It's so relaxing."

"I'm relaxed. Stop worrying about me. I'm having a great time."

"Yeah, this is the life, isn't it?"

They sat there in silence for a few minutes. Dee dug her toes in the sand and attempted to cover the tops of her feet without using her hands.

"Have you heard from that cowboy you met?"

Dee closed her book and looked out at the waves. "No, we didn't exchange numbers." A little white lie. She hadn't told Jancee about the note Grady left her.

"That's too bad. I think a hot cowboy is just what you need."

"Yeah." She smiled at the memory. "He was so . . . I don't know. I can't even put it into words."

"Try." Jancee turned on her stomach and cupped her chin in her hands, like a kid waiting for story time.

"There was just something about him. He was tall and rugged, kind of weather-beaten, you know? And he had these amazing eyes that crinkled up when he smiled."

Jancee held up her hand. "What color? What color were his eyes? I need details."

Dee tried to recall. It seems like something she should know. She closed her own eyes and conjured up his face, but it didn't help. She only remembered how they made her feel. "They were kind. His eyes were kind."

"Good enough," Jancee said.

Dee quirked her mouth and shrugged. "I'm not doing a very good job of describing him, sorry. It's like I knew him in another lifetime."

"I think we should track him down so you can *know* him in this lifetime."

Dee shook her head. "It's better this way. Not ever seeing him again. Like, it was this perfect moment in time, and if he had my number and actually called, we probably wouldn't have anything to talk about. It would ruin everything."

Jancee shook her head. "You're nuts, you know that?"

"I prefer to think of myself as incurably romantic."

"Oh, you're incurable all right." Jancee got up from her towel and plopped into the beach chair next to Dee. "Maybe we can find you some romance here in sunny Florida. See any hot prospects out there in the surf?"

Dee looked out at the surfers. "If I were thirty years younger, I'd say yes. But since I don't relish the idea of being charged with propositioning a minor, I think I'll pass."

Jancee shaded her eyes with her hand and looked up and down the beach. "They're not all kids. I see a lot of more mature guys around us."

Just then, an elderly man coated with tanning oil strolled by sporting European-style swim briefs. Dee looked at Jancee and wiggled her eyebrows. Both of them dissolved into muffled shoulder-shaking laughter.

"Let's keep looking, shall we?" Jancee said.

BY THE LAST FULL DAY OF THEIR TRIP, DEE FELT LIKE she'd lived at the beach forever. She and Jancee had walked the shoreline every morning, watched surf competitions every afternoon, and spent early evenings nursing cocktails and watching pelicans dive into the water for their dinner.

They had just walked back onto the beach after grabbing lunch across the street. Dee was settling herself under the umbrella, while Jancee stretched and looked out at the surfers. Suddenly, Jancee froze mid-stretch.

"Oh my God!" she cried. "Isn't that Bruce Rizzo out there?"

"Where?" Dee looked out toward the surfers.

Jancee pointed. "Over there, blue shorts, black baseball cap."

Dee followed Jancee's outstretched arm. There he was, standing at the edge of the water. Bruce Rizzo. She'd met him when she worked on the Ocean City boardwalk and shared a run-down beach house with Jancee and some other girls during summer breaks from Temple. She and her friends would finish waiting tables at the boardwalk breakfast spots and then hang out on the north end beaches watching the surfers.

Dee had watched Bruce. She could still picture him walking up the beach, shaking the water out of his long hair, his skin tan and gleaming. He'd squat down next to her towel and dazzle her with his smile. "What's going on Dee Dee? Can I have a drink?" Then he would take a swig of her soda and amble off toward the boardwalk to go make out with whoever his girlfriend was that week.

"Bruce! HEY, BRUCE!" Her animated friend waved her arms and ran down the beach. Dee trailed along behind her. They were halfway to him when he finally looked away from the surfer he'd been talking to.

"Jancee? Dee? What the hell? What are you girls doing here?" He looked from one to the other of them with a bemused smile.

"We thought we'd take a little blast-from-the-past vacation and watch some surfing," Jancee said. "What are you doing here?"

"I live here. Moved down about ten years ago. I got tired of the long winters in Jersey, so I sold my business and bought a surf shop here."

"You own a surf shop," Jancee said. "That's perfect."

"Yeah, well, I'd rather be out there in the waves, but it's tough to pay the bills that way." He tilted his head toward the teenager next to him. "This is my nephew, Michael. He's the big surf dude now."

Michael nodded his head at them and pushed tangled wet hair back out of his eyes. "Hey," he said. "I gotta go, Unc," he said to Bruce. "See ya later." He picked up his surfboard and loped off down the beach.

"Wow. I can't believe you two are here," Bruce said. "What's it been, like thirty years?"

"Something like that," Jancee said.

"Remember the year we came down for spring break?" Bruce said.

"Yeah, those were the days." Jancee pushed her sunglasses back on her head. "Remember how terrible the waves were that year? We couldn't catch anything."

"I don't remember the surf being bad. I think you were just too hungover to stand up on your board."

Dee laughed along with them, but she remembered the trip as being nothing but a long-distance version of her unrequited crush. And now, here she stood, somehow morphing back into her self-conscious, clumsy teenage self. She nodded along as Jancee spoke, trying to think of something interesting she could say to the former center of her universe. His skin was leathery after a lifetime of baking in the sun, and his once shoulder-length hair had been replaced with a short cut and a bald spot. Unlike Frank at King of the Road, he didn't try to disguise it with a comb-over, which Dee respected.

"So, what have you girls been up to?" Bruce asked.

"I live on the Main Line in Philly. I've got a little jewelry business, and I just got engaged." Jancee flashed her three-karat solitaire at him. "And Dee here just got divorced, and she's driving eighteen-wheelers all over the country."

Oh God, Dee thought. *I sound like such a loser. Why don't I have a little jewelry business and a big diamond on my hand?*

Bruce whistled. "A truck driver? I can't quite picture that." He looked down at his phone. "Listen, I've got to get back to the shop. You two want to meet me for dinner later? It'd be great to catch up."

Jancee took down the name of the restaurant, and they agreed on a time.

After taking a final look out at the surfers, Bruce picked a faded black T-shirt up off his nephew's beach towel and pulled it on, then adjusted the brim of his baseball cap. He looked from Jancee to Dee and shook his head.

"I can't believe I ran into you two here. And you both look great, by the way." He winked at Dee and then headed up the beach toward the parking lot. "See you girls later."

When Bruce was out of earshot, Jancee turned to Dee. "Did something happen between you two that I don't know about?"

"What? No. Nothing happened. Why?"

"I don't know . . . You didn't say a word the whole time he was here, and I thought maybe he'd been a jerk to you or something. We definitely don't have to meet him for dinner. I'll call and cancel."

"No," Dee said, a little more emphatically than she'd meant. "I mean, that's okay. I was just letting you do the talking."

Jancee narrowed her eyes at Dee. "Oh my God. You still have a crush on him, don't you?"

"Don't be ridiculous. Of course not." Dee flounced into her beach chair and began flipping through a magazine, but she could feel Jancee's gaze still on her.

THEY WERE GETTING READY TO LEAVE FOR DINNER when Jancee broached the subject of Bruce again.

"Isn't it the weirdest thing, running into Bruce here?" She was fastening an elaborate silver and coral necklace from her line around her neck.

"Yeah, it's really strange. I can't believe we didn't spot him before today, though. He had to have been down there watching his nephew, don't you think?"

Jancee nodded as she regarded herself in the mirror. "It'll be great to catch up with him over dinner, won't it?"

"Mm-hmm." Dee sat down on the bed to tie her espadrilles.

"So, what do you think, Dee? He's still looking good, isn't he?" Jancee was clearly ready to play matchmaker. "And that body. Wow. All that surfing must really work the abs."

"Yup, he still looks good." Dee didn't like the direction this conversation was heading. "Did you bring hair spray?"

"Sure did." She reached into her bag and tossed it over to where Dee sat. "Now, what was I saying? Oh yeah . . . you know what they say about old surfers? Old surfers never die; they just ride their longboards."

Dee picked up the hair spray and considered pitching it back at Jancee.

"Get it, Dee? Get it? They just ride their 'longboards.'" She swiveled her hips suggestively.

"Would you please shut up." Dee set down the hair spray and settled for throwing a pillow instead. "You need to get your mind out of the gutter."

♛

THEY MET BRUCE IN ONE OF THE CROWDED TOURIST restaurants on the Intracoastal Waterway. Twinkly lights danced at the ceiling, old-time travel posters covered the walls, and a hula grass bar that ran the length of the room featured a stuffed alligator reclining on a shelf above the beer taps.

"I put our names in already," he shouted. "Looks like it's going to be a while before we get a table, but I promise you the food is worth the wait."

The three of them inched their way to the bar, brushing past an incongruous mix of sunburned college kids and senior citizen snowbirds, all in various states of inebriation. Dee was in a hurry to join them. This evening was beginning to make her nostalgic, and not in a good way.

Finally, Bruce squeezed into a spot at the bar. "Quick, what'll you have?"

"I'll have a light beer," Jancee said. "Whatever they have on tap."

Bruce looked to Dee.

"A vodka martini with a twist," she said.

Dee had finished her first martini and was starting a second by the time their table was ready. It was a booth, thank

God. She was tired of being jostled around by strangers, and the tables on the floor were surrounded by the overflow of people trying to make their way to the bar.

"Wow, what a rush," Jancee said, as they slid into their seats. "I love being in hot spots like this. You meet so many interesting people."

Bruce sat across from them in the booth and told them stories about the years he spent traveling the world as a professional surfer. From what Dee was able to hear above the din, he had loved the travel and the competition, but he'd never gotten the big break all surfers hope for, a major sponsorship. Dee couldn't hear much of what he was saying because it was so loud. And, thanks to Jancee's comedy skit in the hotel, Dee's mind was playing a little track all its own, like an iPod stuck on repeat: "Longboard, longboard, longboard."

When she couldn't stand it any longer, she excused herself from the table and hurried back to the restroom. Pushing past a crowd of girls touching up their makeup, she closed herself in a stall and slapped her hands against her cheeks repeatedly.

"Shut up, shut up, shut up," she muttered.

Back at the table, Bruce was sitting by himself. Their meals had been served while she was gone, and Jancee was up at the bar, getting another beer. Dee slid into the booth, and Bruce leaned forward with a smile.

"Do you want to ride my longboard?"

"WHAT?!" Dee screeched.

Bruce lifted one eyebrow and repeated himself. "Do you want to try my Lanai burger. It's the house specialty." He motioned down at his plate.

"Um, no. No thank you." Dee could feel her face burning, and it wasn't from her slap-happy session in the stall. *Damn you, Jancee.*

The rest of the meal passed without incident. They sampled one another's food and continued attempting to hold a conversation without shouting. Dee finished her martini and stopped acting like a poster child for the socially awkward.

After dinner Jancee caught Dee's eye, raised her eyebrows in some kind of coded message, and put her hand to her head like an actress in a silent movie.

"Oh, I've suddenly got the worst headache. It's just splitting."

Bruce flagged the waitress down for the check. "I'll take care of this and get the car."

"Oh no, don't bother. Our hotel's right down the street and the fresh air will do me good. You two have a good time now. Thanks for dinner, sweetie." She planted a kiss on Bruce's head and was gone before Dee could come up with an excuse of her own.

Poor Bruce, Dee thought. Trapped into spending time with her. She looked longingly at her empty martini glass.

"How about if I show you around town? Some of the off-the-beaten-path areas. We've got an arts district in the old part of town, Canal Street. It's right up the road, lots of little shops . . . pretty cool place." Somehow, Bruce seemed to have forgotten that Dee was certifiable.

"It sounds nice." Dee fiddled with the clasp of her purse. "But you don't have to entertain me. I'm sure you have things to do, and you've got to work tomorrow, right?"

"Are you kidding?" he said. "I'm having a great time. And I want to hear what you've been up to. I think I might have monopolized the conversation during dinner. Once I start talking about my glory days, I can't seem to stop."

"Not at all." Dee smiled at him. "You've got some great stories."

"Come on. Let's get out of here."

They walked all around the palm tree–lined historic arts district, stopping in interesting-looking shops and galleries. Bruce was a perfect gentleman—opening her car door, taking her arm when they crossed the street, even putting his jacket around her shoulders to block the evening chill. Dee knew better than to read too much into his behavior—Bruce had always known how to make a girl feel like a princess . . . at least as long as she was in sight.

For just a moment, Dee allowed herself to daydream about someone who cherished and protected her, as if she were a rare orchid or a delicate piece of china. Someone like the taciturn Kansas cowboy whose face she could barely recall. She shook off the feeling of melancholy and turned her attention to the man by her side, who was currently making a fool of himself mimicking the modern art portraits as they browsed in a gallery where every painting was a variation on the Greek tragedy and comedy masks. Bruce scrunched one eye nearly closed and widened the other. "Do you think the model really looked like this?"

The store manager had been glaring at them from behind the register during Bruce's antics. "We'll be closing in five minutes," he said. Dee nodded at him and choked back a laugh. He had the same bushy eyebrows and Van Dyke beard as the subject of the gallery paintings.

Dee whispered in Bruce's ear. "I think he's the model."

Bruce looked over and gave a little salute. "Thank you, sir. We very much enjoyed perusing your artwork." Then he linked his arm through Dee's and steered her out of the gallery, where the two of them broke into laughter.

"Do you think he's the artist and they're all self-portraits?" Bruce said.

"Maybe," Dee said. "I'm so glad his eyes aren't distorted like the paintings."

"Yeah, that really would be a tragedy."

Dee giggled. "Good one."

They continued walking down Canal Street, but most of the shops appeared to be closing.

Dee looked at her watch. "Oh. I didn't realize how late it was."

"You know what they say, 'Time flies when you're having fun.'" Bruce wrapped his arm around Dee's waist and pulled her in for a quick kiss. "I'm not ready to let you go just yet. Come on, I want to take you to my favorite spot."

The thrill of his touch and the martinis in her bloodstream convinced her to follow his lead and see where the evening would take them. They ducked into a trendy, darkened coffee bar that featured a jazz trio playing quietly on a small stage.

"Okay, for real now, I want to hear what you've been up to. How in the hell did you end up driving a truck?" Bruce said. He held her hand across the table and leaned in, seeming to hang on her every word as she told him about her cross-country trips. All her teenage dreams were coming true! Lost in a happy fog, she made up her mind to take Jancee's advice and say yes to romance. She was a modern woman. She could have sex with no strings. It would be perfect. A one-night stand was just what she needed. She should drink martinis more often.

Then a girl not much older than Katie walked over with their coffees and a big smile.

"Bruce!" she exclaimed. "I didn't know you were coming in tonight."

"Hey, babe! How's the back?" He abandoned Dee's hand on the table and began to massage the waitress's spine. "That was quite a spill you took yesterday."

"Oh yeah, it was crazy, right?" she said. "I'm getting out there again tomorrow, though. Maybe we can hang out after?"

"You bet." He gave the girl a final pat on the rear. "I'll buy you a beer."

He turned back to Dee and reclaimed her hand with a smile. "Having fun?"

"Absolutely. It's just like old times."

Bruce didn't pick up on her sarcasm. "I know," he said, squeezing her fingers. "I'm so glad you're here."

Dee wasn't sure if it was the caffeine or the waitress's frequent stops at their table that sobered her up, but by the time they left the coffeehouse, she was completely clearheaded.

Bruce draped his arm around her as they walked back to the car.

"So what do you say, Dee Dee? Want to come back to my place?"

Dee smiled up into his guileless face. Bruce was who he was, and he took no pains to hide it. He loved women. Women loved him. But try as she might, she just couldn't bring herself to join that conga line. *No riding the longboard for me tonight,* she thought, and began laughing. Laughing so hard, she snorted. Bruce stopped smiling.

"I'm sorry," Dee sputtered. "It's the martinis. I don't even know what I'm laughing about. You must think I'm crazy." She inhaled deeply and tossed her head to clear it. "Sorry," she said again.

"No problem." Bruce's face fell back into its usual happy-go-lucky expression. "So what now?"

"I think I'd better get back to the hotel. We've got an early flight tomorrow."

Bruce nodded. "You got it, babe."

♕

JANCEE WASN'T AMUSED BY THE RETELLING OF THE date. Instead, Dee was treated to a lecture on their way to the airport.

"Once again, you spend an evening with a hot guy and when push comes to shove, there's no pushing or shoving. You didn't even kiss him? For fuck's sake, Dee, you're like a preteen."

"It just turned me off, the way he was carrying on with that girl in the coffee place," Dee said. "I mean, forget 'Flavor of the Month'; with him, it's more like 'Flavor of the Hour.'"

"But you knew Bruce was like that. Bruce has always been like that."

Jancee had a point. But Dee had always been a master of denial.

"I know. I just used to think that, maybe with me, it would be different."

Jancee was a little slow, but at last she caught on. "Oh, Dee." She pulled an exaggerated sad face, looking a bit like one of the paintings in the Comedy/Tragedy gallery. "I'll shut up now."

She didn't really shut up, though. She just switched to a new subject. Her interpretation of this turn of events was that Dee should sign up with an online dating service.

"Look, you know you're interested in finding someone new, and random cowboys and old college flames are not getting the job done. You need some help."

Once they boarded the plane, Jancee began showing her dating apps on the phone. "You've probably heard of this one, Tinder? See, you just swipe right on the guy's picture if you're interested, and left if you're not. I'll bet Katie has it. But it's more for just hooking up, and you're obviously not into that."

Did Katie have Tinder? It sounded like a terrible idea. Like the backstory for a true-crime episode. She rather not know if her daughter used it.

"I'm not interested in any of them. I just want to read my book."

Jancee ignored her. "Ooh, you might like this better. It's called Bumble. It's more female-centered. See? You check out the guys' profiles, and if you're interested, you send them a message. And then they can get back to you if they want to meet. Cool, right?"

"Nope."

"How about this guy? Not bad, huh?"

"Please stop."

"Okay. How about if we just work up your profile?"

"Nooooo!" Nothing Dee said did any good. Finally, she grabbed Jancee's noise-canceling headphones from her lap, clapped them on, and pretended to go to sleep.

chapter

TWENTY-ONE

AFTER PICKING SPOT UP FROM THE KENNEL, DEE walked into a house that felt more like a meat locker. Waiting for the central heating to kick on, she flicked the switch on the gas fireplace and sat on the hearth, Spot curled up at her feet.

It would be time to get back on the road tomorrow. She pulled Grady's note out of her toiletry bag and ran her finger along the phone number. *I can't do it,* she thought. *I just can't do it.* She put the note back in its plastic bag.

She called Katie instead.

"Hey, sweetie. I just wanted to let you know that I'm home."

"How was your trip? Did you and Aunt Jancee have fun?"

"Oh, you know Jancee. Never a dull moment."

"I wish I could've come with you. I'm so pale, I'm practically invisible. I think I'm going to go tanning later on."

"Oh, Kate, don't go doing that. It's really dangerous. It doubles your chance of getting skin cancer." Dee couldn't help herself.

"Mother. Please. I'm not going to go a million times and fry myself. Tell me about Florida. I'm so jealous. What did you do?"

"Mostly, we just went to the beach and out to eat. It was very relaxing. Oh, and Jancee tricked me into going on a date." Dee put her hand to her mouth. Why had she said that? She shouldn't be telling her twenty-year-old daughter about her extramarital dating experiences.

But Katie didn't seem bothered by it at all. "Really? Who was he? How did she trick you?"

"It was a guy I knew in college. We ran into him on the beach and went to dinner, and then Jancee claimed to have a headache and left me alone with him."

"So . . . did you have a good time?"

"Yes. Actually, I did." This was surreal, talking to her daughter about dating a man besides her father. "But he was always kind of a player, and he still is, so I don't think I'll be seeing him again."

"Player?" Katie laughed out loud. "Listen to you, Mom."

Dee flushed with embarrassment. Was she trying too hard to seem hip? "Well, whatever. He dates a lot of women at the same time."

"Yeah, I'm aware of the definition. I'm just kidding with you. It's kind of weird talking to you about this stuff."

Dee knew it. Why didn't she just keep her mouth shut?

"I'm sorry, sweetie. I shouldn't have mentioned it. I didn't mean to make you uncomfortable."

"I'm not uncomfortable. It's just a little weird, that's all. Actually, I kind of like talking to you about it."

"You do?"

"Sure. I want you to be happy."

"I am happy. How could I not be happy with you for my daughter?"

"Yeah. I am pretty awesome." Katie laughed. "Seriously though, Dad's getting married to that girlfriend of his and I want you to find somebody too."

"So, you know they're getting married?"

"Yeah. Dad wants me to be in the wedding." Katie scoffed. "Like that's ever going to happen. I told him I'll go, but I'm not standing up there with her."

Dee sighed. Another subject on the list of things she never thought she'd be talking about with her daughter.

"Listen, Mom, I'm about to get on an elevator. Can I call you back later tonight?"

"Sure, honey. I just wanted to let you know I was home."

Dee sat there for a moment, looking at her phone. Somewhere over the past few months, her daughter had become her friend.

EARLY THE NEXT MORNING, DEE WAS AT THE DISTRI-bution center cleaning up her truck and preparing for another two weeks on the road. As she stood on the step box polishing the side mirrors, Rico wandered over.

"Hey, Queenie!"

Dee frowned down at him. "I'm still not sure how I feel about that name."

"Ah, go on. You know we're all just kidding with you." He knelt down to pet Spot.

"Hmm." Dee climbed down and dropped the rag in her cleaning bucket. "So, how are you making out? You still like being out on the road?"

"Yeah. It's awesome," he said. "My girl, Laurel, doesn't like me being away so much, but we're figuring things out. We've already got enough saved to get an apartment together."

"That's exciting," Dee said. "What does Laurel do?"

"She's a hairdresser. Really talented. She'll have her own salon one of these days. We're saving for that too."

Dee smiled up at him. She really liked this kid. "It sounds like you two have a great future ahead of you."

Rico grinned and pushed the hair back out of his eyes. "Yeah, I think so too. Laurel's looking at secondhand shops for furniture, and her mom's giving us some kitchen stuff."

A memory of the mismatched flatware and hand-me-down dishes she and Dan started out with flickered in her memory. She missed the optimism of new beginnings. And the optimism of youth. She sighed without meaning to.

"How about you? You doing okay out on the road? You sound a little tired," Rico said.

"Oh, I'm okay. If I'm tired of anything, it's of listening to the same twenty songs over and over on the radio. I never realized how limited playlists were until I started driving this truck day after day."

"You should sign up for a streaming service," Rico said.

Dee looked at him blankly.

"Music streaming. You have to pay for it, but it's not bougie."

"Okay, still lost. 'Bougie'?"

"Not expensive." He held out his phone and pointed to an app. "I've got Spotify. There're others, but this one's the best, I think. You put one song or artist you like in there, and it'll bring up, like, a thousand other songs. It's killer."

Dee looked at the playlist he'd opened up. "Is it just hip-hop?"

"Nah. It's got everything." He scrolled on the phone and held it out again. "This is Laurel's stuff."

Now she saw some songs she recognized. She handed his phone back. "Thanks, Rico. That's just what I need. And listen, I might have some furniture for you, if you're interested. I've got my house up for sale and once I get a buyer, there's a lot of stuff I won't be needing."

"That would be awesome."

"I'll let you know as soon as it sells, and you can bring Laurel over to see if any of it will work for you." She loved the idea of helping this young couple get started. Especially since Rico had made her feel like part of the team from day one.

Before starting the truck, Dee set about harnessing Spot in the passenger seat. She'd taken her to the vet before her vacation, just to be sure there were no hidden injuries from the accident, and the doctor recommended she get a seat-belt attachment made just for pets. Never having owned a dog before, Dee was constantly amazed at the number of gadgets you could buy for an animal. Spot didn't seem to like it much.

"You'll get used to it." Dee rubbed the dog's velvety ears. "I'm not taking a chance on you getting hurt again."

Then they were on their way, barreling down the highway. A rush of adrenaline shot through her every time she set out on a trip. In the past, she would have identified what she was feeling as nerves, but she'd successfully talked herself into calling it excitement. When any scary thoughts presented themselves, she met them with rational arguments. She hadn't heard anything about Jensen in months, and having Spot with her really did make her feel more secure. Even though the pup was as docile as any golden retriever, people seemed to avoid getting too close to her.

This week's trip out West would be taking her straight through Wichita, on the same stretch of highway where she'd met Grady. Dee considered going a different way, but Kansas was the most direct route. It's not like she would go looking for him anyway. She couldn't even bring herself to call him. Afraid to find out that the night she remembered lived only in her memory.

The sad truth was, she couldn't put the few hours they'd spent together out of her mind even when she wasn't within a hundred miles of him. It had become a way to pass the time, imagining what a life with him might have looked like. She imagined him teaching her to ride a horse along a sun-dappled trail, or sitting by a campfire under a starry Midwest sky, or dancing. Dancing with Grady. That was her favorite daydream, mostly because she could still remember the feel of his arms around her, leading her in time to the music, making her feel safe.

Sometimes she let herself imagine a physical relationship with him. But her PG-rated daydreams didn't amount to much. Once she got past the memory of him kissing her in the motel lobby, her imagination quit on her. That is, until she found some new music.

After another ten hours of listening to top-twenty hits, she took Rico's advice and signed up for a streaming service. Stopped for the night just over the Indiana state line, she downloaded the app and spent an hour selecting music genres and playlists. The next day's driving flew by despite Indiana's monotonous nothing-but-cornfield scenery. There were so many great songs and artists. She'd never even heard half of them.

As she drove along, looking for a place to stop for the night just outside Wichita, a new song began to play. It caught her attention right away because the guy's voice had the same deep and gravelly timbre as Grady's. She glanced at the display—"Like a Wrecking Ball." But this was no pop song.

Some guy named Church was singing about getting home to his woman after a long time on the road. Listening to the song, Dee's Disney-sanitized daydream took a sudden turn. Now imaginary Grady wanted her in the worst way. He needed her so badly he was going to knock down her door rather than use his key. He had her up against the wall and was doing seductively obscene things to her. The song came to an end just as she found a rest area. Good thing. She needed to get her wool sweater off before she burst into flames.

She took Spot for a walk to cool off and then listened to the song a few more times. Jancee was right. She needed a man.

chapter

TWENTY-TWO

ANOTHER FEW DAYS ON THE ROAD HAD HER IN NORTHERN California wine country. She'd always wanted to visit the area, even more so once she branched out from drinking only white zinfandel. She thought she'd have just enough time to drive through the area and maybe pick up a souvenir bottle of cabernet. Then she got lucky with scheduling. There'd been some kind of mix-up with the logistics team, and the trailer full of almonds she needed to pick up would be a day late. She consulted her travel clippings file and decided to spend the night in Calistoga.

The magazine article recommended the town for people who "just want to chill." After seven days on the road, yeah, that's exactly what she wanted. She found an inn with reasonable rates and a welcoming attitude toward dogs and, after finding a lot where she could park the rig overnight, checked in.

Right off the bat, she loved the place. Amelie, the clerk that took care of her, was cheerful and full of enthusiasm, handing her brochures and pointing out places Dee needed to visit during her stay.

"My goodness, thanks for all this," Dee said. "I wish I was going to be here for more than one day."

"Oh. It's the best," the girl said. She had blond hair with purple highlights, a tiny amethyst stud in her nose, and a flowy bohemian dress that reminded Dee of Stevie Nicks in her heyday. "I moved up here from Southern California. It's a whole different vibe. Everybody's so laid-back."

"That sounds like just what I need right now," Dee said.

"If you're only going to be here for a day, try to at least get over here to Old Faithful." Amelie opened the map and drew a line from where they were to another location. Dee noticed a small tattoo on her wrist. An infinity symbol with the words "Love the life you live / Live the life you love." She'd never before been a fan of tattoos, but this one she liked. Maybe just for the sentiment. At her age, it might be more appropriate needlepointed on a pillow.

"Old Faithful?" Dee said. "I thought that was in Yellowstone."

"Well, that's the more famous one, but ours is cuter. And easy to get to. It's just a five-minute drive from here."

Dee looked at the map. "Maybe I can stop there on my way out of town tomorrow. I'm driving an eighteen-wheeler, so I don't think I'll run over there now."

The girl handed her another brochure. "Here. You can rent a bike."

Again, Dee found herself studying the girl's tattoo. She pointed to it. "I love that," she said.

"Thanks! I got it downtown at Monkey Wrench. They're top-notch if you're looking for some ink."

Dee laughed. "I think I'm a little old for that. But it looks beautiful on you."

"Aww, thanks. You're not too old, though. My mom and I got these matching tattoos after her divorce."

Dee left the office in a fog. She had never ever wanted a tattoo. In fact, she had frequently lectured Katie about the foolhardiness of putting something so permanent on her body. Now, all of a sudden, she wanted one desperately. She wondered if there were narcotics wafting in the air. Maybe the person who checked in before her had been smoking something in the lobby.

She walked downtown with Spot, to a charming main street with early 1900s buildings. Adorable shops with clever names like Stix & Stones and Sugar Daddy's made it impossible to resist shopping. Nearly every store offered dog treats and had bowls of water outside. Spot had to sample all of them. She bought Katie an enormous tie-dye hoodie. It would be huge on her, but that's the way she wore them. For herself, Dee bought a Pura Vida bracelet with a tiny bus charm that sort of looked like her tractor trailer.

After returning her dog to the inn and dropping off her purchases, Dee walked back to the bike shop the clerk recommended, rented a bike, and rode to the Calistoga Spa to see the geyser. Riding past grape arbors and viewing the mountains in the distance, she thought again about the quote on Amelie's wrist. While she didn't love everything about being a truck driver, she was certainly enjoying this.

Old Faithful geyser, however, turned out to be a bit of a disappointment. She walked around the grounds and saw the goats and bighorn sheep, then watched the water spout out of the ground a couple of times. It didn't impress her much. Walking to the exit, she overheard a man talking to the woman next to him. "More like Old Fake-ful if you ask me. I can't believe we just spent thirty bucks on that." Dee agreed. At least she'd enjoyed the bike ride out.

For dinner, she walked back downtown and stopped in a brewery that had high ratings on Tripadvisor. The hostess seated her on the outdoor patio, and she ordered the rosemary chicken with roasted vegetables and a glass of chardonnay. The sun set over the mountains as she sipped her wine, and the patio heater by her table offset the evening chill. Best of all, the chicken dish made up for all the subpar meals she'd eaten on the road. She savored each bite of perfectly roasted brussels sprouts and baby carrots.

As she sat back, enjoying the last of her buttery and not-too-oaky chardonnay, she heard a strangely familiar voice behind her. She took another sip and eavesdropped on the conversation. The man had a melodious voice that she could swear she'd heard before, but where? They were talking about the Grateful Dead. Reminiscing about shows they'd gone to. Suddenly, it came to her. It was Long Strange Trip, the trucker whose videos she'd watched over and over.

She spun around in her seat and looked over at him. He wore a purple tie-dyed T-shirt and faded jeans. He actually looked like Jerry Garcia, an effect Dee suspected was not coincidental.

"Excuse me, are you Long Strange Trip?" As the words came out of her mouth, she realized how odd it would sound if he wasn't the YouTube guy. Becoming less inhibited by alcohol was both a blessing and a curse.

"Yeah!" The guy's face lit up. "How'd you guess?"

"Your voice sounded familiar. I watched your videos over and over before I started driving."

"No way! You're a trucker?"

Dee nodded.

"Well, get on over here and join us. Me and my buddy just got in from Seattle and are washing the dust down, as they say." He shoved an extra seat back from the table. "You waiting on the music to start?"

"What music?"

"They've got a Grateful Dead cover band coming on in ten minutes. They're supposed to be good. Nothing like the real thing, I'm sure, but we'll take what we can get."

Dee looked at her phone. She had nowhere to be. The thought of sitting in this lovely space with its twinkling lights and firepits blazing while talking with some friendly people sounded wonderful. "Are you sure you don't mind me breaking in on your night?"

"Are you kidding?" Long Strange Trip's friend spoke up. He, too, wore a tie-dyed shirt, but he had dreadlocks, no beard, and skin the color of the dark beer he was drinking. "We're team drivers and, speaking for myself, I'd give anything for somebody else to talk to. I'm Jerry, yes, that's really my name, and this is Tony, but you can just keep calling him Strange, 'cause he is."

Dee laughed and pulled up a chair. The conversation flowed easily. They talked her into trying a craft beer. She'd actually enjoyed the one she'd tried in Kansas, though it might have had something to do with the man who bought it for her. This brewery didn't have cherry, so she went with a lager that featured prickly pear.

She told Tony how much she'd enjoyed the videos he posted, then they talked about the trucking industry for a while. They asked how long she'd been driving and what she thought of it. Then they told her how the two of them had followed the Grateful Dead tour in its last five years.

"When they quit touring, we were kind of at loose ends, so we decided to keep driving around and make a living at it." Jerry took a sip of his beer.

"Twenty-five years later, and here we are, still together and still listening to the Dead." Tony smiled and patted Jerry on the forearm, and the two men shared a look. Dee turned her head in the direction of the stage. Realizing that they were a couple unleashed a wave of sadness in her—in a restaurant filled with couples enjoying the evening and one another's company, she was the only party of one. Loneliness engulfed her. She gulped down the rest of her beer and turned back to Tony and Jerry.

"So, what's your favorite Dead song?" Dee asked.

"Hmm, that's a tough one," Jerry said. "I guess I'd have to say 'Ripple.'"

"You should be able to guess mine," Tony said.

Dee smiled. "'Truckin'?"

Tony pointed at her with a thumbs-up gesture. "That's life, ain't it? One long strange trip."

"Let's get another round," Jerry said.

The music started, and for some reason, Dee decided to tell them about her sudden desire to get a tattoo.

"Hell, that's a great idea," said Tony.

"We've both got some tats," Jerry said. "Look at this one." He rolled up his sleeve and showed her an elaborate skull with roses around it.

"Oh, that's"—*creepy*, is what she thought, but she came up with another adjective—"so cool. Very detailed."

Then Tony showed her the tattoo on his upper arm. "It's our truck. Look at the detail on this one! You could get one just like it."

Dee gave him a weak smile. "I was thinking of something a lot smaller."

"Like this?" Jerry said, showing her one of the Grateful Dead's marching bears.

"Yeah, we both got that one." Tony showed her his.

They drank more beer and continued talking about tattoos, then somehow they all ended up at Monkey Wrench, the place Amelie told her about. All three of them got tattoos. Jerry got a compass, Tony got an anchor, and Dee got the infinity symbol quote. It didn't hurt as much as she thought it would. Maybe it was all the beer.

The next day, Dee awoke with a searing pain on her wrist. She looked at the bandage momentarily confused and then remembered the previous night's activities. "Oh for God's sake, Dee. Have you lost your mind?" She spoke out loud, so Spot answered in Chewbacca-speak. Dee shook her head at the dog. "Yeah, where were you last night? You're supposed to be keeping me out of trouble." She peered under the bandage and shrugged. She didn't hate it. She felt a little ridiculous, but what the hell. Her once-boring life was a thing of the past.

chapter

TWENTY-THREE

WEEKS LATER, DEE'S BEGINNER'S LUCK RAN OUT. IT was late when she finally pulled off the highway on the final night of a trip down south. The entire route had been one headache after another—instead of drop-and-hook, she had to wait on trailers being loaded—and the hassles of that were compounded by road construction on seemingly every highway she traveled. The quote on her wrist mocked her. Had she jinxed herself? Then that morning, she'd had a grueling three-hour wait at the Kia plant in West Point, Georgia, to pick up a load of car parts followed by an accident on the highway. If she hadn't been so tired and hungry—she'd eaten nothing but a couple of apples for lunch—and if she'd hadn't burned through even her auxiliary fuel tank when she was stuck behind the pileup on I-85, she would have looked for someplace less dreary than Ruby's Diner to spend the night.

Ordinarily, these little mom-and-pop places were a welcome change from the indistinguishable corporate rest areas that made up her days, and frequenting them made her feel like she was doing her bit to help out the little guy. Katie had convinced her how important it was to "shop small and shop local." But Ruby's had seen better days. Remote and surrounded by forest, it looked like a setting in the movie *Deliverance*. The neon sign she'd seen from the highway should have been her first clue—the *T* and *R* were out, so the sign read "UCK STOP."

More like yuck stop, Dee thought as she stood at the diesel pump refueling. Litter blew around the cracked pavement of the parking lot. A small line of semis stood at the back of the lot, and only a handful of people were in the diner. At least there were no banjos playing in the background.

As she waited for the tank to fill up, she glanced over her shoulder at a lone pickup truck parked just outside the dim circle of streetlight. She had that creepy-crawly feeling of being watched. She told herself she was being paranoid, like a kid afraid of the dark. But it was *really* dark, especially out behind the ramshackle diner.

The two tanks were finally topped off. She climbed back in the cab, pulled off the latex gloves, and wiped her hands with the antibacterial wipes she kept stashed in the console.

"Okay, Spot. Let's get you a walk and some kibble, and then I'll grab some dinner in that lovely establishment over there."

The dog yawned.

The only open spot was at the very end of the lot, next to a line of trees. *At least it's convenient for Spot's walk,* Dee tried to tell herself. And she wouldn't have to wear her eye mask to block light from the streetlamps. There weren't any.

"See, glass half-full, right, Spot?" She used a high-pitched singsong voice with the dog, trying to jolly both of them up.

Maybe Spot was picking up on Dee's anxiety, but she was even jumpier than normal.

"Get busy, and I'll let you back in the truck. Come on, pup."
After putting the dog back in the cab, she walked toward the diner with a feeling of dread. Now that she had a full tank, she could get back on the highway and find a better place to stop for the night. But she was so hungry. And so tired.

There were two men playing cards at a table in the middle of the room, a lone woman seated in the back booth, and a few men at the counter. There was something familiar about the one closest to the kitchen. He was short and wiry like that creep from training, but he wore a trucker hat, and she couldn't see his face. He was the only one who didn't turn to look at her when she walked in. She buttoned her fitted down jacket and wished she'd pulled on a baggy sweatshirt instead.

Taking a seat at the table nearest the door, she tried to look like she belonged. The men had stopped staring at her. And what would Jensen be doing down here in the middle of nowhere? She looked out at the trucks. No fuel rigs. The place was a such a dump, her biggest worry should be food poisoning.

She ordered an omelet and then walked back to the bathroom, trying to get a better look at the guy who reminded her of Jensen. He averted his head as she went by. Was that intentional? She closed the ladies' room door behind her and took a deep breath of disinfectant-scented air. She had to stop letting her imagination run wild. *Be rational. It's been a rough trip. You'll feel better once you're heading home.*

Returning to her table, she again glanced at the men sitting at the counter. Trucker Hat was no longer there. She'd been worrying over nothing, as usual.

A scowling waitress set Dee's plate in front of her. "You want anything else?" The question sounded like a challenge.

"No thanks. Just the check."

The woman slapped it on the table and went back to the counter, where she resumed watching something on her phone.

The omelet was surprisingly good, and Dee's spirits began to lift. A full stomach made everything better. Maybe she should have had that tattooed on her wrist.

As she left the diner and headed back to her truck, she heard the metallic squeak of a door opening. She glanced over her shoulder and saw someone getting out of the pickup parked in the shadows. Instead of walking to the diner as she expected, he started moving in the same direction as her. She should have trusted her intuition. Jensen had been at the counter and now he had her in a place with no one to help her, just like he'd threatened. Was this a coincidence, or had he been stalking her all this time? She had to decide quickly: walk back to the diner and come face-to-face with him or hurry to the truck. Maybe she was still imagining things. He could be a random stranger heading to the trees to relieve himself.

She picked up her pace. Immediately, the footsteps quickened behind her. She began running and heard him running too. It wasn't her imagination. He was chasing her and getting closer. She made it to the back of her truck. A few more yards and she could open the door to let Spot out. Heavy breathing right behind her, she reached up for the handle. Too late, she remembered it was locked. Wiry arms wrapped around her waist and slammed her against the wheel well. Everything went dark.

She regained consciousness face down in the dirt and felt him yanking at her jeans. The sound of Spot barking and snarling echoed above her, but locked in the cab the dog couldn't protect her. Dee scrabbled and clawed at the ground, trying to get away. "No. Let me go." As if in a nightmare, her voice came out a whisper. She drew a breath, and this time managed a real scream. Immediately, her attacker clamped a hand over her mouth. She was trapped. No one could have heard her over the idling trucks. The sound of him unbuckling his belt fueled a desperate attempt to escape. She twisted her head violently, managing to loosen his hand, then she bit down as hard as she could.

"You little cunt," he growled. He threw her on her back and sat on her, pinning her to the ground as his thumbs crushed her windpipe. She scratched at his hands, but it was useless. She had no strength to fight him off.

Through the blood rushing in her ears, she could hear Spot howling and throwing herself against the door. She was going to die. She was going to die in this godforsaken place. What would he do with her body? Would he leave her lying here? Or would he bury her somewhere that no one would ever find her? She should have listened to Jancee and bought a gun. Or listened to her own intuition and gotten back on the highway.

Just as she lost consciousness, she felt a jolt and his grip seemed to loosen. She was floating. So this is what dying felt like. Floating away. Then nothing.

DEE OPENED HER EYES AND SAW A LIGHT. WAS THIS the beckoning light people reported seeing after having been declared clinically dead? Was she supposed to follow it? It seemed more like a flashlight. A big silver flashlight. And behind it was an angel. A Black angel with shiny ringlets and a warm urgent voice.

"You're okay now. Wake up. Come on, mama, wake up."

Could she bargain with this celestial being and get a second chance at life? That's how all those stories came to be in the first place, right? Because the people who died came back to life?

"Am I in heaven?" Dee said, her voice a raspy croak.

"Not any kind of heaven I'd want to imagine," said the voice behind the light. "Can you sit up?"

Dee rolled on her side and pushed herself up, noticing as she did the prone figure of a man with a gaping wound on the back of his shaved head. She put a hand to her throat and looked again at her angel and the bloody flashlight she held.

It was the woman who'd been sitting in the back booth. "We need to get out of here," the woman said. "Do you think you can drive?"

Dee looked back at the man on the ground. "Is he . . . is he dead?"

"I don't think so. Here, let's get you dressed and in the truck. Hurry." The woman pulled her to her feet and helped her with her clothes.

"Shouldn't we call the police?" It sounded like someone else talking.

A quick shake of the head. "No. I don't trust the cops around these parts. And for all we know this skinhead's friends are in the diner over there. Let's go." She pushed Dee toward the front of the truck.

"Wait! I want to see his face." Blood streamed from the back of the man's bald head. *Was it him?* Had Jensen been stalking her all this time?

He groaned as the woman rolled him over with the toe of her boot. "Someone you know?"

Dee looked down, then shook her head. She'd never seen him before. It was a stranger.

"Okay. Get in the truck and calm your dog down."

Too dazed to think for herself, she did as she was told. Spot licked at her face and sniffed her, while the woman grabbed the unconscious man by the feet and dragged him into the brush. Dee watched the scene unfold as if it were something in a movie. A movie she would have walked out of. But there was no walking away from this.

The woman straightened and brushed her hands on her jeans, then returned to Dee's truck.

"This is my truck right next to yours. Follow me back out to the highway and we'll find a place to stop further up the road."

Dee was too rattled to argue. More than anything, she wanted to get away from this place. She brought the engine to life and followed the truck ahead of her. Half an hour later, they stopped at a well-lit super truck stop. If only she'd driven a little bit further before stopping for gas.

They parked on the far end of the lot, a phalanx of other trucks blocking them from the view of anyone on the access road or in the restaurant. Dee couldn't think straight. She had a blinding headache, and the right side of her face throbbed with pain. Something warm and sticky ran down her face and neck. She should do something, but she couldn't think what. With an air of detachment, she watched the woman come around the cab to her door. She stared down at her.

"Open up."

Dee did as she was told.

"Are you okay?"

Dee shook her head.

The woman climbed up on the step box and studied Dee's face. "Can you talk?"

"Yes." Her voice came out in a croak. She hardly sounded human.

"Okay. Listen, I'm going to go in the Quick Stop over there and get some ice. Just sit tight."

Dee nodded wordlessly. She watched as the woman flipped the hood of her sweatshirt up and walked away. She had no idea how long she sat there. Spot leaned against her, shaking. Or maybe it was Dee who was shaking. Nothing made sense. Time had stopped.

Then her rescuer reappeared. "Is your dog going to let me in?"

"I think so," Dee whispered.

"Okay, climb in the back."

Dee sat on the bunk, Spot glued to her, and accepted the large Coke she was offered.

"Drink some of this."

Again, Dee did as she was told. She stared straight ahead as the woman cleaned her face with a damp washcloth. Where had all that blood come from? She didn't flinch as the woman applied antiseptic to her temple and affixed a butterfly closure.

"Name's Sugar, by the way."

"I'm Dee." She put her hand gingerly to her throat, wondering if the damage to her vocal cords was permanent.

"Well, I wish it had been under different circumstances, but nice to meet you. Not too many of us woman truckers out here."

Dee nodded.

"Here, hold this on the side of your head." Sugar put a plastic bag of ice in Dee's hand. She leaned back against the wall of the cab and looked around. "Real cozy in here." Then she rested her gaze on Dee again. "You feeling any better?"

"I don't know," she said in her wrecked voice. "I think I might be in shock."

"I imagine you are, in shock, that is. But I think that's the worst of it." Sugar pulled a phone from her pocket and glanced at the screen. "I've gotta get back on the road. I'm due in Philadelphia tomorrow."

Dee didn't want to be alone. "Can you stay just a little longer?"

Sugar checked her phone again. "Maybe another few minutes."

"Are you sure we shouldn't call the police? I mean, now that we're here and there are all these people around?"

"No way."

"But look at me." Dee repositioned the ice bag. "Anyone could tell I was nearly killed. If we called the police, they'd have to believe us."

Sugar shook her head. "Look, honey, I get that you believe the police are good guys, and maybe most of them are, but unfortunately I might not get the same treatment you're used to."

Another layer of bad feelings swirled into Dee's emotions, a faint whiff of shame for taking it for granted that an innocent person would get fair treatment. She'd sometimes felt embarrassed by the privileges she enjoyed solely for being married to someone wealthy, but she didn't think too much about what life would be like if she were another race. "So, what do we do?"

Sugar put her elbows on her knees and leaned toward Dee with a fierce look on her face. "We do just what we were doing before that motherfucker showed up. Finish this trip. Cover up your neck, wear some dark glasses, and then stay home sick until the bruising clears up. And forget you ever met me. I'm a figment of your imagination, got it?"

Dee nodded mutely.

Sugar sighed and leaned back against the wall. When she spoke again, her voice had softened. "Listen, I'm sorry for yelling at you." She moved the curtain aside and looked out the window. "I need to get on the road now. You lock up and get some sleep."

"I'll never be able to sleep."

"You don't have sleeping pills?"

Dee shook her head.

Sugar pulled a prescription bottle from her satchel and shook some yellow pills into Dee's hand. "Take one of these if you want. They work fast and don't leave you groggy."

Sugar pulled her hood back up, and after checking again that no one was around, she climbed down from Dee's cab and up into her own.

Dee leaned her forehead against the glass, watching the truck pull out, keeping her eyes on the taillights until they disappeared from view. Then she locked the doors and pulled the curtains to the bunk closed. She was still vibrating with fear. Her throat was swollen and achy, and her head throbbed. Her whole body felt bruised. She opened her palm and looked at the pills. No idea what they were. But she needed the oblivion of sleep, so she swallowed one before she could change her mind. What was one more careless act this evening?

In the morning, the bruising was worse. The marks on her neck were purple, and there were black-and-blue crescents under her eyes. She had a pounding headache, and the side of her forehead was swollen. She tried parting her hair so that it covered her temple, but it was matted with blood. The neckline of her shirt was crusted with reddish brown, and more spots were on her jeans. She swallowed the bile that rose in her throat and dug out clean clothes. The bag of souvenirs she'd purchased in Calistoga were still in the truck, so she grabbed the oversized sweatshirt she'd gotten for Katie and ripped off the tags. Then she shoved her blood-spattered things in a garbage bag. Before changing, she snapped a selfie with her phone. If the police caught up with her, she wanted to be able to prove she had been attacked.

chapter

TWENTY-FOUR

HOME HAD ALWAYS BEEN A SANCTUARY FOR DEE, BUT now it became her panic room. As soon as she closed the door behind her, she rearmed the alarm system. Then she sent text messages to Jancee and Katie, whose calls she'd been ignoring. She claimed she had laryngitis, the same lie she'd told Frank when she checked in and asked for a few days off. Like Sugar, she pulled her sweatshirt hood forward to hide her face before going into the office.

"You're sick too? Bob and Vicky are out with the flu, and Angie's helping out with the grandkids, also sick, leaving me to handle the whole damn place." He glanced up from the computer screen. "Well, you look like hell. Sure, take a few days off. Just add it to the shit show this week is turning into. I got Gary out here in Colorado with faulty brakes, Josh in New Mexico with a flipping speeding ticket, a Walmart in Arkansas refusing a delivery." Frank grumbled under his breath and pounded at the keyboard. "Whole damn schedule is blown to pieces."

Rico came in as she left the office. He wasn't as easy to fool.

"What the fuck happened to you?" he said.

"Nothing," Dee said in her damaged voice. "I'm sick. Bad sinus. You better not get too close."

Rico frowned and held the door for her. "What's with the sunglasses?"

"My eyes are really sensitive to light right now." She tugged at her hood and walked past him with her head down.

"Queenie?"

Dee ignored the concern in Rico's voice and hurried to her car. "I'm fine, really."

After a few days holed up in the house, the bruising had faded enough to cover with makeup and her voice was almost back to normal. When she ran out of Sugar's sleeping pills, she began drinking wine until she passed out on the couch with Spot curled up at her feet. But no matter what she tried, her mind replayed the assault all day long and terrifying nightmares haunted her at night.

And what if her attacker was dead? Did that make her an accessory to murder? Or would the law consider it self-defense? She had too many questions, and no one to give her answers. She didn't dare google news reports from Georgia. She'd seen enough CSI episodes to know that checking computer search engines was the first thing the police did when investigating a suspect.

She dug the bloodied clothes out of the garbage bag and examined them. The blood on the shirt was hers, but what about the splatters on her jeans? Did blood spray on her clothes when Sugar swung the flashlight? She knotted the bag back up and took it to the dumpster behind the supermarket late at night. Then she worried that security cameras may have recorded her suspicious behavior. Paranoia engulfed her. What had happened to her perfectly ordered life? She seemed to exist on the other side of the mirror now—a dark jumbled place.

Before heading out in the truck again, she took a ride to Cabela's, the huge hunting and fishing supply store in Hamburg. Not to buy a gun—she was still too afraid of accidently killing someone she knew in a panicked moment—but she thought there might be something less lethal that would make her feel safe on the road. Like mace, or pepper spray, or a Taser. Now that she was a criminal (was she?) she didn't care if it was illegal to carry one in the truck.

Expecting to see a lot of camping equipment and sporting goods when she entered the store, she was unnerved by the vast amount of weaponry—crossbows, rifles, handguns, and economy-sized containers of ammunition surrounded her, along with racks of camouflage-print clothing. "This place is a freaking armory," she said under her breath. "In and out. Just get what you need and get out."

"Can I help you?" Dee jumped in surprise when the salesclerk addressed her.

She cleared her throat. "Yes. Do you carry Tasers?"

"Well, not Tasers exactly," the woman said. "But I'm sure we can find something you can use. We've got a whole line of personal defense equipment right over here."

She led Dee to a counter that contained an array of stun guns, pepper sprays, collapsible batons, and something called a tactical pen that apparently doubled as a stiletto. Hoping to avoid hand-to-hand combat, Dee bypassed the batons and pens and settled on a combination flashlight and 800,000-volt stun gun in bubblegum pink.

"And how about this pepper spray gel?" Dee read from the packaging. "Is it true that it shoots fifteen feet and will blind an assailant for forty-five minutes?"

"I guess so."

"Okay. I'll take both of these."

The clerk raised her eyebrows. "Sounds like you live in a dangerous area."

"My job sometimes has me in some sketchy places."

"Well, if you don't mind me saying, you might want to consider—"

"No guns." Dee cut her off, shaking her head. Was this store operated by the National Rifle Association?

"I wasn't suggesting that. I'm talking about a self-defense course. I mean, this stuff's not going to do you much good if you don't know some basic defensive moves." The clerk handed her a brochure, along with the shopping bag. "This is one that offers three-hour classes at the Y, or you could check with your local police department."

"Thanks, I'll look into it." Dee flipped through the brochure as the woman rang up her purchases.

She had talked to Katie about taking a class before she went to college, but her daughter claimed she was too busy. At the time, Dee could find nothing but martial arts studios offering monthslong training, wearing a *dōgi* and earning belts, so she didn't press the issue. But this program sounded promising—three hours of fending off simulated attacks in the safety of a well-lit building.

As soon as she got home, she got the go-ahead from her daughter and then registered them both for a session when Katie came home at the end of the semester.

WEEKS PASSED. DIVORCE PAPERS WERE SIGNED. PROSPECTIVE buyers traipsed through the house. Dee got back on the road. No one mentioned the small scar that had appeared on her temple or commented on her new accessories—a pseudo-flashlight that always hung from a strap on her wrist and a container of pepper spray peeking from the pocket of her purse.

She kept a close eye on her fuel levels and stopped only at well-lit, busy truck stops. She kept Spot by her side at all times. She'd found a website for emotional support animals and ordered a doggy vest. Sure it was bogus, but no one questioned her, even when using the ladies' room or eating in restaurants.

A little-known fact of life: if you act ballsy enough, you can do pretty much whatever you want.

Another fact of life: no matter how many precautions you take, there are still some things that will surprise you.

chapter

TWENTY-FIVE

"CAN YOU TELL ME WHAT THE HELL YOU'RE MIXED UP with in Kansas?" Frank's voice echoed from the cell phone.

Dee panicked for a split second until it registered that he was talking about Kansas, not Georgia. This didn't have anything to do with the attack. "Kansas? You mean the snowstorm? I know I lost a few hours there, but the roads were impossible. And you're the one who told me to stay in a motel. That's why I expensed it." How could he question her about something he himself had suggested? And why was he bringing it up now?

"This isn't about the snowstorm. I got a message from some guy at Scott Farms looking for you, and I know for a fact that we never sent you there. Are you driving on the side for somebody else, 'cause if you are . . ."

"I don't know what you're talking about!" If he was going to yell, she would too.

"Okay, okay. Just settle down. There must be a mix-up. But this guy from Scott sure seemed to know who you were."

"What guy from Scott? I've never even heard of Scott Farms."

224

"Yeah, me neither. I googled it. It's a ranch in Kansas. And this guy that's calling you is the owner, Grady Scott."

Dee pulled the truck to the shoulder and drifted to a stop. "*Grady* Scott?" she said in a small voice.

"So, you do know him."

"Grady called me?"

"Yes, goddam it, that's what I've been saying for the last ten minutes. Now, tell me what you were doing at that ranch."

"I wasn't at the ranch."

"Dee Levari! Give me a straight answer. Do you know the man, or don't you?"

"Yes. I know him. He's the cowboy in the pickup I told you about. The man who stopped to help me when I got run off the road."

Frank blew out his breath. "You got picked up by a rancher in Kansas. Yeah, that sounds like our Queenie, right there."

"I didn't get picked up! He just took me to dinner."

"For God's sake, Dee, just give the man a call. I'm not a flipping matchmaker here."

Dee sat in the truck on the side of the road, letting the traffic blow past her. She thought she might laugh and cry at the same time. Grady had found her.

"GRADY SCOTT!" HE ANSWERED HIS PHONE ON THE first ring.

Dee froze. What was she going to say to him? She'd forced herself to make the call without obsessing about it, and now her mind was blank. She should just hang up. Say, "Sorry, wrong number."

"Hello?" Grady said.

"Hi. It's Dee."

"Dee? Can you hold on for a second?"

Dee heard him talking to someone in the background. *"I need to take this. Go ahead without me."*

Then he was back on the line with her.

"Hey! How have you been?"

"I'm good. Everything is good."

She was interrupting him. He had an important job. She should have called later. "Are you busy now? I can call some other time."

"No. I was just in a meeting, nothing important."

"Oh." Instead of words, Dee's mind was filled with re-membered sensations. Grady's hand on her back, her forehead on his chest, the pressure of his warm lips on hers. This was a mistake.

"I left you a note at the hotel, hoping you'd call, but they probably didn't give it to you," Grady said.

"No, they did. I just . . . I didn't know what to say. I still don't know what to say, but, you know, my dispatcher told me you called and . . ." Dee drifted off. "I'm sorry."

The line was silent for a bit. When Grady spoke again, his voice had taken on a more formal tone. "It's me that should be sorry, tracking you down like . . . well, I just kept thinking about you. I guess I made that night out to be something it wasn't."

"No. You didn't . . . I mean, it was. It was special to me too. That's why I didn't call."

Grady was quiet again. "I'm confused. You didn't call *be-cause* it was special?"

"I was afraid it would be awkward and then . . . I don't know. I just didn't want to ruin everything. It was kind of perfect."

"I agree. It was perfect."

Dee began to relax. Just the sound of his voice, low and rumbly like a cat purring on her chest, brought back the way she'd felt that night, how comfortable she'd been with him.

"So. How have you been? Did you and Dave end up winning that competition?"

Grady chuckled. "Nah. I lost my touch. Started throwing all my darts over my shoulder into the bar."

Dee laughed.

"I'd like to see you again," Grady said.

"I'd like that too."

"I was thinking maybe I could come out your way."

"You'd come to Pennsylvania?"

"I'm in New York every month or so to see my kids. I thought maybe next time I go to see them, I could make a little detour out your way."

"I didn't know you had kids."

"There are a lot of things you don't know about me. And a lot I don't know about you. Thought we might work on changing that."

Dee nodded and smiled, and then remembered that he couldn't see her. "I'd like that."

They slipped back into the same easy way of talking from the night of the snowstorm. He told her about his children, a boy and a girl—teenagers now—living in New York with his ex. He'd met her when a rodeo tour he'd been on performed in Madison Square Garden. She'd enjoyed being married to him while he was in the limelight, but she grew bored with ranch life when he quit the rodeo.

And Dee told Grady about herself. How much she'd loved raising her daughter and fixing up their home, about living her life without really thinking about what her life was meant to be, until Dan left and forced her to make choices.

They talked for an hour. And then they both grew quiet.

"Where are you right now?" Grady asked.

"In the truck. I'm pulled over in Richmond."

"Virginia?"

"Mm-hmm."

"What are you wearing?"

"Um, jeans and a black sweater."

"Are you wearing those boots?"

"My cowboy boots? Yes." Oh God. Was this how phone sex started?

"They were the first thing I noticed about you, those boots."

She didn't know anything about phone sex, but sweet Jesus, his voice, so deep and gravelly and . . . she drew a shaky breath. Her body seemed to know what phone sex was the moment he said hello. The lyrics from "Like a Wrecking Ball" ran through her mind.

Then her awkward brain took over. "Oh, my boots?" A high-pitched giggle came out of nowhere. "Well, a friend took me shopping in New York? And I thought I might just give them to my daughter? But then it's a good thing I kept them, because my driving instructor at the commercial driving school?" What was going on? She sounded like a Valley Girl! She finished talking all in a rush. "So he insisted on hard-toed shoes, so I started wearing them, and now I'm glad I kept them, though they don't really match everything and sometimes I find them a little uncomfortable." She probably shouldn't have brought up Katie. Or the fact that her boots were uncomfortable. It would probably spoil the mood, if he was trying to set a mood. Actually, everything that had just spewed out of her mouth would spoil a mood.

"Are you okay?" he said.

"Yeah. Sure. I just don't really know how to do this. I guess I'm a little nervous."

"Do what?"

"Um, I don't know." Oh God. She'd been spending too much time with Jancee. *Get your mind out of the gutter, Dee.*

Grady exploded with laughter. "Do you think I'm trying to compromise your virtue over the phone?"

Dee dropped her burning face into her free hand. "Sorry. I don't know what's wrong with me."

Grady was still chuckling. "No. It's my fault. I didn't realize how it would sound when I asked what you were wearing. I just wanted to picture you."

"Oh," Dee said. "So, how about you? What are you wearing?"

Another low chuckle. "A white shirt and khakis."

"Are you wearing your hat?"

"Nah. Not in the office."

"I like it. The hat."

"I'll keep that in mind." Grady wasn't laughing anymore, but it still sounded like he was smiling.

"So. I guess I should get off the phone and get a nap. I need to get up in a few hours and finish my trip."

"Are you going to be home next weekend?"

"Mm-hmm."

"I'm going to be in New York for a few days. How about if I swing out your way on Sunday? Maybe go for dinner somewhere?"

"I could cook something."

"Even better."

Dee cradled the phone to her ear and slipped down on her bunk. She wanted to go to sleep now. She wanted to go to sleep and dream about Grady. Her attempt to stifle a yawn failed. "Sorry. I guess I really need that nap."

"That's okay, sweetheart. Get some sleep and drive home safely."

"Okay. G'night." *Sweetheart.* He called her sweetheart.

"Good night." Grady's voice was a low rumble. "And Dee?"

"Mm-hmm?"

"I wasn't trying to seduce you on the phone, but I can't make the same guarantee the next time we're alone."

chapter

TWENTY-SIX

ONCE HOME, DEE WENT INTO A FLURRY OF HOME-making activity. She hadn't cooked a proper meal in months. Out came all her old favorite cookbooks, which she pored over with a shopping list at her elbow. She decided on chateaubriand with a red wine reduction, scalloped potatoes with a cheesy white sauce, and a vinaigrette-dressed green salad. Along with a bottle of cabernet, she purchased a couple of six-packs from a local craft brewery. For dessert, she planned to make an apple pie with homemade crust and vanilla ice cream. In Dee's experience, there wasn't a man alive who didn't like apple pie.

Susan stopped over on Friday afternoon when Dee returned from the grocery store.

"I may have some good news for you tomorrow," Susan said. "I had a couple through the house last week while you were away, and they really liked the place. They want to come through for a second look tomorrow. Will that work for you?"

"Sure, that will be fine."

Dee lifted the last two bags onto the counter with a grunt. The reusable sacks were great most of the time, but every once in a while, she got a cashier who loaded all the heavy items into the same few bags. That's all she needed, to wrench her back and ruin her romantic evening.

Susan peered into the bags.

"My goodness. What are you going to do with all these groceries? Is Katie coming home?"

Dee pressed her lips together. She hadn't said anything to Susan about Grady.

"Katie won't be home until next week. Actually, I have a date this weekend."

Susan narrowed her eyes. "With who? Don't tell me you've started with that internet dating business, because I'll tell you, I just think that is dangerous. You cannot believe a word those men say about themselves. I just watched *Dirty John* on Netflix. Have you seen it?"

Dee shook her head. "No, Susan, I really don't . . ."

"Well, you should watch it. This poor woman thought she'd met the love of her life only to have him turn out to be a psychopath. He tried to murder her daughter, and the daughter ended up killing him instead."

Why did Susan have to bring this up now? She'd just begun to feel like herself again. She pushed the cloud of panic down and busied herself putting the ice cream in the freezer. "It's not anyone I met on the internet."

"So? Who is he?"

"I met him in Kansas. Remember a few months ago when I told you about going off the road in that snowstorm? Well, he's the man who stopped to help me. His name is Grady."

Susan sunk onto a barstool. "But Dee! You're talking about having a perfect stranger come into your house."

"Grady's not a stranger. We've talked a lot and . . . I don't know how to explain it. I feel like I've known him forever."

Susan shook her head. "I don't like this. When is he coming?"

"On Sunday. He's going to be visiting his kids in New York for the weekend and then he's stopping here."

Susan continued to shake her head as if she'd just learned Dee had a terminal illness.

"Listen, Susan, how about if you stop over and meet him when he gets here. Call me when you see the car in the driveway and bring over some real estate papers for me to sign or something. You'll see. You'll like him right off, I know it." Susan's concern no longer irritated Dee the way it had in the past. Now it just made her feel like someone cared.

"Okay. I'll do that. Maybe we should come up with a signal you could give me if you're feeling threatened."

Dee pulled Susan off the barstool and steered her toward the door. This kind of talk was dredging up all the nasty stuff she was trying to keep buried.

"That's enough. I'm a grown-up, remember?"

"Okay, okay, I'm leaving." She paused on the porch. "And remember, I'll be by tomorrow afternoon with that couple from the Monihan agency."

"That's fine. I've got a hairdresser appointment, so I'll be out of the way, and I'm taking Spot to the groomer for a bath. The coast will be clear."

In truth, Dee had not just a hairdresser's appointment but a whole day at the spa. She was finally using a gift certificate Dan had given her two Christmases ago, and Jancee was joining her. Unlike Susan, Jancee had been giddy at the prospect of Dee having a fling with "the hot cowboy."

"You're on the right track with the mani-pedi. But I think you should go in for the deluxe treatment. Get a full-body sugar scrub to exfoliate and then the seaweed wrap to draw out toxins. And maybe some waxing. Have you ever had a Brazilian?"

"Oh, Jancee, be serious."

"Where did I lose you?"

"At the wax."

"But you are going to get the scrub and the wrap?"

"Maybe."

"Think of it like getting your car detailed before you put it up for sale. You just want to show everything in its best light."

Dee rolled her eyes. "You really know how to make a girl feel special."

👑

SATURDAY EVENING, DEE SAT ON THE COUCH, SIP-ping a cup of decaffeinated green tea and admiring her smooth feet and the deep-red polish on her toes. Spot was snoring next to her, exhausted from the stress of spending the day at the groomer. Dee arched her back and stretched. She wasn't stressed at all.

She should take Katie with her next time. Maybe they could go during her summer break. She picked up the phone and called to suggest it. Right away, Dee could tell there was a problem. Katie didn't sound like herself.

"What's wrong, sweetie?"

"Oh, I'm okay. I just have a stomachache. I probably had too many fries with lunch."

"Do you have any ginger ale? That might help."

"No. I think I'm just going to go to bed."

"That's probably the best thing. Fill the hot-water bottle and take that to bed with you."

"What were you calling about? Is something wrong?"

"No. Everything is fine. I just went to a spa with Jancee and thought that might be fun for us to do together sometime."

"Sounds great, Mom. I'll call you tomorrow."

Dee hung up the phone. Her inner calm vanished, and a nagging worry lodged in the pit of her stomach. What if Katie had appendicitis? Or *E. coli*? She'd seen a lettuce recall in the news recently. She chewed at her cuticle. This part of being a mother never went away. Dee worried with the same intensity about her twenty-year-old daughter as she had when she was nine. And she was fairly certain she'd still feel this way when Katie was forty.

Enough. She gave herself a mental shake and got off the couch. Her daughter had a little indigestion. This should be way down on the list of things to obsess about.

AFTER RISING EARLY THE NEXT MORNING TO GET the pie in the oven, Dee sent Katie a text to see how she was feeling. She received an answer almost immediately.

"Feeling much better. Going back to sleep. Talk later."

And just like that, the shadow of dread lifted. Now she was free to enjoy getting ready for Grady's arrival that afternoon. She baked the pie and left it to cool on the counter, then peeled and sliced the potatoes and left them to soak in cold water. She'd set the dining room table with china and taper candles, debated whether it would look like she was trying too hard, then decided trying too hard was better than the alternative. The only thing missing was a vase of flowers on the table. She'd considered buying them at the grocery store, but had a feeling Grady might show up with a bouquet. She would bet serious money that he was the type to bring a woman flowers.

With the house and dinner under control, Dee set about making herself look as alluring as she'd felt when she left the spa. She took a bath, shaved and scrubbed until she was as smooth as her fifty-three-year-old skin allowed, and then slathered on body lotion. She finished with a dab of Jo Malone's Orange Blossom Cologne on each wrist and between her breasts. After snipping the tags from the black lace bra and panty set that Jancee and the Saks stylist had insisted upon, Dee slipped them on and gazed at her reflection.

Not bad. She'd been unable to eat much since Grady told her he was coming, so her stomach was practically concave. It amazed her that a few little wisps of lace could perk some things up and hold others in like this. And her blowout looked as good as it had when she walked out of the salon yesterday. Skipping the shower in favor of a bath had been genius.

Lying on the bed was the outfit Dee finally settled on after an hour of deliberation. A periwinkle raw silk fitted tunic and slim black ankle pants, with a pair of kitten heels. Jancee hadn't been overly impressed when Dee modeled the outfit on FaceTime.

"I don't know, Dee. I like the color, but don't you think it's a little too covered up?"

"Covered up?"

"Yeah. I think you ought to show more skin. Maybe a little cleavage."

"That's just the problem. I only have a little cleavage."

Jancee laughed. "You completely underestimate your feminine powers."

"Yeah, sure."

"I'm just joking with you. You look beautiful. That cowhand is going to sweep you off your feet the moment he walks in the door."

"He's not a cowhand. He's a rancher."

"Whatever. Either one sounds sexy."

BY FOUR O'CLOCK, DEE WAS PERCHED ON A BARSTOOL at her kitchen counter, bouncing her foot. Grady was not due to arrive until six. There was nothing to do for the next two hours but sit here and morph into a bundle of nerves.

At a knock on the door, she sprung from the stool like someone pinched her. Was he early? She smoothed the front of her tunic and walked toward the door, with Spot skittering on the hardwood floor next to her. She was forgetting something. She put her finger to her lips. She'd forgotten lipstick. She glanced at her reflection in the foyer mirror. No makeup! She'd forgotten to put on any makeup.

Dee froze with indecision. Should she run upstairs and brush on some mascara and a little lip gloss? Another rap came at the door. She grabbed her sunglasses from the foyer table, jammed them on her face, and opened the door with a crazed smile.

It was Susan.

"What the heck are you doing in there?"

Dee pulled off the glasses. "Oh my God, Susan. You scared me. I thought Grady was early, and I forgot to put my makeup on."

Susan regarded her with a frown. "What kind of man is this that can't see you without makeup?"

"It's not that he *can't* see me without it. I'd just rather have it on. And you're a good one to talk. I've *never* seen you without makeup."

Susan pursed her lips. "I guess you have a point."

"Come on in," Dee said. "I thought you were going to come over when you saw his car."

"Well, I'm still planning to do that. But I have some good news and I wanted to give it to you right away. We have a full-price offer on the house!"

"Oh my gosh! That's great."

"I knew it was a done deal as soon as they walked in yesterday. The husband was upstairs measuring the bedrooms, and the wife was telling him where she wanted to put the Christmas tree. Best of all, it's a cash deal, no contingencies."

"That's great. Did you talk to Dan yet?"

"Not yet. I wanted to tell you first. I'll give him a call, and assuming he's okay with the offer, I'll pop over later with the papers for you to sign." She pushed Spot's nose away from her crotch.

"One more bit of advice. If I were you, I would put Spot out in the backyard when your friend arrives."

Dee bit her lip. Susan had a point, but not solely because the dog got in people's personal space. Ever since the attack, Spot had been leery of men, growling low whenever they passed.

chapter

TWENTY-SEVEN

WHEN GRADY ARRIVED, DEE WAS STANDING IN THE middle of the living room in her bare feet, scrolling through Spotify, trying to find a good music selection. She'd been standing ever since Susan left to prevent creases from forming on her slacks.

At the sound of the chimes, she slipped on her shoes and ran to the door, pausing at the last second to collect herself. And double-check that she had, indeed, put on her makeup. She threw open the door, and it was as if her porch opened onto the last moment they'd seen each other in that Midwest motel lobby. His arms were filled with a riot of sunflowers, lilies, roses, and twigs with berries.

"Hi," Dee said, her voice a breathy imitation of Marilyn Monroe's. *Where was that coming from?*

"Hi." Grady grinned down at her.

"Won't you come in?"

Argh! What was wrong with her. *Won't you come in?* She sounded like a butler. Blood rushed to her face as she stepped back to let him in.

"I'll just get a vase for those."

She turned toward the kitchen. She hadn't even said thank you or told him how beautiful they were.

"The flowers are beautiful. Thank you." *Oh God. She should have had a drink.* She was behaving like a moron. Dee pulled the largest vase she had out from under the sink and then nearly dropped it on the counter with her shaking hands.

Grady set the flowers and his hat down on the kitchen table, strode over to her, and took both of her hands in his. He was smiling down into her eyes, and the warmth from his hands seemed to travel up her arms and into her nervous system like a sedative. "What's wrong?"

Dee shrugged her shoulders and glanced up at him. "The truth is, I'm a little nervous."

Grady held her eyes. "Don't be. It's just me." He brought her hands to his lips and then froze when he saw her tattoo. "What's this?"

"Oh." For the first time, she regretted her impulsive decision in California. Katie and Jancee loved it, and Susan either hadn't noticed or had decided to keep her opinion to herself. "I, um, just got it on a whim. It's a little tacky, I know."

He ran his finger over it and Dee shivered. "I think it's kind of hot," he said.

"Oh my God." She put her hand to her face and then gave him a gentle shove. "Please, just go sit down."

Grady pulled out a barstool, and Dee shifted into hostess mode. She didn't know what she was doing when it came to dating, but if she was cooking a meal for someone, she was in her element. "Would you like a drink? I have both red and white wine and some craft beers." Dee opened the refrigerator and read the labels. "Yards IPA and Tröegs DreamWeaver Wheat. And there's a bottle of scotch somewhere around here."

"An IPA would be great."

Dee poured Grady's beer and slipped her professional-grade apron over her head before pulling the tenderloin from the refrigerator.

Grady whistled. "You look like you know your way around a kitchen."

Dee smiled. "I just know where to shop. Don't jinx me, now." She hesitated with the pepper mill poised over the roasting pan. "You do eat beef, right?"

"I'm a rancher," he said. "If I didn't eat beef, I think I'd get laughed out of Kansas."

While Dee cooked, Grady told her about life on the ranch and they traded stories about their children. The doorbell rang as Dee finished putting the tenderloin in the top oven to slow roast and the potatoes in the lower oven on convection.

"Excuse me a minute."

Dee opened the door and Susan sailed past her, waving papers from the prospective buyers.

"Hello, Dee," she trilled. "I have these contracts for you to sign."

Dee scurried behind her into the kitchen.

"Oh my. Hello. I didn't realize you had company, Dee." Susan's voice had taken on a weird cadence, like a film star from the 1940s.

"This is my friend, Grady," Dee said. "Grady, this is my neighbor, Susan."

Grady stood and shook Susan's hand. "Nice to meet you."

"Likewise, I'm sure." Susan looked Grady up and down as if she were filing his image away for a police lineup. "Well, I'll just leave these papers and you can get them back to me tomorrow. I've highlighted the places that need a signature." She sniffed at the air. "Mmm. Something sure smells delicious. Well, I'm off. Bye now!"

The door slammed, and Dee and Grady stood there in stunned silence. Then both began to laugh.

"Sorry," Dee said.

"What was that?" Grady said.

"Hmm. How should I put this?" Dee paused and cast her eyes at the ceiling for an answer. "She's a friend but also a one-woman neighborhood watch."

"Did she give you a 'stranger danger' lecture before I arrived?"

Dee smiled and fought back a shiver. "How did you guess?"

Dee poured herself some wine and grabbed another beer for Grady.

"We could sit out back on the patio if my dog behaves."

"Spot? She and I are old friends."

The dog was lying with her nose pressed pathetically against the glass door.

"She's been a little protective lately."

Luckily, Spot seemed to remember him, sniffing his boots for a few seconds and then curling up on the doormat.

Dee brought a timer outside with her and set it on the patio table, then joined Grady on the wicker glider. He nodded toward the timer. "You think of everything, don't you?"

"Let's just say I learn from my mistakes. Once, we had a barbecue and I completely forgot about the cake I was baking for dessert. It looked like a slab of charcoal when I finally took it out."

Grady nodded and took a swig of his beer. "Here's to learning from mistakes."

The golden hour approached. As the sun slipped behind the hills on the horizon, wispy clouds turned watercolor shades of pink and purple. Sunset had always been one of Dee's favorite times, and having Grady alongside her made it even better.

He leaned forward and rubbed behind Spot's ears with both hands. The dog looked about ready to climb into his lap.

"So, a dog named Spot. Like the old-school storybooks?"

"I was trying to be clever."

"Have you thought about changing your name to Jane?" Grady said with a smile.

"No, but my ex-husband is a dick." Dee clapped her hand over her mouth. *Where did that come from?* What about her resolution not to bad-mouth her ex?

Only Grady didn't seem too shocked. In fact, he was laughing. "Ouch. I set you right up for that one, didn't I?"

Dee could feel her face burning. "I'm sorry. That was rude." She'd known she was going to screw things up one way or another.

Grady shook his head. "Believe me, I've heard worse."

In spite of her comment about Dan, the evening seemed to be going well. The chateaubriand was the exact amount of rare that Grady claimed he preferred, the potatoes cheesy and browned on the top, the salad crisp, and the apple pie still warm in the center. Dee even remembered to take her apron off before she sat down to dinner.

But once they finished their meal, she was once again adrift in insecurity. Grady stood and carried their plates to the sink, and Dee began to load the dishwasher. Grady stopped her.

"Okay, you're done. When I was a kid, my mother's rule was the cook didn't do cleanup, and that always seemed fair enough to me. You are officially off duty."

With that, he picked her up by the waist and deposited her on the counter. Then he rolled up his sleeves, put her apron around his neck and set about scrubbing the roasting pan and casserole dish crusted with cheese. Dee stared at the muscles in his forearms as he worked in the sudsy water. It was the sexiest thing she'd ever seen. Grady looked up at her out of the corner of his eye and flashed his dimples at her.

"You know you're almost irresistible in that apron, don't you?" Dee said. She had consumed two glasses of wine, so anything she thought was now coming directly out of her mouth. She wished she could find a middle ground between mute idiot and no filter whatsoever.

Grady nodded, and his laugh lines deepened. "That was the plan."

When he'd finished with the dishes, he tossed the apron over the back of a barstool and moved to stand in front of her, his hands resting on the counter alongside her hips. Perched next to the sink, she was eye level with him. Thanks to the wine, she didn't think twice about putting her hands up on his shoulders. She noticed then the crisp fabric of his blue pinstripe shirt and a straight pin he'd missed near the collar. Her heart twisted at the thought of him buying a new shirt to wear for her.

"Thank you for dinner," Grady said. His face was inches from hers.

"You're welcome," Dee said.

Grady leaned in closer.

"And thank you for doing the dishes," Dee said.

Grady's dimples twitched. "You're welcome."

"I'm glad you're here," Dee whispered.

And then he kissed her while lifting her off the counter. Some instinct she didn't even know she had compelled her to wrap her legs around him as he carried her to the couch in the living room. There were no thoughts, no doubts, no fears zapping around in her brain anymore. Yoga instructors were always yammering on about finding your bliss. Well, Dee finally found hers. Bliss had a sandpapery jaw and warm insistent lips and hard muscled arms. She wanted to be consumed by him. She didn't care that his fingers were unbuttoning her top. She wasn't wondering if he liked her black lacy bra. She wasn't thinking at all. She was simply melting into the moment.

Until Grady reached down and began to unbuckle his belt. The jingling metallic sound flashed her back to the night in Georgia and the monster who had appeared out of the dark. She couldn't breathe. Had to get away. Escape. Dee shoved Grady's chest in a panic, sending them both tumbling to the floor. She jumped to her feet, hyperventilating.

Grady sat up and ran a hand over his close-cropped hair.

"Sorry, sweetheart. I guess I got my signals crossed up there."

"No. It's nothing you . . . you didn't do anything wrong." Dee's voice was shaking, her hands trembling so badly that she couldn't get her blouse buttoned. She gave up and pulled it together, crossing her arms in front. "I just . . . I guess I'm not ready for this."

She couldn't tell him. Couldn't explain what had happened. She'd promised Sugar she would keep her mouth shut.

"Can I get you some coffee, or a drink?" Dee moved toward the kitchen.

"Sure," Grady said. "Coffee sounds good."

They sat at the kitchen table trying to make small talk for a while, but the magic was gone. The silences between them were no longer companionable. They were loaded with things that needed to be said but couldn't.

"I think it's about time I got on the road." Grady reached across the table for his hat and stood.

"But I thought you were going to stay."

"Some other time." He smiled down at her and gently brushed her cheek with his knuckles. "You don't need to be afraid of me, Dee. I'd never hurt you."

Her eyes filled with tears. "I know that."

chapter

TWENTY-EIGHT

WHILE IT'S ALWAYS FUN TO REPLAY A TERRIBLE DATE with your girlfriends—turning something miserable into a joke—when the date was wonderful until you did something to screw it up, reliving it is simply mortifying.

"So, how did everything go last night?"

Dee was emptying the dishwasher when Jancee called to interrogate her the next morning.

"Is he still there?"

"No. I'm alone," Dee said. "And it looks like I'll always be alone."

"Oh, girlfriend," Jancee said. "What happened?"

"I don't know. Everything was great until after dinner. When we were messing around, I just . . . I sort of freaked out." Dee couldn't tell Jancee the whole truth, but she had to unburden herself a little bit.

"Was he being kinky or something?"

"No. He wasn't doing anything wrong. We were just on the couch making out . . ." Dee paused. Was there a way to talk about physical relationships that didn't sound like a high school conversation? "Anyway, I guess I felt trapped and had some kind of panic attack . . . and shoved him away."

"Shoved him?"

"Yeah, like, shoved him onto the floor."

"Well, that's a little extreme. But it's kind of understandable. I mean, you haven't been with anyone but Dan in forever. Maybe this guy isn't really your type."

"No. That's definitely not it. He's perfect. I'm the problem."

"So, did he leave mad?"

"I don't think so. He seemed . . . sad." Dee's chest ached at the memory of him brushing her cheek and reassuring her. "And I'm sad. It's just a mess. I make a mess of everything."

"I'm sorry, Dee."

For once, Jancee had no snappy comeback or well-intentioned pep talk.

Susan called next, whispering into the phone like a double agent. "Is everything okay over there?"

"Yes, everything is fine. I'm by myself."

Susan's voice rose to its normal volume. "I thought you might be since I didn't see his truck. I just wanted to make sure I wasn't disturbing anything if I pick up those papers. Did you have a chance to look them over?"

Dee's gaze went to the table where Susan's folder lay next to the vase of flowers Grady brought. "I'm sorry, Susan. I forgot all about it. If you have a minute, I'll sign them while you wait."

"I'll be right over."

Susan helped herself to coffee, while Dee skimmed the paperwork and began signing in the designated spots.

"Are you sure you're okay?" Susan said.

Dee capped the pen and leaned back in her chair. A momentary flash of déjà vu overtook her when she glanced out the window and noticed the quivering new leaves on the maple tree. Life was blowing by, seeming to increase in speed with every passing month. "Things didn't go the way I'd hoped last night. It seems I'm not quite ready for dating after all."

Her old friend nodded sagely. "I guess I know something about that. After John died, I went out with a few men, but there just wasn't any spark. I finally decided it wasn't worth the trouble."

So there you have it, Dee thought. She was destined to live out her years like Susan, all alone, day upon day upon day. The decision to become a truck driver was just another link to her solitary destiny.

Susan slapped the table. "But what the heck am I talking about? I was much older than you and set in my ways. You need to jump back on that good-looking horse that threw you and ride him."

"Susan!" Dee laughed in shock.

"That's right, I'm a bawdy old lady. When you get to be my age, you can say whatever you want."

chapter

TWENTY-NINE

NOW THAT THE HOUSE WAS UNDER CONTRACT, DEE had plenty to keep her busy between road trips. The biggest challenge—getting rid of twenty-five years of stuff. Using the Marie Kondo method, she found that very few of her possessions brought her joy anymore. She wanted to shrug them off like a heavy coat on a spring day.

It was the first weekend of Katie's summer break, and Dee had two days before she was back on the road. Rico and his girlfriend were coming over to see what they could use, but first Dee wanted Katie to take a look and choose anything she might someday want. Her daughter was unsentimental now, but what if she grew older and regretted not holding on to the buffet in the dining room that had belonged to Dee's grandmother? Or the Persian carpet from the living room where she used to lay on her stomach as a child and make up stories, imagining the intricate designs as animals or people?

Or maybe she'd want these Hummel figurines that Dan's mother bought them each Christmas. Dee took one out of the china cabinet, a little girl and her dog. No. Katie definitely wouldn't be interested in these dust collectors. Dee didn't like them herself, but she'd felt compelled to display them year after year so that Linda and Jim would see them when they visited. She put the Hummel back in the cabinet. She had always liked Linda, despite her terrible taste in home decor.

Dee leaned against the doorway to Katie's room and surveyed the explosion of clothing, shoes, and hair products that littered the floor. "Okay, missy. Time to get to work."

Katie groaned from somewhere under the jumble of bedding. "Why do we have to do this at the crack of dawn?"

"I don't know what time zone you're in, but no one considers this the crack of dawn. It's nearly ten o'clock, and I have Rico coming over at three."

The bedding shifted and Katie sat up, rubbing her eyes. "I promise you I'll be dressed and have my room cleaned by the time your friend gets here. But I'm really tired. Finals were awful this semester."

Dee picked her way across the room and sat down on the bed. Spot followed her in and, as usual, sat at her feet. "Getting dressed would be nice and so would cleaning up this pigsty, but what I really need you to do is go through the house with me and let me know what you'd like to keep."

Katie yawned. "Nothing. I don't have room for anything. My campus apartment is tiny, and I doubt I'll be living anywhere much larger for a long time."

"I know. I didn't mean for you to take anything now. I just thought you might want to have some things, like family heirlooms, you know? For when you get a house of your own someday. We can put them in a storage unit until you're ready for them."

Katie reacted as though Dee had suggested they scrub all the toilets in the house with a toothbrush.

"Ugh." She tucked a pillow behind her with a dramatic sigh. "What things?"

"Well, I thought you might like to have the living room rug and maybe the buffet in the dining room. And I have these Post-it notes for you to stick on anything else that catches your eye." Dee handed the neon-yellow notepad to Katie.

Katie took it and flipped the pages with her thumb a few times. "Okay. I guess it would be nice to have the rug someday. I don't know about the buffet. I don't think I'll ever want a formal dining room."

"Yeah, I know that's not the style anymore, but I thought you might be able to use it like a foyer table. I saw some things on Pinterest where they stripped the finish with oven cleaner and gave it a more modern distressed look."

Katie pursed her lips. "Okay. Maybe you could show me later."

Dee looked around the room. It had been after midnight when Katie got home. She couldn't imagine how she managed to make such a mess already.

"So, Mom." Katie hesitated. "Where are you going to live after this?"

Dee shrugged. "I haven't made up my mind yet. We can just rent something short-term for a while."

"You could always come crash in my apartment."

Dee patted what she thought was Katie's leg, buried under the covers. "Thanks, sweetie. Susan across the street offered to let me live there for a while too."

"You're going to live with Mrs. Myers?" Katie's tone was incredulous. "I didn't think you even liked her."

"She's been a really good friend to me since your dad left. I think maybe I just never took the time to get to know her."

Katie picked at a piece of lint on her pajama top. "But I thought you said she was a busybody."

Dee sighed. She now felt guilty for every awful thing she'd ever thought or said about Susan. Why had she been such a bitch?

"I had no idea I was so mean about her. Yes, she is pretty opinionated, but it comes from a good place. She's usually just trying to be helpful. And I'm not going to take her up on the offer to live there any more than I'm going to move into your place. What do you think about staying at the Residence Inn for the summer? They have a pool."

Katie threw the covers back. "Actually, Mom, I've been meaning to talk to you about that. I got an internship with the engineering department this summer, so I won't really have a summer break. I have to go back next Sunday."

"I didn't know you were looking into internships already," Dee said, trying to ignore the sinking feeling in the pit of her stomach. "I didn't intern until my junior year."

"Oh no. You have to start a lot earlier now, especially since I'm doing study abroad next year. I know some kids who even interned as freshmen. I was lucky to get this spot without having anything else on my résumé. And it's paid."

Dee was torn between feeling sorry for herself and achingly proud of her daughter. She reached over and gave Katie a long hug. "I'm happy for you, sweetie."

"Thanks, Mom."

"Okay. I'll go put more coffee on. Up and at 'em." Dee clapped her hands and tried to ignore the loneliness rising inside her. She'd really been looking forward to having Katie around for a few months. Heading to the door, she nearly stepped on Spot, who was now snuggled under a pile of Katie's laundry. At least there was one living thing that wouldn't leave her side.

She paused at the door. "Will you still have time to do the self-defense class with me on Saturday?"

"Absolutely! I think that's going to be fun."

By the time Rico and Laurel arrived, Katie had not only cleaned her room and put sticky notes on a few things, she'd helped Dee pack up the office and the china cabinet before going to the mall to meet some friends. At three o'clock sharp, Rico and Laurel drove up in a borrowed pickup truck. Rico introduced Dee to Laurel, for once referring to her as Dee instead of Queenie. Dee remembered Laurel. She was the pretty dark-haired girl who'd driven Rico to orientation.

"We have $300," Rico said. "Which isn't a lot, I know. But we were hoping it might be enough for a couch, if you have one. And maybe some kitchen chairs?"

Dee shook her head. "Rico, I'm not taking your money. You and Laurel are welcome to anything you want. The few things I'm keeping have yellow Post-it notes on them."

"No, Queenie!" Rico sounded angry. "I mean, Dee. No way. I'm not here for a handout."

"It's not a handout. You have no idea how much . . ." Dee's voice choked up. For goodness' sake, would she ever stop crying like this? She cleared her throat. "If it weren't for you, I don't think I would have made it through training."

Laurel squeezed his arm, clearly proud of him.

Rico rolled his shoulders and cracked his neck. "Thanks," he said. He reached over and gave Dee a quick hug. "Thanks a lot."

Seeing Rico and his girlfriend tease and laugh with each other as they walked through the house made Dee well up with something like maternal happiness. She'd liked this kid since the moment she met him. If she'd had a son, she would have wanted him to be just like Rico. She noticed Laurel gazing at him with a smile while he told Dee about their apartment. They were so clearly in love. As happy as she was for them, it made her even more unhappy with the state of her own love life.

Katie was eating out with her friends, so Dee decided to skip cooking and nibble on raw carrots and cheese and crackers for dinner. Protein, vegetables, and starch. Seemed like a balanced meal to her. Then she fortified herself with a glass of wine and called Grady.

She apologized again for shoving him off the couch. She thought about lying to him and coming up with some excuse for her behavior, but he didn't seem to need an explanation. He was his usual good-natured self, joking with her that landing on the floor the way he had reminded him of his years in the rodeo.

"I'll tell you what, you're pretty strong for a little filly."

"Should I be insulted that you're comparing me to a horse?" Dee twirled the wine in her glass. She loved listening to his voice.

"Nah. Beautiful animals, both of you."

They laughed and talked until Grady had to leave for dinner at his brother's. Dee put down the phone and slid her wineglass in a circle on the granite countertop. If only she could snap her fingers and forget what happened in Georgia, just somehow excise the section of her brain where that memory lived. She wanted to see Grady so much her chest ached. But what if she freaked out again when he touched her? What a fucking nightmare. She chugged the rest of her wine and went to bed.

chapter

THIRTY

SINCE KATIE'S SUMMER BREAK WAS CONDENSED TO A week, Dee called Dispatch and talked her way into a short three-day jaunt to New England instead of her scheduled cross-country route. Then she made the most of their time together. She cooked her daughter's favorite meals—lemon chicken with olives and orzo and lasagna with Italian sausage—and she froze portions for Katie to take back to school. Katie skipped going out with her friends so the two of them could watch movies curled up on the remaining couch. And then it was Saturday, the day of their self-defense class.

They sat in a circle in a sectioned-off area of the Y's basketball court. Worn navy gym mats designed to cushion falls from back-handsprings and cheerleading pyramids covered the floor. Dee hoped they were thick enough to prevent injuries for middle-aged women like herself and not just prepubescent gymnasts.

There were four other women besides Dee and Katie in the class. Two were another mother-daughter duo. They didn't go into detail, but they alluded to the daughter's ex-boyfriend and some veiled references to stalking. The other two were a pair of thirtysomething coworkers from Philadelphia concerned about a recent spate of muggings near their office building.

Linda, the instructor, looked about Dee's age and seemed ready to lead them through a series of yoga asanas. She sat cross-legged with her hands loosely clasped in her lap, nodding encouragement as each woman spoke.

"And what brings you to our class?" Linda asked Dee.

"Well, I think it would be good to know some techniques to get out of any dangerous situations I might find myself in, because I drive a truck and sometimes I'm by myself, well, I'm always by myself, but sometimes in bad areas . . ." This was getting too close to the truth. She changed the subject. "But mostly I came because I want my daughter to be safe at college. Even though I tell her not to, she's always going to the library by herself late—"

Katie broke in. "Mostly we came because my mom's a truck driver."

This got an awkward laugh from the group. They were probably relieved that Katie rescued them from hearing any more of Dee's long-winded explanation.

Linda nodded and looked around the circle. "These are all good reasons to learn self-defense," she said. "But before we start on the actual techniques, I want to talk a little bit about how we, as women, sometimes let the societal norms we've been taught put us in danger."

Dee felt a little door in her brain closing. She didn't want to listen to a lecture; she just wanted to learn how to escape from the clutches of a murderer. She studied Linda's outfit instead. She wore a coral Lululemon wrap top, and her wavy long gray hair was stacked in an effortless messy bun on top of her head. Dee wondered how her hair would look styled like that. She'd have to let it grow for at least a year.

Linda continued to talk and Dee half listened. "How many of you have ever felt uncomfortable with something a man said or did, but didn't do anything for fear of hurting his feelings? Maybe you've had a stranger stand too close to you in a public place or ask you inappropriate questions; maybe someone's acted in an overly familiar way? Any kind of behavior that kind of creeps you out."

Linda took in the shrugs and nods of the group.

"The first part of self-defense training is learning to be more assertive," she said. "We are especially prone to nonassertive behavior in situations involving acquaintances or when we 'aren't sure' something is wrong. Our feminine training leads many of us to want approval, be helpful, kind, and quiet. But those very behaviors are what predatory men depend on to find victims."

Linda rose from the floor in one fluid motion. She was definitely moonlighting from her real job in a yoga studio. "I'd like us all to do a little role-playing now. I'm going to attempt to start a conversation with each of you, and I want you to respond in the way that you would if you were being bothered by a stranger."

"What are you reading?" Linda sidled up behind Katie and leaned over her shoulder, as if trying to see a book she was holding. Katie suppressed a giggle.

"Um, *Harry Potter and the Goblet of Fire.*"

The other girl her age snorted with laughter. Linda waited for the girls to stop laughing.

"Okay, the idea is to prevent a conversation from starting. Imagine you are feeling threatened by this person's behavior.

You're on a nearly empty bus, it's late, and he's standing too close to you. Let's try this again."

"What are you reading?" Linda said.

Katie shot Dee a "little help here" look.

Dee shrugged. She had no idea what the correct response was.

"Please leave me alone," Katie said, looking at the floor.

"That's better," Linda said. "But you want to be more assertive. Drop the 'Please' and look directly at me."

Katie did as she was told.

"Better," Linda said.

Next Linda approached one of the Philadelphia coworkers.

"Hey, girl, you sure fill out those jeans nice!"

"Get away from me, you filthy jerk," the woman yelled.

"Okay," Linda said. "Very assertive, but you want to avoid escalating the situation by being insulting in return. Simply say, 'Leave me alone.'"

Here Linda paused to hand out a packet of assertiveness guidelines, and they spent a half hour practicing being confrontational.

"Name the behavior," Linda called out. "Criticize the behavior. Identify the action you want."

This was all well and good, but it wasn't making Dee feel any safer, just surlier. Maybe sometimes strangers were just being friendly and trying to make an innocent connection. How threatening was it, really, to ask someone what they were reading?

"You're staring at my chest, and that is really offensive," Katie recited. "I want you to stop."

Dee took a deep breath and concentrated on not rolling her eyes.

Finally, they moved on to the physical part of the program. The shuffling of paper broke the room's silence as the women paged through their packets to the self-defense techniques. There were descriptions of each type of physical attack, the Double Front Wrist Grab, the One-Hand Wrist Grab, the Front Choke . . . Dee's hands began to shake as she read the supposed way she could have gotten away from her attacker—according to the printout, she should have jabbed him in the eyes, shot her arms up between his to break his hold, kicked him in the groin, and hit him in the face with the heels of her hands.

Hysteria began to engulf her. This was ridiculous. She remembered the overwhelming strength of the man who grabbed her. She'd barely had the power to scratch his hands before she passed out. Wrong workshop. She'd chosen the wrong workshop. Maybe the police-sponsored class with the padded suits would have been better. This class was going to do nothing but give Katie a false sense of security. It would probably make her even less cautious when she went out at night.

Dee lifted her eyes to the rectangle of sky visible through the gym's ceiling-high windows. Breathe. Concentrate on all that blue. But the vibration of anxiety increased until she could hear nothing but a roaring in her ears. She let her glance fall back to what was going on in class just in time to see Linda demonstrating a choke hold on Katie and instructing her in the multistep fiction of getting out of it.

"Stop it! Let go of her!"

Linda dropped her hands and took a step away from Dee's mama bear–like charge. Katie's shocked expression did nothing to put the brakes on her runaway temper.

"This is all bullshit. None of it would work, not even a little bit. I can't believe I just paid $300 to be told I can defend myself by being rude to strangers and kicking men in the balls. Have you ever been attacked? Have you been in the grip of a man who's twice as strong as you and really trying to hurt you? Because you can't fucking get away from someone like that. You can't."

Ironically, Dee's outburst had fueled her with so much adrenaline, she felt as though she actually could fight off an attacker, or ten. The other women in the class were trading brow-raised glances. Clearly, they thought she was unhinged.

Linda crossed her arms in front of her chest. "Perhaps this isn't the best workshop for you, Ms. Levari. You can request a refund on your way out."

"Fine. I'm happy to go. Because this was a complete waste of time."

She stalked out the door without looking back, for the moment forgetting that Katie was even there.

Seated in the Volvo, she began to reconsider her behavior. Had she been maybe the tiniest bit out of line? She spotted Katie standing just outside the building with her back turned, talking on her cell phone. Was she calling one of her friends? Dan? A psych ward?

Katie got into the car without a word.

"I'm sorry about that," Dee said.

No response.

They were pulling into the driveway at home before Katie spoke.

"I don't know what's going on with you, Mom, but I think maybe you need to go talk to someone." Katie's voice was matter-of-fact, but her arms were crossed tight across her chest, and she didn't turn her head in Dee's direction.

"Katie, I said I was sorry. But that class was a huge waste of money. It just made me angry."

"No shit?" Katie turned toward Dee. Was that fear in her eyes? Or disgust. "Maybe the class was lame, but I can't believe the way you went off on that woman. Aren't you the one who taught me to treat other people the way I would want to be treated?"

Dee nodded and willed herself not to cry. She'd made a fool of herself and embarrassed her daughter. She was not going to make things worse by shedding tears and manipulating Katie into feeling sorry for her.

"You're right," she said. "That was inexcusable. I don't know what's wrong with me."

Katie blew out a breath.

"Look, Mom, I know this year has been rough. It seemed like you were handling things, but maybe you've just been, I don't know, bottling things up. Remember when you and Dad took me to that therapist in high school? I didn't want to go, but you made me, and it did help."

In the strange calculus of her mother's brain, the memory of Katie's dark emotional period made Dee's current troubles seem immediately less daunting. Her daughter was happy now, other than thinking her mother was a psychopath, and in Dee's long-ago prayers she had promised she'd never ask for another thing.

"I'll do that," she said, "call a therapist. Aunt Jancee recommended one to me a while back."

"I got the contact information from her," Katie said. "I'll text it to you."

"Was that Aunt Jancee you were talking to outside the Y?"

Katie looked down at her phone. "I didn't know who else to call. You really scared me." At this, her voice broke. "I never saw you act like that before."

QUEEN OF THE ROAD

"I'm sorry, honey. I know I embarrassed you. I'll pull myself together." She patted her daughter's arm, not sure if a hug would be welcome.

Katie grabbed a napkin from the glove compartment and blew her nose.

"It doesn't matter. I'll never see any of those people again." She got out of the car and hurried to the house, Dee trailing behind her.

A tense silence filled the house. Katie crossed the foyer to the stairway and paused with her hand on the railing.

"Promise me you're going to get help."

Dee nodded. "I promise."

Katie's face crumpled, and she ran into Dee's arms, both of them sobbing for a long time. Dee with embarrassment and regret. And Katie? Perhaps she was crying over her lost innocence, the realization that her mother was far from perfect, and could, in fact, be a total jerk.

chapter

THIRTY-ONE

THE NEXT MORNING, DEE CALLED JANCEE'S THERA-
pist and scheduled an appointment. She also ran to the local
bookstore and bought out their self-help section.

Midlife crisis? *Check.*

Surviving divorce? *Yup.*

How to be happier? *Why not?*

Post-traumatic stress disorder? *Ya think?*

Katie had avoided Dee after they got back from the Y, going out to dinner with a friend and then directly to her room.
Now it was nearly noon, and she was still asleep. Or hiding. It
was just as well. Dee couldn't face her anyway.

She tucked the PTSD books in her travel bag and stacked
the rest on the kitchen counter where her daughter would be
sure to see them. Then she left a note about the meals she had
packaged up in the freezer and drove to a coffee shop in town
to wait.

A call from Jancee came through as Dee sat drinking her
latte. Dee silenced the ringtone and considered not answering.
She was so tired of lying to people.

"Hey." Dee turned toward the wall for privacy as she spoke, though she doubted anyone would be able to overhear above the clattering dishes and babble of conversation around her.

"Hey. Are you okay?" Dee's heart twisted at the concern in Jancee's voice.

"Yeah. I'm fine. I just really blew it yesterday. I, um, I've been keeping a secret that's really screwing me up."

"Dee, you know I'd do anything for you, right? If I can help—"

Dee cut her off. "No, Jancee. You can't help me with this. I'm going to talk with your therapist in a few weeks when they can fit me in. Maybe I'll get some kind of prescription from my doctor. But there's nothing you can do."

Jancee was quiet for a few moments. "Something happened to you after we got back from Florida, didn't it?"

An icy finger ran down Dee's back. "Yes." She couldn't elaborate, but she wasn't going to lie anymore.

"Okay. I'm not going to push you on it, but promise you'll call me if you change your mind. I know a lot of people. If you're in any kind of trouble, I can help."

"I don't deserve you," Dee said.

Jancee gave a subdued laugh. "Usually you mean something else when you say that to me."

"I love you, Jancee." She ended the call and stared into her cup. She really hoped this therapist could straighten her out.

An hour later, Dee got a call from the psychologist's office asking if she wanted to come in that afternoon. The receptionist said they had a cancellation. Dee thought maybe they had someone named Jancee calling the office harassing them.

♕

DEE SAT IN A PAISLEY UPHOLSTERED CHAIR WITH A cup of herbal tea, while Stephanie (she'd insisted Dee call her by her first name instead of Dr. Bonner) sat in the opposite chair with one leg tucked up under her, leaning forward and listening intently. She seemed engrossed with Dee's story, only interrupting to clarify something she'd said. It was refreshing to talk to someone without worrying that she was monopolizing the conversation or being boring. She did tend to ramble, but years of having Dan literally walk out of a room while she was talking to him had her convinced that her communication skills were lacking.

Dee found herself recounting not just her meltdown in the self-defense class, but the reason for it. She'd planned to limit how much she revealed in her first session, and then decide whether to be completely honest. But once she started talking, it was like releasing the floodgates. She couldn't hold anything back.

Maybe it was the therapist's matter-of-fact acceptance of everything Dee said. No exclamations of "Oh my God!" or "That's awful!" to trigger an emotional reaction like she would have had if she'd unburdened herself with Susan or Jancee.

It also helped knowing that the story wouldn't go any further. There were rules of confidentiality. Weren't psychologists even prohibited from testifying against their clients in a courtroom? Maybe she was confusing it with attorney-client privilege. She paused and took a sip of tea.

"Um, Stephanie? I guess I should have asked this before I started talking, but you're not going to report any of this, are you?"

Stephanie shook her head, setting her crystal earrings ringing.

"Of course not. However, at some point, you may want to get to the bottom of what really happened that night. You can get some legal representation and—"

Dee shook her head. "No, I can't do that."

"Okay, let's table that for now. I'm not going to push you into anything."

Stephanie's office was flexible with scheduling, and they even managed to fit in a few video sessions while she was on the road. Eventually, they began delving into her childhood and family trauma to get at the root of what the therapist called her "suppressed rage." Dee had never considered the possibility that her lifelong fear of abandonment stemmed from the fact that her mother died when she was so young. And that her father had basically shut down after her mother's death, leaving Marian to take over the parenting. This realization made her see Marian in a whole new light. She was still a pain in the ass, but now she was an understandable pain in the ass.

Stephanie encouraged her to look upon this phase of her life as an opportunity.

"In spite of everything you've been through, you strike me as a generally optimistic and positive person," she said. "I think you have a promising future still ahead of you."

LEAVING THE OFFICE BUILDING ONE JUNE AFTER-noon, Dee stopped on the sidewalk and tilted her face to the sunshine. A cardinal chirped from a nearby tree and the smell of lilacs floated on a breeze. She had a promising future. And it was time to deal with the past.

She sat down on a nearby park bench and composed a text message to her sister.

I've been doing a lot of thinking recently and I'm just now realizing how much responsibility you took on after Mom died. This is long overdue, but thank you for all you did. I'm sorry for being so unappreciative all these years. Love you.

She hit Send and stared at the text box. Delivered. Blue dots bounced across the screen and then disappeared, more blue dots bounced across and disappeared, but ultimately Marian didn't respond. A familiar bubble of annoyance rose in Dee's chest before she reined it in. She couldn't control anyone but herself. She'd done the right thing by expressing her appreciation, and she couldn't, and shouldn't need to, manage how Marian received it. She practiced the calming 5-3-1 breath Stephanie taught her to use. The first few times she'd tried it, she'd had the queerest feeling, like she might actually forget how to breathe. But now that she'd mastered the simple exercise, it really did calm her down. Who knew?

When she got home, Marian's gray sedan sat in the driveway.

Dee pulled in alongside her and gave a small wave. Marian hesitated, then waved back and climbed out of her car. She wore stained sweatpants and a faded blue tank top, her salt and pepper pageboy yanked back in a ponytail. Dee had never seen her sister so unkempt.

"I thought I'd stop by . . ." Marian paused and held up her cell phone. "Thanks for the message." She looked down at her clothing, perhaps noticing Dee's shock at her appearance. "I was outside gardening."

Dee nodded and pulled the sleeve of her blouse down to cover her tattoo. She didn't want to hear what Marian thought of it. "Of course. Like I said, it was long overdue." She glanced at her house. "Do you want to come in and have some coffee or something? Things are kind of a mess right now, but the coffee maker is still hooked up."

"Yes, that would be nice."

They climbed the steps to the porch in silence. Marian cleared her throat as Dee unlocked the front door. "I've always loved this front porch of yours," she said.

Dee smiled. It had been a long time since Marian had said anything positive to her. "Thanks, Mare. I'm really going to miss it."

While Dee scooped coffee grounds, Marian wandered around the empty living room with Spot trailing after her. "You've always been such a homebody. I can't believe you're traveling all around the country now."

Dee leaned back against the counter as the coffee maker gurgled to life. "Yeah, I can hardly believe it myself. I think I always had this idea that if I made everything at home perfect, nothing bad could happen. But, of course, that wasn't true."

"No. Bad things happen no matter what we do." Marian walked back into the kitchen and bent over to awkwardly pat Spot on the head. "She seems like a nice dog."

"Another thing I never thought I'd do—own a dog. She's really good company, though. Especially in the truck."

Marian didn't seem like herself. Dee couldn't put her finger on it, but something in her manner seemed almost fragile. Had she been waiting for a simple thank-you for thirty years? That seemed unlikely. The room filled with an uncomfortable silence.

"Drinking coffee in the afternoon doesn't keep you awake at night?" Dee said.

"No. Nothing keeps me awake."

"Me neither. I guess sleeping is our superpower." She forced a little laugh.

"That's a pretty pathetic superpower," Marian said, but she smiled as she said it.

"That it is." Dee turned away and filled two disposable cups with coffee, handing one to Marian. "Sorry. All the mugs are packed away."

Marian shrugged and, like Dee, stirred a generous amount of cream into her cup. "I don't mind."

"Shall we go out on the patio? The buyers asked to include the outdoor furniture in the sale, so that's about the only place left to sit."

They sat alongside each other on the cushioned glider. Spot lay down in front of them and rested her head on Marian's foot. Even the dog seemed to sense something odd.

Marian took a sip of coffee and looked out across the garden. "So, I've been seeing a therapist."

Dee raised her eyebrows. "You have?"

Marian nodded. "Rebecca kind of insisted."

"Rebecca? Why?"

"Well, she's pregnant—"

"That's wonderful!" Dee interrupted.

"Yes, but she started therapy herself because she didn't want to be"—Marian's voice cracked—"a mother like me."

"Oh, Mare. I'm sorry."

Marian sniffed. "Yes, well, as it turns out, the way I tried to protect my kids ended up pushing them away instead. I just didn't want to be weak, like Dad."

Weak? Dee had never thought of her father as weak. She'd thought of him as the strong, silent type. He'd always held a job and paid the bills and never had too much to say. But he'd grown even quieter after their mother died. In a way, Dee had thought it was kind of romantic, how he never got over losing her. Only recently had she realized how unfair it was to saddle Marian with the job of keeping a house and taking care of her sibling. As a child, Dee had, selfishly of course, seen the situation only as it related to her—her sweet and playful mother had been replaced by a bossy older sister.

"Dad really left you in the lurch after Mom died, didn't he?"

"Yeah. He did. I mean, I didn't even question it. How crazy is that, to expect a fourteen-year-old to take on all that responsibility?"

"I'm sorry I was such a brat."

"You were so young. I think Dad seemed like some kind of hero to you, but he was a mess after Mom got sick." Marian turned to look at Dee. "Do you know he drank until he passed out every night? Every. Single. Night. He literally drank himself to death."

"No." Dee shook her head. "He had a bad heart. It was a heart attack." She remembered her father drinking beer after dinner, but he'd never been loud or abusive. He'd never seemed drunk.

"I'm sorry, Deirdre. I tried to tell you this before. The drinking caused the heart trouble. It got worse after you went away to school." She looked down at her coffee. "I went to the doctor with him. His cardiologist warned him, but he wouldn't stop. I tried to get him to go to AA but . . . not hard enough. I should have insisted, made some kind of ultimatum."

Dee put her hand on Marian's arm. "It wasn't your responsibility."

Marian covered Dee's hand with her own. "Thank you. That's what my therapist tells me. Maybe someday I'll believe it."

"Well, *my* therapist tells me I have suppressed rage and a fear of abandonment since we lost our mom so early. So I guess we've both been screwed up since puberty." Dee hoped Marian wouldn't see this admission as a ploy to grab attention—a "can-you-top-this" attempt to be the bigger victim. She simply wanted to connect with her sister on their shared experience, something that was only possible for siblings. She all but held her breath waiting for Marian's response. After years of disconnect, she hoped they were finally on the same wavelength.

After a few moments of silence, Marian dissolved into peals of laughter, sounding almost like her childhood self when they'd been best friends sharing secrets and squabbling over toys.

"You're in therapy too?" Marian swiped under her eyes. "I don't know why that strikes me as so hilarious; it's actually kind of sad. Think of the trouble we could have avoided if we'd dealt with all this years ago."

They sat on the patio reminiscing about their childhoods and catching one another up on the current lives of their children, talking until the sun had set and the mosquitoes began to swarm. Dee had forgotten how much fun her sister could be when her sharp intelligence was tuned to witty banter instead of biting criticism. She'd missed this. As if she'd gulped down a cold glass of water and only then realized how thirsty she'd been.

Dee walked Marian to the door. "I'm going to be moving into an apartment in Manayunk. I hope you'll come down to visit."

"Manayunk? Why on earth would you move to Manayunk? You'll be paying a fortune to live in an overpriced suburb of Philly. I saw on the news it was named one of the most dangerous cities in the country."

Dee blinked. Her bossy and opinionated sister was back.

Marian bit her lip. "I'm doing it again, aren't I?"

"I think you're trying to keep me safe," Dee spoke carefully, only recognizing the truth as she said it. "But you don't need to do that anymore."

Marian pulled Dee in for a stiff hug, patting her on the back tentatively. "I would love to come down for a visit. Just send me your address and say when."

Dee stood at the door, waving, as Marian backed out of the drive. It felt as if the world had shifted a bit on its axis, righting something that she had given up on long ago.

chapter

THIRTY-TWO

DEE AND GRADY SPOKE ON THE PHONE ALMOST DAI-
ly. Dee would tell Grady about the strange things she saw on
the road, like the tree stump in the Pine Barrens of New Jersey
that had been decorated to look like the Jersey Devil, or the
sad-looking discarded set of Santa and his reindeer left out
with the trash, or the trucker she'd seen dressed like Elvis in
his Las Vegas years.

Grady, in turn, told Dee all about his days on the ranch.
Along with the expected chores of mending fences and farm
equipment, and having cattle herded from one pasture to
another, he was now busy filling out a slew of government
paperwork and conducting inspection tours to get the ranch
certified organic.

"You know, since I've gotten so good at showing people
around the ranch, how about if you stop here for a visit next
time you're in the area?" Grady said. "I'll give you the grand
tour. We could do a little horseback riding, maybe work on
your dart game."

Dee was parked outside the Dispatch office. As much as she wanted to see him again, it seemed safer to just talk on the phone. Then she didn't have to worry about freaking out if he touched her. Maybe she'd be ready after a few more months of therapy.

"I don't know, I've never ridden a horse. Well, except for a pony at a fair when I was a kid, but I don't think that counts, and you know, the trainer or whatever was leading her by reins, so it's not like I was really riding. And then I think it bit someone . . ." Dee trailed off. She was rambling. Maybe she would just bore him into oblivion and then he wouldn't care if he saw her again or not.

"Ponies are a pain in the ass," Grady said. "But you don't need to worry. I've got a gentle mare for you to ride. Wouldn't hurt a fly. You didn't think I was going to put you on one of those wild-eyed broncos from the rodeo, did you?"

Dee forced a laugh.

"Or we could skip it. Forget the horses. Forget the darts. I'll give you the tour in the truck."

"It's just a busy time right now. With me moving and everything . . ."

The excuse sounded lame, even to Dee.

"I see." Grady sighed. "I'm beginning to think maybe we're looking for different things out of this, well, whatever this is."

"I just need some time," Dee said. "It's just—"

But what could she say? *I am attracted to you, but I'm traumatized from the time I was attacked, and maybe I had something to do with killing a man or maybe he's hurting other women because I didn't call the police.* No. She couldn't talk to him about it.

"Maybe you're not used to being with a man like me," Grady said. "Is that it? I'm a little too rough around the edges for you?"

"I don't even know what to say to that."

"Listen, I get it. You were married to a doctor, for Christ's sake. I would say I'd change, but that didn't work out so well last time I tried it."

Dee's temper flared.

"Are you calling me a snob? You think I think I'm better than you?"

"That's not what I said." Grady's voice sounded tired.

"It's pretty much exactly what you said."

"Well, Dee, I don't know what else I'm supposed to think. You sent a crystal-clear message the last time we were together."

"I told you, it's not you," Dee said. "I just have to work through some things."

"The old 'It's not you, it's me' deal, huh?"

"You don't understand." She didn't know who she was more annoyed with, Grady or herself.

His voice lost all its warmth. "You're right. I don't understand and you won't explain it to me, so I guess we're at an impasse."

She should just blurt it out. Tell him all the grisly details and make him feel terrible for accusing her of playing games.

"I've got to get back to work. Take care of yourself, Dee."

He hung up. And Dee went a little bit berserk. After slamming the phone repeatedly against the steering wheel while screaming a stream of obscenities, she hurled it through the open driver's side window, narrowly missing Rico, who was walking across the parking lot.

Rico shaded his eyes with his hand and looked from the phone up to Dee in the truck. "You drop something, Queenie?"

Dee gave a quick nod of her head. "Sorry."

Rico scooped up the phone and strolled around the truck to let himself in the passenger side. He pulled Spot into his lap and set the broken phone down on the console.

"Want to tell me what's going on?"

"Nothing's going on." Dee's voice was raw from screaming. "I'm just having a bad day, that's all."

Rico raised his eyebrows. "Seems more like you're in trouble. And I say that as a guy who was mixed up in some bad shit back in the day."

Vaguely, Dee wondered if there was ever a boy who grew up *without* getting himself into trouble of one sort or another. "You're right," she said. "But I can't talk about it. I owe somebody my life and they asked me to stay quiet."

She frowned at Rico's smirking face.

"I know it sounds dramatic, but it's the truth. Anyway, I can't stop worrying about it and I'm acting weird around Grady, and I can't tell him why. And now I think he broke up with me, or not broke up. God, I don't even know if we were, what, in a relationship?" She dropped her forehead on top of her hands on the steering wheel. "I'm too old for this."

"So, the guy from Kansas isn't messing with you?"

Dee sat up and stared at him. "What are you talking about?"

Rico's dark eyes bored into her; his joking manner gone. "My sister used to go with a guy who beat on her. I know what it looks like."

Dee shook her head. "I'm not dating anyone who's beating me up."

"Then what was up with your face a few months back? And the fact that you're even jumpier than usual?"

Great. In addition to making Grady think she was repulsed by him, her odd behavior had people assuming he abused her.

"Listen, I wish I could talk to you about it, but I can't. I gave my word."

"Okay. I can respect that. But if protecting someone else is screwing up your life, maybe you need to reconsider your promise."

Dee chewed at her cuticle. Nothing like a little self-mutilation to help solve a moral dilemma.

"You need to come clean to your man," Rico said. "If he's a good guy, he'll understand."

He nodded toward the phone before he got out of the truck. "You should take that into the Apple Store. They might be able to fix the screen or at least get your contacts off it."

THIRTY-THREE

DEE MOVED INTO HER MANAYUNK APARTMENT AT the end of July. It had a great view of the Schuylkill River from the balcony, scads of boutiques and trendy restaurants within walking distance, and Jancee lived just around the corner. She wanted to love it. On paper, it was the perfect place. She listed all its wonderful features in her head: The view! The rooftop pool! The first-floor health club! A dog park for Spot! But when she sat on her new outdoor sectional nursing a glass of wine and watching racing crews row their shells in the river below, she felt like a visitor in someone else's life. She wondered if it would feel less foreign if she wasn't on the road so much. Or if she finished unpacking. But she left the boxes stacked and took on as many cross-country trips as she could to avoid facing the truth—she would never again know the contentment and rightness of a true home.

She'd taken Rico's advice about visiting the Apple Store to have her phone repaired, but she didn't call Grady to explain herself. What if he was so angry, he wouldn't take the call? Instead, Dee wrote him a letter. Her perfectionist tendencies came out in force as she reconsidered each word and revised it over and over. It took her a week to write. She scribbled thoughts down between driving shifts and reconsidered every sentence while she drove. Once home, she unpacked the box holding her office supplies and transcribed the letter onto the embossed stationery Dan's mother had gifted her for every birthday. Other than writing Linda thank-you notes, this was the only time she'd ever used it. She looked up the address of Scott Farms and dropped the pale-blue envelope in the mail. Then she waited a week. Two weeks. A month. He didn't call.

On one of her rare free weekends, Katie came to see the new apartment. Leading up to the visit, Dee had been apprehensive. She was afraid that she might have permanently altered their relationship with her meltdown. And she worried that she wouldn't be able to cook a decent meal in her tiny kitchen with half her cooking utensils still packed away. Moving boxes were stacked three high in every room.

She needn't have been concerned. Over a dinner of spaghetti with Rao's jarred sauce and garlic bread from the freezer section, Katie chattered about her internship with the engineering department and the work they were doing in sustainable architecture. She was especially excited about helping with the design of a green roof project.

"It's a great way to conserve water," Katie said. "The rooftop vegetation captures storm drainage water, and because it's such a good insulator, it can reduce summer temperatures in urban areas. Did you ever hear of the heat island effect?" Dee shook her head and studied the poised young woman across from her, whose passion and optimism were focused on making the world a better place. One of the most gratifying parts of being a parent had to be seeing a child grow into the adult version of themselves.

By the end of the evening, Dee had a decent understanding of ecological design and the need for it. A subject that would normally make her eyes glaze over somehow became fascinating, simply because it interested her daughter. Fortunately, another of Katie's attributes was her forgiving nature. She never said a word about Dee's rage-fest at the self-defense class. Nothing in her demeanor gave any indication that she held a grudge about the incident, or indeed, even remembered it.

IN THE MIDDLE OF SEPTEMBER, DEE SET OUT ON A route that took her straight through Wichita. She didn't call Grady when she started out. Why should she call him? Obviously, his feelings had changed. If he wasn't interested anymore, he wasn't interested. Nothing she could do about it.

But as soon as she crossed the Kansas state line, she found herself punching the address of the ranch into the GPS. Maybe the letter had been lost in the mail. Pulling off the exit, she saw a sign for the ranch. She froze at the stop sign and thought about driving straight across onto the access road that led back to the highway. Letters didn't get lost in the mail. Just because she wanted to believe it didn't make it true.

A car came up behind her and blew its horn. With a resigned sigh, she steered the truck toward the ranch. Rejection would sting, but she had to know for sure.

She pulled up the tree-lined driveway and looked back and forth between a low-slung brick office building and the barn across the way, trying to decide where to start her search. Then, out of the corner of her eye, she noticed men in the field working on some piece of equipment attached to a tractor.

One wearing a cowboy hat stood up and turned toward the truck. From this distance, Dee couldn't make out the expression on his face. What if he didn't want anything to do with her? Coming here was a mistake. If he still cared, he would have called her.

She forced herself to climb down from the truck and walk his way. With a sinking feeling, she realized she'd been hoping he'd take one look at her, wave his hat in the air, and run through the field of alfalfa like something in a country music video.

Instead, a grim-faced Grady hoisted himself over the fence and stood facing her. She didn't know what to do. Maybe he thought she was crazy and made up everything in the letter. And then another horrifying thought occurred to her. What if he'd read the letter and turned it over to the authorities?

"I, um, I was on the highway." Since he didn't look happy to see her, Dee decided to act like stopping by was an impulse. "I saw a sign for the ranch, so I thought I'd say hi, but I see you're busy . . ."

"So, you were just in the neighborhood?"

"Sort of." Dee shrugged.

Grady pulled off the leather work gloves he'd been wearing and slapped them against his thigh. He looked as uncomfortable as Dee felt. "If you'd called first, I would have gotten myself cleaned up."

His boots were caked with mud, and his arms and face were streaked with dirt and sweat. The T-shirt he was wearing was the pinkish-gray one he'd had on the first night she met him. Or maybe all his shirts looked like that.

Dee didn't care. For the first time in her life, she made the first move. She reached out with both hands and pulled his face down for a kiss. And Grady, bless his heart, didn't miss a beat. He wrapped his work-hardened arms around her and pulled her to him.

Kissing made words unnecessary, but like all good things, it couldn't last.

"God, I've missed you," he said, brushing the hair back from her face.

He seemed to be clueless as to the reason for their separation.

"Didn't you get my letter?" Dee said.

Grady looked away from her gaze.

"I didn't open it," he said.

Dee shook her head in disbelief.

"Look, I'm an idiot, okay?" Grady said. "I thought it was a 'Dear John' letter. And I just, well . . . I tossed it in a drawer."

Seriously? She went to all that trouble, pouring her heart out on paper, and now she was going to have to wing it?

"It was a letter telling you why I've been, um, afraid of getting, you know, more involved . . . physically."

Dee could feel her face burning. She couldn't talk about this without getting flustered.

Grady was looking down at her, dimples twitching. "If you are trying to drive me crazy, you're doing a great job."

Dee managed to free herself from his embrace without resorting to any of the methods outlined in that ridiculous self-defense class. Then she pulled her phone out of her pocket and brought up the photo she'd taken the morning after the attack. Without a word, she handed it over to him.

Grady's smile faded, and his face grew hard.

"Who did this to you?"

"I don't know who it was, some stranger at a truck stop in Georgia."

"For God's sake, Dee." Grady's voice was gruff. "Why didn't you say something?"

He pulled Dee to him and held her, tucking her head under his chin.

Could she leave it at that? Now that Grady knew this much, maybe she could put the nightmare behind her.

"Did they catch him?"

If only she could come up with a half-truth that would make this go away. A little white lie. But no, she didn't want to carry it around anymore.

"I don't know." Dee took a step back and forced herself to speak. "There's more I need to tell you."

Grady's eyes held hers as he nodded encouragement.

"Someone came along when I was being attacked. He was choking me, and I blacked out. When I woke up, there was a woman there and she had hit the guy in the head with a flashlight. And then we just left."

"You didn't call the police?"

She shook her head. "I know I should have. But I was so shaken up, and Sugar, that's the woman who saved me, she said we had to get out of there. She said the guy might accuse her of attacking him and that she would be the one to get in trouble."

Dee took a breath and continued. "So now I don't know if he's dead and the police are looking for who killed him, or what if he's not dead and he's out attacking somebody else? But I promised Sugar I would keep my mouth shut, and how can I take a chance on getting her in trouble when she saved my life?"

"Okay, that is a lot of shit to be dealing with, no question." Grady pushed his hat back and wiped his brow with a bandanna pulled from his back pocket. "But you do have to deal with it. You can't put something like that behind you until you've faced up to it."

"But I promised to stay quiet. She saved my life. I'm not going to take a chance on getting her charged with murder."

"Okay. Let's think on this for a bit."

They walked over to a weathered picnic table under a shade tree and sat on the tabletop with their feet resting on the bench, looking across the field to the men still working on the tractor. After they'd sat there for a while in silence, Grady looked at his watch.

"You know, I always think better on a full stomach. How about if I grab us some lunch from the office over there?"

Dee didn't see how eating was going to help anything, but she nodded. "Okay. I'll get Spot out of the truck and let her run around."

They split a turkey sub that Dee was pretty sure Grady had intended to eat in its entirety, along with Cokes and a bag of chips.

Grady wiped his mouth on part of the paper napkin he'd ripped in half. "How about if you go down there and tell the authorities your side of the story and leave Sugar out of it. Just tell them you came to and didn't know what happened to the guy. That you panicked and left."

Dee tossed a leftover chip to Spot.

"What if they think it's suspicious? And ask me more questions."

"Cops think everything is suspicious, that's what they're paid to do. You just stick to your story."

"But what if they can tell I'm lying?"

"You're not lying. You're telling them what they need to know."

Dee rested her elbows on her knees and leaned forward, mimicking Grady. Their two pairs of boots were an interesting contrast lined up on the bench, his worn and muddy brown and hers barely scuffed bright turquoise and black. Dee snapped a photo with her phone.

"Not much of a matched set, are we?" Grady said.

"I think I'm kind of over the whole matchy-matchy thing," Dee said.

"Glad to hear it." Grady slung an arm across Dee's shoulders. "How about if I go down there with you and we see what we can find out?"

Her split-second reaction was a feeling of relief. *Yes. Please. Help me fix it.* She was so tired of dealing with things on her own. But she fought against the instinct.

"No. I'm not getting you mixed up in this too. I need to take care of it myself. I'll do the right thing. As soon as I finish this trip, I'll fly down there and get it straightened out."

Dee began to search for flights on her phone, but Grady reached over and covered the screen with his hand.

"It's okay to let someone help you out now and then, Dee," he said. "It doesn't mean you're weak."

Her eyes were now swimming, and she couldn't have seen anything on the phone anyway. *God.* When had she turned into such a crybaby? "No, I appreciate it, but I got myself into this mess. Everybody told me it was dangerous, but I had to be pigheaded about it and prove . . . I don't even know what I was proving."

"Looks to me like you were proving you could take care of yourself and do a difficult job," Grady said. "Getting attacked like that was just a piece of bad luck. It could have happened to anyone."

Dee nodded and blinked back the tears. She took a deep breath. It felt as though a strap that had been constricting her lungs had suddenly disappeared. "I would love it if you came with me."

"Consider it done." Grady squeezed her shoulder and put his elbows back on his knees as he glanced over at the men in the field. "When do you have to get back on the road?"

"Oh, um, I have to be in Oklahoma City at noon tomorrow, so I'm just parking at that Flying J out on the highway tonight."

"So, you have a few hours to kill?"

"Yeah, but I know you're in the middle of"—she motioned toward the men in the field— "well, whatever you're in the middle of. I'll just head out now and . . ."

Grady reached over and took her hand. "The only thing I'm in the middle of is talking to you. Those men can repair a thresher without any help from me."

"Oh," she said in a small voice. When she decided to come here and level with him, she hadn't given much thought to what came afterward. "So, what do you want to do?"

He jumped down from the table and stood in front of her. "I'd like to take you horseback riding and show you around the ranch."

Dee gulped. What she told him when he'd first invited her to the ranch was true. She hadn't been on a horse since she was a kid, and even then she'd been terrified, sitting on the back of a broken-down nag being led around a corral at the county fair. "Did you say you have a really gentle mare for me to ride?"

His eyes softened as he looked down at her. "The gentlest."

"Okay then, let's go!" She sounded a lot more thrilled than she felt.

Grady chuckled. "Such enthusiasm! Just give me a minute, cowgirl. I want to let the men know I'm leaving." He started toward the field and then stopped and turned back to her. "We can go in the office over there first to look at flight schedules. Business before pleasure, as they say."

Dee watched as he continued to the fence, putting his hands on the top rail and vaulting his legs over to the side in one fluid motion. She had no idea farmwork was so acrobatic.

chapter

THIRTY-FOUR

THEY FOUND FLIGHTS THAT WOULD GET EACH OF them to Atlanta around the same time the following week, and then Grady introduced Spot to his border collie, Bo. Dee hadn't yet taken Spot to her apartment's dog park and didn't know how she would react, but the dog's social skills were far superior to her owner's. The two animals sniffed each other for less than a minute and then took off, running around the fenced enclosure near the barn and playing tug-of-war with a discarded piece of harness.

As they walked toward Grady's pickup, he stopped and looked down at himself with a frown. "Do you mind coming to the house for a minute so I can grab a quick shower? I hate to even get in the truck with you like this."

Dee shook her head and smiled up at him. "I'd love to see your house."

They drove to a sprawling timber-framed ranch home with a deep-green metal roof and a wide wraparound porch furnished with a porch swing and cushioned Adirondack chairs.

"Is this where you grew up?" Dee said.

Grady stood next to her, looking at the house. "Yup. The original homestead is still under there, I just did some renovations after I bought it from my folks. Dad had a stroke a couple of years ago, so he and my mom moved into an assisted living community in Wichita."

"I'm sorry. That must be hard." Since both Dee's mother and father had died without going through the declining health of old age, she'd never been put in the caretaker position. Losing your parents sucked no matter how it happened.

Grady jutted out his bottom lip and nodded. "But it's okay. The place they're living in is like a country club, and they both seem happy." He tilted his head toward the house. "Come on in and make yourself at home. There's iced tea in the refrigerator along with some of that cherry lager I remember you liking so much. I'll be back before you know it."

Dee helped herself to a glass of tea and then settled in to wait on an oversize leather sectional facing a floor-to-ceiling stone fireplace. The kitchen was in view across the way, and soaring beams held up a tongue-and-groove ceiling. The house looked like Grady, massive and rugged yet somehow refined. A framed photo of two little towheaded children sat on a side table next to where she sat. She picked it up for a closer look. A boy and a girl sat on a split rail fence in matching overalls and blue-checked shirts.

True to his word, Grady returned showered and dressed in clean jeans and a black T-shirt as she was studying the photo. How did men manage to finish grooming so quickly? He walked over to where she sat and nodded at the picture in her hands. "Those are my kids, Rachel and Bryce, and that's them now." He pointed to a collection of professional photos arranged on the fireplace mantel.

"They're beautiful," Dee said.

"They are, aren't they?" A shadow crossed his face. "It's been rough having them so far away all these years." He blew out a breath and reached for Dee's hand. "You ready to hit the trail?"

"As ready as I'll ever be," Dee said, glancing up at the photos again as she stood. She couldn't imagine how a man like Grady, who appeared to be nothing but kind and conscientious, turned into an absentee father? She wanted to blame it all on his ex-wife, but from her own experience she knew things were rarely that one-sided.

They drove to the stables and Grady introduced her to Polly, the sorrel mare she would be riding. The horse nickered and trotted over to Grady as soon as they approached the corral. "We've got a platform over here that will make it easier for you to mount her," Grady said. "You two get acquainted while I saddle her up."

Big brown eyes with amazing lashes stared back at Dee. She had such a sweet, trusting face. She reminded Dee of Spot. How could she be afraid of this beautiful creature? She reached out and patted the horse's neck while Polly regarded her with a docile expression.

Grady returned with a saddle and blanket, and Dee watched as he went to work. The muscles of his broad back tensed and his biceps bulged as he effortlessly lifted the saddle into place. She couldn't tear her eyes away from his torso. It was like an anatomy lesson. Or some other kind of lesson. She put a hand on the fence to steady herself.

"Okay, let's get you on board," Grady said. "And here"— he placed a cowboy hat on her head—"we don't want any sunburn on that pretty nose."

Dee put her hand on top of the hat and wrinkled her nose at him, half-afraid that she was in the middle of a lucid dream.

Once Dee was in the saddle, Grady brought out his own horse, an enormous black one with a white stripe on its forehead. It tossed its head and neighed in an aggressive way. She was happy to be sitting on her sweet little mare.

Grady saddled the big horse up, and Dee indulged in her new favorite hobby of anatomy study. What were all those muscles? Biceps she knew, and kind of had a thing for, but what were those big muscles running across Grady's back? Lats? Lateral something. She shivered and forced herself to look out across the field.

Grady didn't need to use the platform to get on his horse. He just put a boot in the stirrup and threw his other long leg over the saddle. Dee felt like such a weakling. She couldn't even manage a regular push-up when she worked out. She had to cheat and use her knees.

Before they headed out on the trail, Grady went over the basics of controlling the horse. Then he put his hand to his chin and squinted at her. "You look real natural in that saddle. Like a little jockey." He clicked his tongue to the horses, and they started through the gate. Dee concentrated on holding the reins loosely, while she gripped the sticking-up part of the saddle like her life depended on it. As far as she could tell, it was the only thing keeping her from bouncing right off the horse.

"Whoa." Grady stopped their progress and came up alongside her. "Try to relax a little bit. You're doing fine, but you need to ease up on the pommel there."

"The pommel? That's this thing here?"

Grady looked like he wanted to laugh, but didn't.

"But I'm afraid I'll fall off."

"You're not going to fall, I promise. Instead of relying on your hand strength . . ." He reached over and patted her knee. "You want to use your legs. Imagine you're gripping the saddle with your thighs."

Dee's mouth was dry, but she swallowed anyway. These anatomy lessons were getting to be a bit much.

The ranch was awe-inspiring. Dee always thought of herself as more of a beach girl, but the wide-open skies and shifting clouds were winning her over. Reddish cows with white faces lowed in the distance as two men on horseback guided them into another pasture. "Those are Herefords over there." Grady gestured to the cattle the men were herding. "They're our biggest source of income."

"They're so cute," Dee said.

Grady cocked an eyebrow at her. "Yeah, they're cute. That's mainly why we raise them."

The trail they were on meandered along the rail fence and in and out of pockets of trees. Dee grew more comfortable on the horse, even leaning forward to pat Polly's neck whenever they came to a stop.

They were riding along a ridge that overlooked the whole property. Grady pointed out the various outbuildings and another home in the distance where his brother and his family lived. "I'm not a proud man, but, well, I am proud of this ranch. My great-grandfather started it, but Joe and I have been doing things a little differently, keeping up with the times, you know. We take good care of the animals and try to be as sustainable as possible. I think I told you about getting certified organic." He stopped talking and reached over to pull Polly's harness so that the horse didn't walk directly under a low-hanging tree branch. "And just last month we applied to join a program out of New Zealand to vaccinate our cattle and reduce the methane they produce. We want to be good stewards of the earth, you know?" He stopped talking and looked away from her. "Listen to me. I can't help myself from going right into tour-guide mode."

He reminded Dee of a little boy, so earnest and animated. She loved getting to know this side of him. "Please, don't stop. I'm enjoying it."

Grady smiled over at her. "Don't flatter me too much or I'll have you falling asleep in the saddle."

"I promise, I'm not humoring you. My daughter is a passionate environmentalist and she's got me converted. I'm fascinated by what you're doing here."

They rode for two hours and never left Scott Farms' property. Dee asked how many acres it was, just because she knew that was a standard of measurement for land.

"Close to forty thousand," Grady said.

Dee nodded like she knew what that meant. Really big, she assumed.

They got back to the stables and Grady helped her off Polly. Another man wearing a cowboy hat with a long dark braid down his back walked out of the building.

"Hey, boss! How are things looking?"

"Lookin' good, George. Lookin' good. You men are doing a real fine job out there. George, this is Dee. Dee, George, our ranch foreman." Grady inclined his head toward the horses. "You mind getting these two cleaned up and fed for me?"

"Sure thing," George said.

Dee wondered how many employees Grady had, but she didn't bother asking. The answer wouldn't mean anything more to her than the acreage had.

George walked off with the horses, and Grady looked uncomfortable for the first time since they'd set out on the trail. "So . . ." He paused and looked off toward his pickup. "I'm going to propose something here, but I don't want you to get the wrong idea." He took a breath and stuck his thumbs in the pockets of his jeans. "I was thinking you might want to come to dinner with me back at Dave's and then stay the night. Not with me," he hurried to add, "in the guest room."

Dee began nodding before he'd even finished talking. The thought of leaving him gave her a hollow feeling in her chest. "I would love that."

He grinned down at her and offered his arm. "And I have something I think you're going to like before dinner."

Her heart fluttered. Why was her mind turning everything into something suggestive?

They stopped by her truck to get her things and then collected Spot and Bo, to take them up to the house. Grady showed Dee to the guest room with its attached bath, and both went their separate ways to clean up for dinner.

Dee showered and dressed in a clean pair of jeans and picked out the nicest top she'd packed, a turquoise silk tank with a matching pashmina. She tried not to think too much about the fact that she'd packed something she would never normally wear on the road. *Fine.* Yes, she'd been hoping this might happen.

The guest room was light-filled and comfortable with white painted furniture and honey-colored plank floors. A vintage quilt covered the bed. Dee fingered the hand-stitched blocks of fabric, wondering if it had been made by one of Grady's grandmothers. Then she went downstairs where Grady sat at the kitchen island, halfway through a beer. Seriously, how did he get ready so quickly?

He grinned as she walked into the room. "How about a drink?"

"I'd love one."

With a flourish, Grady produced a bottle of Kim Crawford from the refrigerator.

"I didn't know you liked wine."

"Um, no, not really a fan. I got this back when . . . well, I bought it hoping you might stop in sometime. I remember you saying you especially liked this kind."

She smiled up at him. "It's my favorite."

Grady brushed his finger across her wrist tattoo when she reached for her glass. "Is this true? Are you living the life you love?"

She studied the tattoo, afraid to meet his eyes. "I am today."

They finished their drinks on the porch swing, watching the sun set over the gently rolling hills in the distance with Spot and Bo lying alongside each other at their feet. Dee had never seen Spot so worn out. After the last flush of pink left the sky, Grady put the dogs in the house and fed them, then came back out with Dee's wine in a bag of ice. "Thought you might enjoy this more than beer or the bottom-shelf wine that Dave carries," he said.

"Are you sure he won't mind?"

Grady looked at the bottle and seemed to consider the question. "Tell you what, however many glasses you drink, I'll pay him what he charges for his wine."

Dee grinned and shook her head at him. "You're going to pay Dave a corkage fee?"

Grady grinned back at her. "Sure. I'll tell him it's a good way to class up the joint."

Grady and Dee sat at the bar and ordered burgers and Dee withstood a little good-natured kidding from Dave about being a wine snob. They didn't play darts or dance this time. It was late and Dee was tired from riding the trail. "I had no idea horseback riding was so exhausting," she said.

Grady rubbed his jaw and nodded. "Yeah, it uses muscles you probably don't even know you have. You might be sore tomorrow."

Gah! Her brain was doing it again. *Shut up!* She took a big gulp of her wine.

BACK AT THE HOUSE, GRADY SHOWED HER WHERE EV-erything could be found in the kitchen, just in case she wanted something to eat or drink in the middle of the night. Dee had *never* wanted anything to eat in the middle of the night, but she appreciated the gesture.

The dogs were curled up together on the rug in front of the fireplace even though there was no fire going. It was probably Bo's usual place to sleep, and Spot was just going with the program. What an agreeable dog. Dee loved her. Dee loved this house and the ranch. Dee loved Dave's bar. Dee loved everything tonight. Dee had maybe had too much wine to drink.

She looked over at Grady getting her a glass of water to take upstairs. She loved this man. She shook her head. *No.* Don't think it, because then you'll go and say it.

He showed her back to her room and set the glass of water on the nightstand. "There's a sound machine over here in case there're any noises outside keeping you awake. Or if I snore." He smiled and shrugged. "I live here by myself, so I'm not sure, but it's a definite possibility."

"Thank you. I'm so tired, I'm sure I'll be asleep before you could even begin to snore. If you snore." She tried to wink at him. She'd never been very good at winking.

He laughed and leaned down to lift her chin in his hand. Then he kissed her as he had the night they met, but this time it wasn't a quick brush of his lips. Dee put her hands behind his head and pulled him to her. He kissed her mouth, her throat, her clavicle; her silk top slid off her shoulder and she didn't even notice. She wanted to kiss him all night. She wanted to do more than kiss him.

But Grady put his hands on her shoulders and stepped back, gently straightening her top as he moved away from her. "Good night, Dee," he said in his rumbly voice. Then he walked across the hall to his room.

Dee shut the door and leaned against the dresser for a few moments before getting ready for bed.

She lay there under the quilt wide awake. She felt the presence of Grady across the hall like a homing device. She stared at the clock on the bedside table. An hour passed.

The door to his room stood slightly ajar. She hesitated for just a second and then pushed it open. Grady lay on his back with his arms crossed behind his head, those biceps that drove her crazy visible in the moonlight. Like her, he was still awake. Without a word, she crossed the room. His eyes held hers as she stood next to the bed, unbuttoning her sleep shirt and letting it drop to the floor, then she slipped under the covers next to him.

He rose up on an elbow and studied her face. "You sure you're ready for this?" His voice sounded even huskier than normal.

She leaned forward and kissed his lips. "I'm sure."

He pulled her over on top of him, then reached up to hold the hair back from her face. He gave her a crooked smile. "How about if I let you take the lead, darlin'."

She bit her lip and nodded, then leaned down and kissed him again as his hands traveled from her face down her body. Everything in her past ceased to exist. The future meant nothing to her. The only thing on her mind was how much she wanted this man.

THE NEXT MORNING, DEE AWOKE TO AN EMPTY BED. She lay there for a few moments, disoriented, and then everything that happened the previous evening washed over her. She shivered at the memory and ran her hands over her body under the covers. She was still naked. She pushed herself back against the pillows on the headboard, pulling the comforter up to cover her chest. Spot, who'd been curled up on a rug by the door, stretched and came alongside the bed, resting her head on the mattress. "Hey, Toto." Dee scratched behind the dog's ears as she looked around the room. "Looks like we're still in Kansas."

Sunlight streamed through sheer curtains at the windows. Shiplap covered three walls, built-in Edison lights flanked the king-size bed, and an oversize painting of a breathtaking prairie sunrise hung on the opposite wall. A blue flannel robe sat folded at the foot of the bed.

She slipped into the much-too-big robe, belted it, and went down the hall to brush her teeth with Spot right behind her. Then she followed the aroma of bacon and coffee to the kitchen. Grady stood at a butcher block island in the center of the vaulted room, whisking eggs in a stoneware bowl. He looked up and smiled as she padded into the room in her bare feet.

"Morning, sweetheart." He left the eggs and met her halfway across the room with a kiss. "Sleep okay?"

It took her a few seconds to answer because her body wanted to skip the social niceties and drag him back to the bedroom. She felt her face flush as she remembered the things they'd done. She smiled, but she couldn't meet his eyes. "Yes, I, um, slept really well."

"Me too."

She glanced up at him and saw his dimples dancing. "Oh God." She laughed and covered her face with her hands. "Don't look at me."

"Come on." He put an arm around her shoulder and kissed the top of her head. "Get over here and have some breakfast. We need to get you on the road if you're going to be in Oklahoma City by noon."

chapter

THIRTY-FIVE

A WEEK LATER, DEE AND GRADY MET AT THE ATLANTA airport, Grady flying in from Wichita and Dee from Philadelphia.

Even with Grady by her side, Dee approached the upcoming task with all the reluctance one felt for complicated dental work, or maybe a more serious surgery that carried the possibility of death. Not that she was given to overdramatizing things.

"Maybe we could just forget about this and book another flight."

They were standing in the line for rental cars, but Dee's attention was on the nearby overhead display of departing flights.

"There's one that leaves for the Bahamas in an hour," she said, only half in jest.

"I think we'd best get this cleared up first." Grady smiled down at her. "Although now that you mention it, I wouldn't mind spending some time on a beach with you and a couple of margaritas."

"Maybe we can find a tropical version of this," she said, reaching up to tap the brim of his cowboy hat. "A straw one, like Kenny Chesney's."

The rental car attendant nodded to them.

"Come on, sweetheart." Grady took Dee's bag and started forward. "The sooner we get this over with, the sooner we can plan our vacation."

TWO HOURS LATER, THEY PULLED INTO THE RUN-down truck stop where the attack took place. Dee had consulted her truck log to get the exact location of the exit, even though she was certain it was seared into her memory like a virtual GPS. Ruby's Diner and the gas station next to it looked every bit as dilapidated in the daylight as they had in the dark. Faded red paint peeled from the diner's asbestos shingles and a ripped canvas awning flapped over the entryway.

Grady turned off the ignition and looked over to Dee. "Is this the place?"

Her mouth was too dry to speak, so she just nodded while pulling a notebook and pen from her purse along with a baseball cap and her reading glasses. They had decided to go to the diner first and pose as reporters working on a story about roadside crime. Grady peeked under the brim of her ball cap. "We're not going undercover here, Jump Street."

Maybe he wasn't, but Dee was taking no chances on being recognized. What if the man who attacked her worked here? Maybe he'd recovered and was in the kitchen flipping pancakes.

They took a seat at the counter and ordered coffee. Grady studied their surroundings with an expression she couldn't read. She imagined it might have been how he looked just before they let the bull out of the pen when he was riding in the rodeo. Like he was ready for anything. She felt safer just having him beside her. She opened her notebook and tried to look like a journalist.

Dee cleared her throat as the waitress poured their coffee. "We're working on an article for the newspaper about crime along the interstate," Dee said. "Do you mind if we ask you a few questions?"

The server returned the coffee to the hot plate with a bang. It was the same brittle and irritable woman who'd waited on her the night she was attacked. Permanent frown lines bracketed her mouth as she spoke. "Who'd you say you wrote for?"

Dee adjusted her reading glasses and let her hair fall forward as she scrambled to think of a name. "The *Atlanta Press*." Was that even a real newspaper? She should have prepared a better backstory.

"Never heard of it. Got any identification?"

"Identification?" Dee repeated.

"We're freelancers," Grady said. Dee shot him a grateful look. At least one of them was good at thinking on their feet.

"Whatever," the waitress said. "You here about that guy they found in the woods?"

Oh God. He was dead. "Was he, um, the victim of a violent crime?" Dee's voice rose unnaturally at the end.

The woman stared at her a second too long. "No. He just walked out there and knocked himself in the head for kicks."

A bell rang in the kitchen, and she left to pick up an order.

"She's not very friendly, is she?" Grady said.

Dee shook her head. "Maybe we should leave."

He blew on his coffee before answering. "The only way out is through."

"What does that mean?"

Grady chuckled. "I don't know. Something my dad used to say. Basically, you have to do the hard stuff to get some peace."

The server returned with her order pad, but she didn't ask what they wanted right away. She studied Dee's face. "I remember you. Weren't you in here the night that guy got it?"

"What? No, I've never been here before." Her voice was too high. Despite all the practice over the past few months, her skill at lying failed her when she really needed it.

"Humph." She continued to stare at Dee. "What'll you have?"

Grady took over. "We're thinking about pie. What do people here like the best?"

Dee turned to look at him. Was he insane? They needed to leave. This woman suspected her.

She left to get their two orders of pecan pie, and Dee whispered to Grady. "Are you crazy? We have to get out of here."

Grady rested his forearms on the counter. Even though his posture appeared relaxed, he somehow still seemed tensed. He reminded her of Spot when she was poised to spring on a vole in the backyard. "Leaving would raise more suspicion. Let's just find out what happened and then we'll go from there."

The waitress returned with the pie, and Grady took over their journalistic duties.

"So, tell us more about the guy y'all found in the woods. That kind of thing happen often round here?" Somehow, Grady's voice had taken on a slight southern accent. Not enough to make someone think he was putting it on, but enough to try and make this woman a little less hostile. He brought a generous forkful of pie to his mouth and gave the waitress a thumbs-up.

She didn't stop scowling, but she wiped her hands on a towel at her waist and leaned back against the sink. "Yeah, there was a guy found in the woods behind here a few months ago, clocked in the head. Somebody called in a tip and a swarm of cop cars showed up. So, the guy's in the hospital for weeks, and come to find out, he's some kind of drug dealer. Cops think it was a falling-out with the syndicate. They got the other guy's blood, so they'll probably find him eventually."

Dee picked up her coffee with trembling hands. *Blood.* It was her blood. She felt like she was going to throw up. They had to leave.

The waitress looked out the window and then over toward the kitchen. There was no bell, but she walked back anyway.

Dee pulled off her pointless reading glasses. They were giving her a headache and had fooled no one. She gripped Grady's wrist. "We need to leave. That was my blood. They think I—"

Grady nodded. "Let's go." He threw some bills on the counter and put a hand on Dee's back as they started toward the door. "I'll call my brother. He's got a close friend who's a defense attorney. We'll ask him what to do." He was leaning down, talking to her in a low voice as they walked, and she was keeping her eyes on his to keep from losing it. Neither of them saw the two sheriff's deputies standing at the door of the diner.

"Where do y'all think you're going?" One of the identically dressed men stepped forward. They were wearing hats and reflective sunglasses, even though they were inside.

Grady stood up to his full height and nodded at the deputy who'd spoken. "We're just heading back on the highway, Officer. I highly recommend the pecan pie."

"Is that a fact? Well, we're not here to have any pie, we're here to ask you two a few questions."

"Of course. How can we help you out?" Grady said. His voice was conversational, but Dee sensed the tension in it.

"You don't sound like you're from around here. What brings you to Ruby's Diner?" What the deputy said also sounded conversational, but the fact that he was blocking the door and holding a hand on his holster made it less so.

"Well, sir, we just came to Georgia for a visit and thought we'd take a drive out into the country. This looked like as good a spot as any to stop for a bite to eat. And like I said, the pecan pie was a real treat."

The deputy who had been speaking took off his sunglasses and narrowed his eyes at Grady. "Do I look stupid to you, Yankee?"

"Not at all, sir."

The deputy took a step closer. "So, I'm going to ask you again, where you from?"

Dee felt a scream rising in her throat. She should never have brought Grady here. She'd turned him into a target. She jumped in to answer the question.

"We're from . . . I'm from Philadelphia and . . . and my friend here is from Kansas." Her voice was shaking so badly, even she wondered if she was telling the truth.

"I ran the plates on that rental car out there. You mean to tell me you and your *friend* here flew into Atlanta this morning and just decided to take a two-hour drive?"

Dee glanced at Grady. His face had turned hard and angry. The diner, which had been noisy with the sound of silverware and lunchtime conversation, fell silent as every table turned to watch the drama unfolding before them.

"Last I checked, Officer, this is a free country. There's nothing illegal about driving around it if you have a license. You want to see my license?"

"I don't think you better be reaching for your wallet." The deputy's mouth twisted in a sneer. "That's how a lotta people end up shot."

The deputy nearest the door coughed.

"Jesus! Are you for real?" Grady shook his head.

"Just keep your hands where I can see them."

"Yes, sir."

Dee heard the mocking tone in Grady's voice and hoped the deputy didn't. "Excuse me, Off . . . Officer." Her shaking voice veered into stuttering. "I . . . I think . . ." She took a breath. "I think I can clear this up."

He turned his sneering gaze toward Dee. "Why don't you do that, ma'am, seeing as how you meet the description of a person of interest in a crime that occurred here a few months back."

"Are you accusing her of something?" Grady said. "Because the fact of the matter is, she was the *victim* of a crime here."

The deputy flicked his eyes at Grady. "We'll be the ones to decide that. Keep talking, ma'am."

Grady shook his head. "This is bullshit. I'm calling my attorney." As he lifted his phone and began to tap the screen, the deputy struck it from his hand and sent it flying across the room into the wall.

A curtain of rage fell across Grady's face. "I can't fucking believe you just did that."

A few shocked cries had rung out when the phone flew across the room, and now people were mumbling to one another. She had to do something to defuse the situation before this idiot with a badge decided Grady was a threat and Tasered him . . . or worse. Why did all men, even kind, compassionate, educated men like Grady, turn into saber-rattling cavemen

when they were confronted by an asshole? Maybe anger re‑
leased a megadose of testosterone that they were powerless
to override. She'd come in here with Bruce Banner and now
found herself standing next to the Incredible Hulk.

"Grady, stop. I can handle this."

He turned his furious gaze on her. "Oh, you can, can you?
Well, be my guest." Then he looked back at the deputy. "Do
you mind if I retrieve my phone, Officer?" Sarcasm dripped
from his voice.

"I want you to stand right here where I can keep an eye on
you." Deputy Bad Cop motioned to his cohort by the door.
"Sully, get his phone."

Dee cleared her throat. "I was here in February and a man
attacked me in the parking lot."

"He attacked *you?*" The deputy gave a mocking snort. "Then
how is it we found him half-dead in the weeds back there?"

"Jesus fucking Christ!" Grady exploded next to her. "Stop
talking Dee. You should have a lawyer with you, and he knows
it."

She knew Grady was trying to protect her, but some part
of her (the stupid, impetuous part that got her into a truck in
the first place) wanted to blow it all up. She wanted to tell the
truth and be done with it. She didn't care if she had an attor‑
ney. She hadn't done anything wrong, and none of this was her
fault, and it wasn't fair. Dee looked at him and shook her head.
"I just want to get it over with."

Grady clenched his jaw and spoke in the same angry voice
he'd used with the deputy. "Dee, listen to me. I know you
want to handle this on your own, but you *need* an attorney."

"I'm sorry, Grady. I never should have dragged you down
here. It would have been better if I'd come by myself."

Grady blinked like she'd slapped him. "Fine. Handle it yourself, then."

"Get him out of here, Sully."

"You need an attorney, Dee," Grady yelled again on the way out the door. "He hasn't even read you your Miranda rights."

Miranda rights. She had a vague recollection from some long-ago cop show. Her dad watching late-night TV. *You have the right to remain silent. Anything you say can and will be used against you . . .* But she wasn't going to incriminate herself because she hadn't done anything wrong, damn it. And then she remembered Sugar. She couldn't tell the truth. Maybe she hadn't done anything wrong, but the truth would implicate the woman who saved her life.

With a sinking feeling, she watched as Grady got in the rental car and drove away. Was he really leaving her here by herself?

"Okay, ma'am. Now that your friend won't be interrupting us, how about you explain to me what you were doing here in March?"

Dee turned a furious gaze on the deputy. All the anger she'd felt toward men over the past year—her ex-husband, the bigoted Jensen, the monster who'd attacked her in this parking lot, and now Grady, abandoning her in the middle of nowhere—combined in an explosive force she could barely contain.

The deputy seemed to register the change in her, clearing his throat and pausing before repeating his question. "Tell me what you were doing here in March."

Dee crossed her arms in front of her chest without breaking eye contact. "I want an attorney."

chapter

THIRTY-SIX

OFFICER JAMISON, DEE NOTED THE NAME ON HIS badge, had placed handcuffs on her before putting her in the squad car. Now she sat in an interrogation room in the municipal building with the handcuffs attached to a heavy wooden chair. Black ink stained her fingertips, and her thumb throbbed from a blood draw administered by a nervous young officer. She twisted around and looked at the closed door behind her. There was no clock in the room, but it felt like she'd been locked up for hours.

To her left a large mirror took up most of the wall. She resisted the urge to look at her reflection. It had to be a two-way mirror, and it sickened her to think of who might be out there observing her. She tried to calm herself down with Stephanie's breathing exercise, but she couldn't concentrate. Her heart raced, and jumbled thoughts careened through her mind. How could Grady leave her like this? What kind of court-appointed attorney would this backwoods town have to represent her? Wasn't she entitled to a phone call or something? Could Rummel help her with this? If they hadn't taken her purse and cell phone, she would have called Jancee. Jancee would send an entire law firm down.

Jamison reentered the room with a toothpick clamped in his teeth, carrying a sheaf of papers and an old beige cassette recorder. He set both on the desk and sat down in the wheeled office chair across from her. Unlike the hard-backed torture device she sat in, the deputy's seat was padded and adjustable. He took his time getting himself situated and then turned on the recorder and tapped the papers in front of him. "Know what I got here?"

Dee shrugged.

"Lab reports, Ms. Levari. That was your blood we found on the assault victim. I guess he put up quite a fight."

She closed her eyes and drew on the last remaining scrap of self-control she could muster. "You honestly believe I—" she gestured to her five-foot frame "—beat up that man?"

"Damned if I know." He gnawed on the toothpick in his mouth. Dee wished he'd choke on it.

"Now, I'll admit Davey Turner—that's the name of the victim—he ain't nothin' but trouble, but we been giving him a little bit of rope to lead us to the big-time. Maybe you got caught up in this through no fault of your own. Maybe somebody was using your truck to smuggle drugs unbeknownst to you, huh?"

Dee turned around to look at the door again. "Where's my attorney?"

Jamison turned his hands up. "Beats me. He don't get paid enough to hurry."

"What about my phone call? Aren't I entitled to a phone call?"

Jamison took the toothpick out and studied it. "Technically, yes. But you know, going strictly by the book, things take forever. Like I said, I don't even know when Morgan is going to come in. The guy's got quite a caseload. You might even have to spend a night or two in jail here."

Dee stared at the man across from her. He'd once been someone's little boy. How did an innocent child turn into a churlish, self-important, and ignorant adult like this? Was he not given enough attention growing up? Was it the result of dealing with violent criminals day after day? Dee tried to summon up some compassion for the guy, but it was a hard sell.

The beginnings of a headache throbbed behind her eyes, and she needed to use the restroom—she'd had enough coffee to fill her bladder, but not enough to stave off caffeine withdrawal. Fuck it. She was going to give this jerk what he wanted.

"Fine. I'll give you a statement, but I want to make it clear that I am making it under duress. I asked for an attorney, and none was provided." She lifted her chin and stared at the deputy defiantly.

He chewed at his toothpick and returned her stare. "Well, go on then. The recorder's running."

Dee indulged in a momentary fantasy of lunging across the desk and raking her nails across Deputy Jamison's smirking face. Then she fixed her gaze on the far wall and began speaking in a monotone. "The man you found attacked me in the parking lot when I left the diner and went to my truck. He slammed my head against the wheel well and knocked me out. That's where all the blood came from. When I came to, he was trying to rape me. When I fought back, he choked me. I don't know who came along and knocked him out, but I'm glad they did or I'd be dead."

The deputy rocked back in the chair and put his feet on the desk. "Now that's a real pretty story right there. You think it up while you were locked up in here?"

"If you get me my phone, I'll show you the picture of what he did to me."

"You expect me to believe that you were just in the wrong place at the wrong time?"

Dee blinked at him. *Yes.* That's exactly what she expected because that's what happened. But she didn't waste her breath saying it.

"So, who was it that came along to *save you?*" He made air quotes.

"I don't know. I came to on the ground and that . . . Davey whatever . . . was lying next to me with a gash on the back of his head. All I wanted to do was get away from him. I didn't care who hit him then and I don't care now." Dee's voice began to rise. "For all I know it was an act of God. Actually, I think it would be just great if the Almighty started smacking around violent people in the middle of their attacks."

As Dee finished speaking, she heard raised voices approaching in the hallway.

"Jesus H. Christ! Can I not leave this fucking place for five minutes without things getting screwed up? Goddamn it!" The voice was right outside.

Jamison sat back up in the chair and took the toothpick out of his mouth.

The door banged open.

"What the hell's going on in here, Jamison?"

"Afternoon, Sheriff." The deputy looked like a nasty dog that just got smacked in the nose with a newspaper. "I was just questioning a witness in the Turner case, sir."

The sheriff walked around the desk and picked up the tape recorder. Then he looked over at Dee. He closed his eyes and took a deep breath through his nose. He turned back to

Jamison, and when he spoke, his voice was unnaturally soft. The phrase "suppressed rage" popped into Dee's head. "You're questioning a witness, are you? Where's her attorney?"

Jamison kept his eyes on the desk. "I don't think she wanted one."

The sheriff rewound a bit of the tape and hit Play. Dee's voice rose from the speaker:

"I didn't care who hit him then and I don't care now. For all I know it was an act of God. Actually, I think it would be just great if the Almighty started smacking around violent people in the middle of their attacks."

He hit Stop and looked over at Dee. "Well, that would sure make my job a hell of a lot easier." He picked up the tape recorder and dropped it in the trash can in the corner.

"Get out." The suppressed-rage voice was back. "And send TJ in here to get the cuffs off this woman."

Jamison slunk out the door, and the sheriff lowered himself into his seat, gripping the arms of the chair so tight his knuckles were white. A muscle in his jaw twitched.

The redheaded kid who'd taken her fingerprints and blood came in and carefully removed the handcuffs. He didn't meet her eyes.

"Wait outside the door, TJ." The sheriff lifted his glasses and wiped a hand across his face, then put them back on and looked over at Dee.

"I'm Sheriff Haskell." His voice sounded tired. "I'd like to apologize for the behavior of my deputy. I got elected eight months ago running on a platform to reform policing in the county, and it looks like I still have my work cut out for me."

Dee nodded. Working in law enforcement had to be the most thankless job in the world. Especially for anyone with scruples.

"Would you like a cup of coffee?" Haskell said.

"Yes, please. And could I have my phone back? There's something on it I want you to see."

"TJ!" he barked.

TJ opened the door looking even paler and blotchier than he had earlier.

"Bring us two coffees with cream and sugar on the side. And get Ms. Levari's personal effects."

The door closed, and Haskell leaned back in his chair. "Your friend, Mr. Scott, had his attorney call us. Unlike this Super Trooper I got working for me, I don't believe that you are mixed up in any crime syndicate. That idiot thinks he's going to bring down another Pablo Escobar with a two-bit criminal like Davey Turner." He motioned to the papers on the desk. "I'd just like to close the books on this one. Turner's in jail awaiting trial now because we had ten outstanding warrants on him when he was found."

TJ came back with Dee's purse and suitcase, along with the coffees.

Dee checked her phone. No messages from Grady. No suitcase but her own. She closed her eyes for a moment. *There were no knights in shining armor. There never had been and there never would be, at least not in her life. It was time for her to stop wishing for a fairy tale.* She scrolled to the photo app and brought up the selfie she'd taken of her bruised face, then handed the phone to Haskell.

He studied it without comment and handed the phone back to Dee, along with his business card. "Can you send me a copy of that?"

"Yes." She emailed the photo to the address on the card and then poured cream in her coffee and took a sip.

Haskell started massaging a spot at the base of his thumb like he had carpal tunnel. "Would you mind giving me the short version of what happened that night?"

Dee took a breath. She was so tired of reliving it. "I stopped at the truck stop for dinner, planning to sleep in my cab afterward . . ."

Haskell looked up from his thumb. "You're a truck driver?"

"Yes."

He nodded. "Okay, go on."

"When I left the diner, Turner followed me and slammed me into my truck. When I came to, he was trying to pull my clothes off, and when I fought back he choked me until I passed out. I came to again, and he was next to me with a gash in his head."

The sheriff looked at the report in front of him. "That checks out. Turner had a bite mark on the right hand, and both his hands and arms looked like they'd been scraped up with fingernails. Yours?"

She nodded.

"And you don't know who hit him?"

Dee couldn't meet his eyes. "No."

"Ms. Levari, I'm convinced that you're an innocent victim, but I don't think you're unaware of who saved your life. Much as I'd like to believe your theory about God coming down to take care of things, you and I both know that's not it. Someone called 911 with an anonymous setting on their phone to report an injured man at the back of Ruby's. And I don't believe it was you."

"Someone called 911?"

"As I said, I just want to close the books on this. If no one had called, you might be culpable for reckless indifference. But they did. So, who called it in?"

Dee bit her lip. *Sugar.* She'd saved her life and then saved the life of a criminal. "Some woman. I don't know her name, and I can't remember what she looked like. She hit Turner with a flashlight when he was choking me, then she helped me in my truck and I drove away."

Haskell brought his tented fingers to his lips and nodded his head for a bit. "Works for me." He stood up and shook her hand. "You're free to go. We'll need you back down here for a trial if they add your attack to Turner's rap sheet. That will depend on the DA." Haskell took his glasses off and began polishing them.

She was free to go. Just like that. But she didn't feel free to go. She felt like she'd been pushed out of an airplane with no parachute. "Did you say Mr. Scott's attorney called?"

Haskell looked down at the papers on the desk. "Yes, he called a few hours ago and left a message. I called him back just before I came in here."

Dee checked her phone again. There were no messages or missed calls from Grady. He had his brother's attorney-friend call on her behalf. At least he did that much before he left. She drew a shaky breath. She'd never even told him she loved him. She wished she had now, even if he didn't say it back or feel the same. She just wanted him to know. She blinked back the tears in her eyes. Time to pull herself together. Again. She'd go get cleaned up and then call a taxi or something to take her to the airport. "Which way is the ladies' room?"

Haskell pointed.

She tucked her hair behind her ears and pulled up the handle on her roller bag. She could do this. She'd get to the airport and buy herself a Starbucks Venti latte, maybe she'd even treat herself to a brownie, and she'd be okay. If this year had taught her anything, it was that she was a survivor. She had her daughter, she had devoted friends, she even had her complicated sister back in her life. She'd fly back to Philly and start all over.

"Good luck to you, Ms. Levari," Haskell said.

Dee nodded to him and opened the door. She kept her head down and willed herself not to start crying. After she freshened up she'd feel better. She just had to find the ladies' room. Glancing across the hall, she saw a worn pair of cowboy boots. She lifted her eyes and a small cry escaped from her lips. There stood Grady, arms crossed over his chest, leaning with one boot propped against the green-painted cinderblock wall.

He was here. But it might not mean anything. He'd been raised to finish things. Maybe he stayed to make sure she got to the airport okay.

He lifted his head when she stepped into the hallway, and a slow smile spread across his face. "You sure do make a guy wait around an awful lot."

Dee ran to him, and he grabbed her in a hug that lifted her feet off the ground.

"I thought you left," she said.

"I wouldn't do that to you, Dee." The way he said it, it sounded like a vow.

She stepped out of his arms and gave him an uncertain smile. "You didn't call. Or text." She looked at her phone. Had she missed a message from him?

"My phone's busted." He pulled the shattered device from his pocket. "And I couldn't remember your number."

"But you were so mad when you left."

Grady looked off down the hallway and sighed, then back at Dee. "I have a temper, sweetheart. I'm working on it."

"I have a temper too."

Grady frowned. "I find that hard to believe."

Her relief at finding him waiting for her faded. This was never going to work. They lived too far apart; they both had tempers. Once he found out all about her, he'd leave. She couldn't look him in the eye. "This"—she gestured around with her arm, encompassing the little southern town and the situation she'd gotten them into—"this isn't everything. I have a lot of baggage, Grady. Maybe more than you want to deal with."

He scoffed at her. "Baggage is my middle name."

Dee forced a smile. "You really don't know me that well. And I mean, how would you even get to know me—we live a thousand miles apart. But I'm kind of a know-it-all, and I'm particular about things . . ." She swallowed over the lump in her throat. "Once you know me better . . ."

He dropped his joking manner and grew serious. "We're not kids, Dee. You don't get to this point in life without making some mistakes. There are a lot of things I wish I'd done a better job with, but that's not how life works. We can't go back and change the past, but we can learn from it, right?" Dee lifted a shoulder in response. "And yeah, right now there's a lot of distance between us, but I think we can figure something out." He cupped her face in his hands and made her look at him. "I'm not going anywhere."

Tears spilled onto her cheeks, and he brushed them away with his thumbs. She wanted to trust him, to see a future with him, even if she had no idea what that would look like. She studied his face, the chiseled jaw and warm eyes that had undone her from the first moment she'd met him. There was reassurance in his gaze, but now she sensed the years of pain and regret etched alongside the smiling creases of his eyes. Could the two of them overcome their pasts? Did she have it in her to risk one more blind leap?

She gave Grady a tremulous smile. "I believe you."

He closed his eyes for just a moment, and when he opened them, the shadows were gone. "That's my girl," he said. He leaned down to kiss her, and Dee melted into him, reaching her arms around his neck and running her fingers through his close-cropped hair. She would be the most Zen person in history if she never had to stop kissing this man. She let go of the rage she'd felt toward Deputy Jamison; she stopped worrying about what the future held, she even forgot, momentarily, where she was.

Then Sheriff Haskell stepped out of the interrogation room and collided with Dee's suitcase. Dee and Grady broke apart. Dee stared, horrified, at the sheriff, who had tripped and now crouched with one knee on her carry-on.

Haskell stood up and cleared his throat, then righted the suitcase and wheeled it over to where they stood. "Don't you two have a flight to catch?"

"Yes, sir, we do," Grady said.

"Best get on the road, then," he said. He nodded to Dee and Grady in turn, then walked down the hall and into his office.

Dee looked at Grady with wide eyes and swallowed a giggle, as if they were high school kids who got caught making out by their lockers.

Dimples twitching, Grady gave her another quick kiss. Then he straightened his hat and tilted his head toward the exit.

"Let's go home," he said.

Home. Dee's favorite word in the English language. Four letters that held within them the promise of safety, contentment, and love. She didn't bother asking if he meant Philadelphia or Kansas. She grabbed his hand and pulled him toward the exit.

The End

About the Author

HEIDI HEATH TONY IS A LIFELONG READER WHOSE previous writing gigs include ghost-writing for Miss America's blog, fascinating bill inserts for an electric utility, and many, many articles about critical subjects like Delaware's Punkin Chunkin festival and how to score free drinks in Atlantic City casinos. She and her husband live in the Pittsburgh area with their children and grandchildren nearby, but she will forever be a Jersey girl in her heart.

Queen of the Road is her first novel. If you enjoyed this story, please leave a review or rating on Goodreads or Amazon.